"Henry is an engaging, resourceful hero of this picaresque tale
. . . [*Mad Boy*] is a wartime coming-of-age story filled with
nonstop action and genuine pathos."
—*Kirkus Reviews* (starred)

"*Mad Boy* is a terrific achievement. There's a vicious black
humor at work here, underpinning the larger bend of the story
in a way that keeps you guessing. As each new character arrives
fully formed, like they've stepped out of the archive, you wonder
how Arvin will keep it all together. The best part is, he does."
—Rohan Wilson, author of *To Name Those Lost*

"Surreal at times and brutally realistic at others, this novel is a
strange amalgam of *As I Lay Dying*, *The Adventures of
Huckleberry Finn*, and *The Red Badge of Courage*."
—John Gibbs, Green Apple Books, San Francisco

"A unique, endearing and truly marvelous story."
—Sheryl Cotleur, Copperfield's Books

"*Mad Boy*'s hero is an unforgettable creation, and his adventures move at the most satisfyingly calibrated speeds. You'll
want to race through the book to see what Henry does or
whom or what he encounters next, but you'll also want to slow
down to savor the storytelling magic."
—John Francisconi, Bank Square Books

"Humane and brutal but never false, Nick Arvin delivers an
illuminating critique of American history and myth."
—Mario Acevedo, bestselling author of *The Nymphos of
Rocky Flats*

ALSO BY

NICK ARVIN

In the Electric Eden
The Reconstructionist
Articles of War

MAD BOY

Nick Arvin

MAD BOY

AN ACCOUNT OF HENRY PHIPPS
IN THE WAR OF 1812

A NOVEL

Europa
editions

Europa Editions
214 West 29th Street
New York, N.Y. 10001
www.europaeditions.com
info@europaeditions.com

Library of Congress Cataloging in Publication Data is available
ISBN 978-1-60945-458-6

Arvin, Nick
Mad Boy

Book design by Emanuele Ragnisco
www.mekkanografici.com

Cover illustration: detail from "Bombardment of Fort McHenry
by the British," engraving by John Bower (public domain)

Prepress by Grafica Punto Print – Rome

Printed in the USA

For Cade

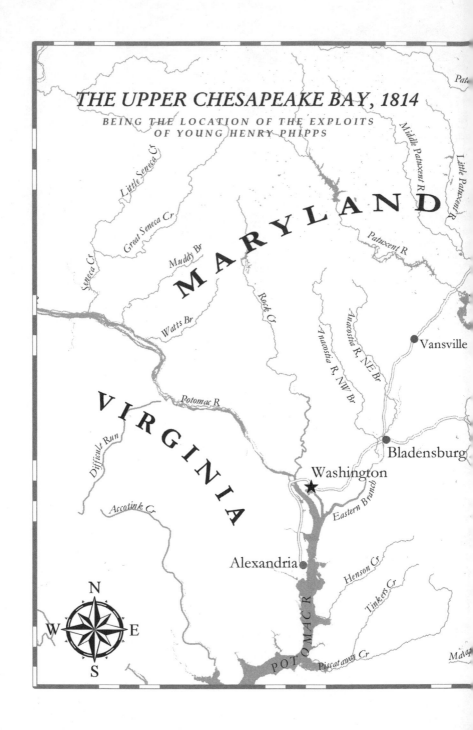

THE UPPER CHESAPEAKE BAY, 1814

BEING THE LOCATION OF THE EXPLOITS
OF YOUNG HENRY PHIPPS

MARYLAND

VIRGINIA

Pat...

Middle Patuxent R.

Little Patuxent R.

Little Seneca Cr

Great Seneca Cr

Seneca Cr

Muddy Br

Patuxent R.

Rock Cr

Watts Br

Anacostia R. NE Br

Anacostia R. NW Br

Vansville

Potomac R.

Difficult Run

Bladensburg

Accotink Cr

Washington

Eastern Branch

Alexandria

Henson Cr

Tinkers Cr

POTOMAC R

Piscataway Cr

Mat...

N
W   E
S

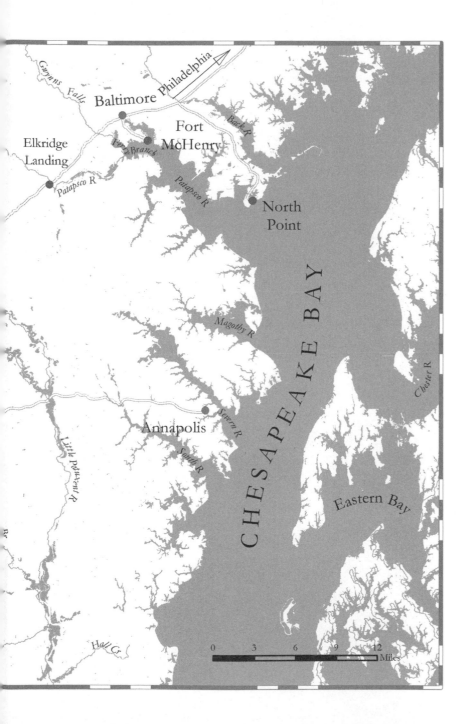

Henry Phipps runs through the shadows under great trees. He's angry. Someone has lied—the slave Radnor has lied to Henry, or someone has lied to Radnor: some liar has lied to someone a terrible lie. He runs through wet heat and spongy mud, through clouds of gnats and sprays of pale flowers, a small boy, lean like a figure cut from a length of wood too thin for the intended shape. He wears a shirt that's scarcely more than sacking with buttons, trousers patched in several places and cinched by a rope belt, boots with a hole in one toe, no hat.

When a bramble scratches his leg, he stops to yell at the plant and kick it. Then he runs on.

Old forest still covers much of the land between the Chesapeake and the Potomac, and America has been at war with Britain for two of Henry's ten years, mostly losing. From ahead drifts the sound of an English voice, which Henry would notice if not for the noise of his own breath, rushing blood, fury.

Why would Radnor lie? Who would lie to Radnor? Henry cannot fathom. He jumped to his feet and raced away before Radnor finished explaining. Henry wants to talk to Mother; Mother will know what to do. Henry is so outraged and wrathful that he gives only contempt to the idea that what Radnor said might be true—that Henry's brother, Franklin, is dead.

He runs under hickories and sycamores, not slowing as the land slopes upward, trying to go yet faster against the ache in his legs.

He careens into a clearing, stumbles, stops. Before him is a round-eyed, jug-eared man holding a musket and wearing a brass-buttoned wool jacket, well-worn, dirty ruddy-pink. Behind this man, scattered about the open meadow, are some three dozen soldiers in similar coats, like a flight of faded cardinals.

They are of course redcoats. A couple of months ago Henry's father was sent to the debtor's prison in Baltimore, but previous to this setback Father had often traveled to Washington, Alexandria, Annapolis, and Baltimore, where he drank whiskey and played faro. He always returned poorer but bearing the latest news, and for two years the news has been of the redcoat raids up and down the Chesapeake, capturing food and goods, destroying farms, taking away slaves.

The jug-eared redcoat, who looks not yet eighteen, yelps, fumbles for the musket on his shoulder, catches a heel, falls on the seat of his patched trousers.

The other redcoats turn and stare. The humid air lies quiet. The ironwork of the British muskets shines like Spanish dollars. The stocks are painted vermillion. Among the British—surprising Henry amid his surprise—are a few black-skinned soldiers. The redcoats span a long, narrow meadow, cut across by a zigzag fence. Out of sight, behind the trees, is a house, and Henry knows the family there a little: the Jeffery family, they keep several cows, pigs, goats, and an uncommon number of turkeys, which they chase across their tobacco field to peck the horn worms.

One of the redcoats has straddled a she-goat with enormous conical teats and slashed her throat. As he stares at Henry, the throat drizzles, and the goat appears both sleepy-eyed and irate.

Some twenty yards behind the jug-eared soldier, who still sits in the grass, stands a redcoat with a gold epaulet, a brass-tipped black leather scabbard, and a jacket that is redder than the others. In each hand he grips a headless chicken. "Hello there, boy," he calls. "Hold up." He looks at the chickens, as if unsure whether to drop them, or throw them, or some other course of action.

Henry, in his surprise, laughs.

Then he turns, jumps for the bushes, and tumbles downhill.

He ends up with his face in branches and dirt. He proceeds sideways through scratching brambles, hoping the redcoats will assume he would continue straight down. He wriggles into a hollow beneath an evergreen and lies panting and trying to swallow his panting.

Behind him the redcoats yell insults at one another. Henry hears the jug-eared soldier call, "Oh, close your hole, egg sucker!" He plods loudly into the brush and trees. "Why run away, boy?" he calls. "Because you're a spy? A stupid one? Come out, stupid spy! Come out, so I can kill you!" Henry watches him aim his musket to the left, then the right, sigh, turn, amble away.

Henry shifts a branch to see the others. This is exciting. Father said that the British would never come this far inland— but for Father to be proven wrong is a circumstance with many precedents. The British have a trio of donkey carts, loaded with cornmeal, tobacco, dead livestock, whiskey. The redcoats smash up the rails of the fence to make a path for the carts, and they move on in the direction of Mr. Suthers's house. A black soldier leads the way. Henry wonders idly how long it will take for the Jefferys' livestock to find the hole in the fence and wander off.

He trails behind the redcoats for a half mile, then turns toward the cabin and Mother, thinking again of what Radnor said. Immediately he's angry, fears he may weep, runs.

In the grove of black walnut that Henry's great-great-grandfather planted a hundred years ago the sun casts shivering fawn-spots on the earth. Henry runs through, footfalls padded by moss. Great-great-grandfather believed his heirs would appreciate the nuts and might use the wood for gunstocks or fencing. He would have been disappointed. His progeny did nothing with the walnuts and instead established and advanced a nearly mythical reputation for dissolute laziness, dependence on neighbors' charity, and love of whiskey and gambling. Henry's great-grandfather and grandfather sold away slaves to pay debts, and the Phippses remained too placid or shiftless or—arguably—stupid to rebuild their accounts by working the land or nail-making or shingle-cutting or rope-walking or some other craft. After Henry's grandfather died of a wart that became gangrenous, the estate passed to Henry's father. Father, in due time, gambled away the land. General opinion held that the only wonder was it had taken so long.

Father was forced to move the family out of the big house to the cabin, and Henry took his first breaths in a borning room built on the side of the cabin. It is the cabin he approaches now. The borning room is gone, after its roof leaked for years, and finally its rotted walls were pulled apart for firewood. What remains is the one-room cabin with the hearth along one wall, beds along two others, a table and benches in the middle. The cabin is built into the side of a hill, and the cabin roof merges directly into the grassy hilltop. Henry has carried buckets up the hillside many times to extinguish fires in the cabin's bark roof and in the clay-and-stick chimney. Most of the cabin has burned and been replaced at one time or another, except for the back wall, which is integral with the hill and faced with granite. When Mother is sick with the black spirit, she lies abed on her side, facing the granite stones, gripping her left thumb in her right hand. Where the chinking between the granite stones has come free a worm or grub or root sometimes noses through.

Nearby a square-doored cellar is dug into the hillside, and

next to it stands a chicken hutch. Slouching opposite the hill is a barn—someone many years ago laid the stone foundation for a proper barn, but the barn itself is a low, leaning, sagging-roofed, provisional structure. A couple dozen chickens peck in the sun-blasted dust, while off to one side lies a vegetable garden surrounded by a jumbled fence of sticks and bits of string, which the rabbits wander through at will. Beyond, wrapping around one side of the hill, is a field of several uneven acres where the biggest stumps have never been removed. Shafts of corn stand out here and there, but much of it is weeds.

As Henry comes up, Mother stands in the garden. She's not working, only standing, talking to herself.

Henry, who has not considered that what Radnor said might be true, sees Mother, and is forced to consider. It is in the way she shapes her body, somehow proudly downward. Grief and fear clamp a hold on Henry. Grief for his brother, but also the choking fear that this may make Mother ill.

But she turns to him, says his name, and he knows, by the fact that she speaks, that she will not be sick, not right now.

All this he sees in a second as he rushes across the yard.

He becomes furious again. When Mother tries to clutch him, he escapes to run round and round the garden, screaming.

"Eat, Henry," Mother says, dipping a bowl of succotash from the kettle. She brings it to him at the table. "Eating can only do you good, and we must have our strength for traveling."

They will go to Baltimore, she said when he stopped running and screaming.

Mother talks without stopping. "Eat all you can. I hate to think what we will leave behind. But this is not the place for us anymore, is it? That's plain. 'For everything there is a season, and a time for every matter under heaven.'"

Henry only recently came to understand that although Mother sometimes quotes the Bible, she doesn't particularly believe in it. It's ridiculous, she told him, but it's handy. Henry eats his succotash. He has already decided that he thinks Franklin is still alive.

A mounted soldier riding messages from Washington to Annapolis stopped at the Sutherses' house yesterday and left a letter, addressed to Mother. No one in the Suthers household bothered to pass the letter along until today, when they sent Radnor with it. Written by a soldier in Franklin's regiment, the letter said, *General Winder has ordered no news of a military nature of any kind should be provided to civilians in this time of war, but I am writing to you in confidence because I believe that you must be informed that your son, Franklin Phipps, has been captured in desertion in the city of Alexandria and sentenced by the courts-martial. He will be put to death by the firing squad before the assembled 5th Maryland regiment at sunrise the morning of the 23rd of August. I am very sincerely sorry. Franklin is a good man and valorous, albeit at times hesitant in certain operations of the mind.*

Today is the 23rd of August. Mother did not receive the letter until midmorning.

After she read the letter to Henry, he stood stupefied, then began stamping his feet and sputtering. He told Mother about the British he had encountered. Franklin's regiment would need to go fight the redcoats, Henry said. They wouldn't have time to shoot Franklin. Mother said it didn't take long to shoot a man, but Henry said that because it was an execution they would want to make a spectacle of it, everyone in clean uniforms, drums and bugles, polished buttons and bayonets and swords, officers very solemn, and so forth. "They'll put it off," Henry says, "and when there's fighting, Franklin will make himself a hero, and they'll forget all about the execution!"

"I don't know," Mother said. "I don't know whether to hope you could be right. Because if he's dead, it'll be worse for having hoped."

Now she studies a pan in her hand, then throws it with casual violence at the corner of the cabin. "Won't be taking that." Henry watches, concerned that she may yet fall ill. He has never been able to predict the sickness, although he has always believed there must be signs for it, the way sparrows flit low to the ground before a storm. If only he knew what to look for—a movement of her fingers, a twitch of her eyelid, a pinch of her lips?

Regardless of any doubt about Franklin's fate, she remains filled with the idea of going to Baltimore. "Franklin's regiment is stationed near Baltimore. If he's not dead, then he'll soon return there. We'll find news of him there. And we need our family to be together again," she says. "Also, if the British are near, and if there will be fighting, we had best move on before worse fortune strikes." Henry wants to go to Baltimore, too. He wants to see Father.

Mother is a tiny woman—to make her laugh, Franklin sometimes lifts her and sets her on his shoulder, where she perches as if seated in the branches of an ambulating tree. She always wears the same gingham dress, always clean and neat, the only assuredly clean and neat item in the household. When she married, her parents gave her an enormous bolt of fabric, which she keeps hidden to prevent Father from selling it for a gambling stake. Whenever a dress begins to show wear, she cuts and stitches another to the same pattern. She hems it a little short, showing the outward turn of her ankles—she stands bowlegged, as if astride a log of considerable circumference. She holds her shoulders high and back in a prideful way. Her family were boatbuilders and fishermen. She is the second to youngest of three brothers and six sisters, and her parents paid little heed to where she married off. Father always said, with an awe that gave it the weight of truth, that she was the prettiest of the sisters.

Now she paces. The cabin floor is packed dirt, hardened with river clay; sometimes, on a Sunday, Mother works swirling, flowery patterns into the floor with a sharp stick. But now the only pattern is the pattern of her pacing. Behind her glows the green window, glassed with upside-down bottles, over Henry's bed. The window was a birthday present for Henry. Father could always find bottles.

She picks up things, sets them down or casts them aside, talks about what she has packed, what she will pack, what she has left out, what she will leave out, talks on and on. Except when the black spirit is on her, Mother always talks, whether or not anyone is listening, her presence extending itself in an ongoing chatter or mutter or murmur, often unintelligible. Father said that it was a wonder her teeth didn't get sunburned. He once brought home an enormous conch shell that he won at faro and gave it to Mother—she often spoke of missing the sea, said she wanted to be buried at sea, with her family around—and the endless sound inside the shell reminded Henry of Mother's talking.

Henry eats, and she paces and talks of Baltimore. "The land here may never belong to the Phippses again. When your father's luck does turn, who can say if Suthers will sell? In Baltimore we will have more opportunity. I will take in wash or sewing; you will find work on the docks, perhaps. We will sell corn cakes or candles or bits of string. We may befriend rich men and beg aid . . . "

Henry is thinking of Franklin, big bull Franklin. Why, even if they did shoot him, it'd be like shooting a bear that won't slow unless you hit it just right. What had Franklin deserted for anyhow? Franklin wouldn't be afraid of fighting. It makes Henry angry, that Franklin would do this and make Mother upset. Henry thinks of what he will say to Franklin, how he will talk about dishonor and Franklin will feel bad, because Franklin is hopeless about honor.

An hour later, the thing happens that is the worst thing. Mother is still talking, although not about Franklin—she hasn't mentioned Franklin since she read the letter. Perhaps not mentioning Franklin is why the sickness hasn't come over her, it is a means of keeping it away, and Henry has decided that he must not say a word about Franklin. She talks instead of the uncommon number of dragonflies that swarmed yesterday evening as she picked green beans, scores of them flocking, with darting blue bodies and shining wings. "Rushing hither and thither, one to another," she says, "like gossips at a fair."

The worst thing begins with a noise, short but loud, of creaking timber. Henry and Mother look at the ceiling, spanned by rough-hewn, burn-scarred timbers. The big timbers have survived all the roof fires, and the cabin is old, no one is certain how old. Looking closely, a little rot can be seen, so mostly no one looks closely. Mother says, "That's curious." She falls quiet, listening. Her silence is nearly as alarming to Henry as the noises overhead.

The creak sounds again, even louder, becomes a quick shriek, which ends with a sound of detonation. A wide section of roof swings as if on a hinge, a huge strange shape slides through, bleating, and Mother disappears.

Henry stands from the table. What is it, bleating? It sprawls massively on the floor. Henry has the idea that Mother stepped behind it, but he sees she's not there. She's underneath it. It is a cow.

Mother's underneath a cow.

Henry cries out, rears back, punches the cow, hard, on her thick moist nose.

A cow has come over the hill, onto the cabin roof, and fallen through, her big dark empty cow eyes rolling. But why? There's never been a cow on the roof before. Then he remembers the redcoats, knocking down fences.

Henry punches again, and the cow makes a weird loud croaking noise, thrashes, twists, heaves, rises. To Henry's outrage, the cow appears unharmed. He swings open the door, punches the cow on the neck to turn her, then again on her rump, to move her. With shivers and lurches, pissing as she goes, she works her way out the door and is gone.

Mother lies on the dirt floor, legs bent one way, head another, body twisted between like rope, eyes open, not stirring. Above her, the roof jaws down. Bark shingles lie scattered around.

Henry gulps a breath. "Get up!" he yells. "Up up up! Stand up! Mother, don't you lie there, get up!"

She does not move.

Henry sits on the dirt floor. "Up," he says more softly, in the tone of a recommendation. "Try to get up. Get up."

Presently he stops speaking, only stares.

He thinks, for a moment, of nothing at all.

Much as if he is also dead.

A breeze sways the cabin door to creak on its leather hinges, and lifts a smell—the smell of Mother's loosed bowels.

Henry stands. He gets a grip under her arms and with great effort drags her shoulders up onto her bed, lifts her feet in, straightens the twist from her torso. He draws off her dress, then her soiled underclothes. He gazes a moment at her nude slack form. He flings the undergarments out the door, then puts water on a cloth, cleans her, throws the dirty cloth into the yard, puts a blanket over her nakedness. He tries to close her eyes, but they will not stay closed. She seems to stare over his shoulder.

He takes her gingham dress off the floor, twists it in his hands, presses it to his face—it smells of smoke, sweat, earth. He holds it out, considers. She did the washing only a couple of days ago. It looks nice. Mother's a small woman, and the dress is nearly his own size.

The dress seems to fit rather well.

He peers down at himself in awe. He twitches a little to see how the dress moves, and how the light from the doorway picks out the blue threads.

He minces a couple of steps, but quickly stops. No, this isn't how Mother moves. He nudges aside fallen shingles and tries again. He lifts his legs in arcs, imitating the sway of her bowlegged step.

He moves to the hearth where the fire is still burning, puts in a log, and jabs it twice with the poker—one of Mother's mannerisms. A fire, she would say, needs food, like anyone else. He lifts the succotash aside, lids it, takes his bowl off the table, sets it in the soaking bucket. He sways to the water bucket, drinks from the dipper.

When happy, Mother's mutter ran fast and percussive, a sound like the birds in the trees or the frogs in the swamp, so constant that he could choose at any time to ignore it or to bring it into focus and wonder over it. Sweet-fern tea, she would say, is the best thing for ague. When numbed with palsy, roll a ball of rosemary between your hands. If you have gravel in the urine, juice wild garlic into cider. Onto a filmy eye, blow powder of human dung. For the King's Evil, take warm ass's milk. For rabies, eat the liver of a drowned puppy . . .

He sways to the shelf on the wall to straighten things. He takes an armful of shingles off the floor, casts them outside. The chickens pause to cock an eye at him. In the quiet he looks down. Sees himself.

He yanks off the dress and glances left and right: no one has seen him, except the chickens. He rubs the dress between his fingers, feeling the softness. He steps inside, folds the dress, sets it on the table. He picks through variously rusting and damaged tools piled in the corner, takes out a shovel.

Don't! Mother cries.

Henry stops, bewildered.

Don't you think of burying me in this filthy swamp dirt!

"Mother?" Henry says.

Motionless on the bed she says, Put away the shovel.

"What I'm going to do," Henry says, at once confused to hear her, pleased to hear her, and cross to hear what she is saying, "is I'm going to dig a hole, then put you in it."

I am not meant for the dirt. I want my family, and the sea, as you well know.

"Oh, be quiet!" Henry jabs the shovel at the floor. Maybe the cow was such a surprise that she doesn't understand she's dead. "You're dead!" he informs her. "You shouldn't argue with me when you're dead! You're meant for the worms!" He glares at her. She gazes back. He holds her gaze, swears that he will not be the first to turn away.

You promised to return me to the sea.

"How did I promise? When? Anyhow, that was before you were dead! Now you're dead, and everything is different!"

And I will have my family around.

"Dead! Dead! Dead! Quiet!" Henry shouts.

I never wanted to go down in the dirt, she says. And you have always known it, because I have always told you. Don't be indolent and unloving and a betrayer of your own blood and mother.

Henry runs straight out the door with the shovel, scattering the chickens, intending to dig a hole, but he can hear her calling, so he runs into the woods, where, hearing her yet, he drops the shovel and covers his ears, but still hears her nattering. It seems fainter, though. He sets out running.

He runs between the trees of the apple orchard—neglected many years, the weeds and woods growing in, he likes to come here in spring and sit among the blooming trees to listen to the riot of bees. But now the blossoms are gone and the apples still green and hard. He keeps running. He decides to go to the big house that once was his ancestors' house, now Suthers's house. He feels doubtful of approaching the elder Suthers sister, because she always disliked Mother—why, Henry didn't understand. But he might ask one of the slaves, Radnor or Charles or Hollis, for help. Perhaps he can borrow a cart, to transport Mother to the ocean. Perhaps then she will shush.

Ahead, voices.

Not so headlong this time, Henry slows, listens, stops, smells woodsmoke, glimpses the flicker of a fire, steps off the trail, creeps up to Sutherses' fields. The fields run a wide expanse of many acres with the Sutherses' house set at the far side and the barn and the slave shacks away in the corner nearest the swamp. The house is two stories and blazing white, but much else shows decay, with several of the slave shacks long abandoned and half of the fields fallow. But in the others grow rows of head-high corn and some beans, turnips, parsnips, cabbages, carrots, beets. Suthers's business lies in Alexandria, and he rarely spends time at the plantation. It serves to show that he will own a plantation if he wants, and as a place to keep his family out of the way.

The redcoats are setting camp in the fields, with tents already up and cooking fires going. Henry spots the same trio of donkey carts he saw before, and even more soldiers, at least sixty. The redcoats have trampled a great deal of the crop, and many of them roam in and out of the house, carrying rolls of tobacco and bottles of whiskey and wine. Henry wonders if Suthers's daughters and the slaves have fled. Mary already left weeks ago for Alexandria, disappointing Franklin terribly. Some of the redcoats, well into Suthers's whiskey, are clapping and yowling like a pack of cats.

A soldier emerges from the house with a chemise on a pole and waves it about, to general applause. Two officers argue over a horse taken from the barn. One pushes the other in the chest, and they fall to wrestling in the dirt. Another soldier grabs two piglets from the pigpen, slices their throats, then swings the gate and throws rocks to make the others run. They squeal and trot a few steps, then stop, sidle back to the dead pigs, mill about.

A noise behind.

Henry turns too late—a redcoat, girthy as a tanner's vat, rushes him and gives a tremendous shove. Henry flies backward, lands on his back in the dirt of the field. The fat redcoat runs up, adds a kick in Henry's stomach, shouting, "Ho! Ho! It's the one who knocked you onto your arse, Bradley! The scary boy!"

Henry struggles to breathe, works himself to sitting as several soldiers gather and gaze at him. "He didn't knock me over." The jug-eared one, Bradley, comes up, puffing. "I tripped, coincidentally." With him is an officer with a face full of carbuncles and a scarce fuzz on his upper lip. "Look at those mean rat eyes," Bradley says. "That's a spy, if I've ever seen one. Let's kill him."

"I'm no spy," Henry says.

"Just what a spy would say!" Bradley cries victoriously.

This makes Henry angry. He climbs to his feet, but the kick in his gut hurts so that he can't straighten and his head throbs. He tumbles over in the dirt. Surprised, he laughs.

"He's laughing at you, Bradley."

Bradley glowers. "Let's poke a bayonet in him and be done."

"That's maybe a bit much, isn't it?" the officer says.

"Spies are to be executed. That's the King's law."

"Well, in that case, maybe a firing squad."

"I'd like to borrow a cart," Henry says, "to take my dead mother to the ocean."

They gawk.

"He *is* only a boy," the officer says.

"Kill him before he can spy again," Bradley says. "A lifetime of infamy ahead, if we don't kill him now."

"Boy," the officer says, "how old are you?"

The younger he seems, the less likely they are to kill him, Henry supposes. He says in a piping voice, "Why, I'm only but six years of age."

Everyone laughs.

"For a spy, he's a poor liar," the fat one says.

"Lock him in the house," the officer says.

Bradley sighs.

"But I have to go back," Henry says. "Mother's dead."

The officer, however, is turning to a commotion among the tents—a dog chasing chickens. Two of the redcoats seize Henry by the armpits and haul him toward the house. "No no no!" Henry cries. "Mother! I have to go back!" He kicks left and right, until one of the soldiers grunts with annoyance and slams a fist into the side of Henry's head, and the world swings like a hawk wheeling.

Henry sits on the floor of a small room, sized for a narrow bed and a chest of drawers, although it holds neither bed nor chest, but only a single small desk with two drawers and a printed portrait of George Washington held to the wall with pins. Light enters by a window built high into the wall, two feet wide but no taller than a pack of cards. Henry cannot possibly fit through.

Henry can hear Mother's endless mutter so very faintly that he isn't sure if he is imagining it. He feels terribly alone. He huffs. Tears trickle down to spot the floor.

But presently his misery makes him angry. He hits the door and lifts onto his toes to peer out the window. On the field under dying sunlight the soldiers have settled around their fires with bottles of whiskey, rum, and wine. The black soldiers are a strange sight, firearms and military accoutrements having been kept well away from the slaves in Henry's experience. He can see about a half-dozen blacks, all imbibing whiskey alongside the white soldiers, except for one who sits quietly, not drinking—Henry realizes he knows him, Radnor, Suthers's slave who came to Henry in the morning to tell him about Franklin. At that time Radnor had been wearing a linsey-woolsey smock; now he's in a too-small redcoat over a pair of brown trousers that look like they may have been taken from Suthers's wardrobe. The sight of Radnor in a redcoat is as strange to Henry as anything that he has seen this day, and he stares for a long time.

Mr. Suthers said there was no reason to hire an overseer to manage only three field slaves, so he had Mrs. Suthers manage them. When she died, the eldest of the daughters took to giving orders. She said she gave Radnor more liberty than she ought, but Radnor wouldn't run off because he wouldn't leave behind his mute brother Charles and his blind brother Hollis, and he couldn't escape for long while dragging those two behind.

Hollis, Charles, and Radnor have been at the farm all of Henry's life. Father, a Federalist living in the land of Republicans, said that the slaves ought to be free like any other men, for slavery was an immoral institution. Henry figured that he agreed with Father about this, but he stopped repeating it after he had been informed by the second youngest of Suthers's sneering daughters that that *was* what a Phipps would say, since the Phippses had been forced to sell their slaves long ago and now lived like vermin. Let all the slaves be freed, why not, when it wouldn't cost the Phippses a thing? Let everyone live like vermin. Henry said that his grandfather had sold the slaves *because* he knew that owning a man was immoral (this was a thing that Father had suggested once, although even he offered it without much conviction). The second youngest sister said that that was a lie, but if it were true, look what happened to the Phippses. Why would anyone else do such a thing?

Henry booted her in the shin so that she ran off shrieking,

but afterward he did notice that Father never talked about freeing the slaves with anyone who was likely to disagree. And Father, who liked to go and converse with the slaves for a few minutes and afterward proclaim their marvelous intelligence, and Mother, who pursed her lips and said that she pitied them, and even Franklin, who in his slow way endeavored to treat unequivocally with any matter he saw as touching on honor— none of them would have thought for a second of helping a slave to escape, any more than they would have thought of loosing the neighbor's goats.

But, evidently, the British would. Henry studies Radnor's dour face, trying to understand. Henry's first thought was that the redcoats must have purchased Radnor from Suthers, but then he supposes that the redcoats are simply taking Radnor, the same way they are taking the horses, pigs, whiskey, and such. The puzzling question is, what is Radnor now? Is Radnor no longer a slave? Is he British? Henry knows that the British don't have slaves, so Radnor wouldn't be a British slave. And where are Hollis and Charles? Is Radnor leaving behind Hollis and Charles? The eldest Suthers daughter said he never would.

He cannot see Hollis and Charles anywhere, but the brothers are said to have Cherokee blood, and Henry knows they can be as silent and invisible as Indians—even Hollis, despite his blindness—with great skill at roaming in the dark. Sometimes all the slaves in Maryland and Virginia seem to be wandering about at night, evading the slave patrols with little trouble. Henry, who also likes to be out in the night, has seen them and sometimes he has heard Hollis playing the Jew's harp, and Radnor softly singing:

Who stole the pigeon pie
And hid him in the bag o' rye?

Charles, the mute, had once appeared silently behind Henry in the center of an open field and tapped his shoulder. Henry felt his heart might never start again. It was Charles's idea of a joke. He bent to grab his knees, convulsing with his weird coughing laugh.

If Radnor is with the redcoats, Henry thinks, then Radnor can explain to the others that Henry is not a spy. He shouts and bangs on the window, but Radnor doesn't notice, too far away. No one notices. Henry turns to the door and shouts and kicks. He hears soldiers moving around the house, sees a line of lamplight come and go under the door, but no one pays him any heed. Henry shouts and kicks until he is hoarse and both feet hurt. He sits, falls back, lies flat on the floor, panting.

Perhaps he should try to sleep, pass the night. But he fears that Mother will be angry at being left alone. And a whispery sound catches his ear.

"What?" he says.

He's sure it's her. He listens hard, but he can't quite grasp the words. He knows, however, her tone of complaint. He jumps to his feet. "Mother! Stop, stop, stop!" Now that he hears her, he doesn't want to hear her, not in that carping voice. "They've locked me in!" He rattles the door to show her.

Still he can hear her. In a fury he pulls the desk from the wall, topples it over, yanks out the drawers, throws them down. Something clinks on the floor, and he discovers it is a half-dollar, which had been hidden in one of the drawers. Typically this find would be thrilling, but now it is bitterly useless. Mother's voice won't stop. He pockets the half-dollar and stomps around, wondering what else he can find. He feels along the baseboards, then into the gaps between the floorboards. The only light is an egg-shaped moon in the window, and he must seek with his fingertips. There are several pebbles wedged between the boards. One he draws out and examines in the dismal light until he is sure: a worn flint.

He pulls the George Washington off the wall and tears it into thin pieces. He breaks a desk drawer into smaller and smaller pieces, assembles a pile of paper and tinder. Tediously, he works the little flint against one of the steel pins that held the George Washington on the wall. It requires many attempts to throw a spark, and the spark dies before it reaches the paper. He keeps trying. Spark. Spark. Spark.

A spark touches an edge of paper and embers. He puffs the faintest puff of air to give it life. Puff. Puff. Puff. The ember expands over the fragment of paper, bridges to the next.

He adds paper and breath until a yellow fingernail of flame appears. He adds fuel. The flame opens like a tiny fist. Soon it touches the wall. He breaks the legs off the desk, puts them into the flame.

The fire flickers up, drops, regroups, then curtains upward to blacken the ceiling. Smoke fills the room, and Henry puts his mouth to the gap at the bottom of the door to breathe.

It grows extremely hot, however, and Henry begins to think he will be cooked through. Someone beats on the door, then runs off. With a clatter, several pair of boots return down the hallway. A key works in the lock. Henry draws back and crouches, holding his breath. The door swings in. When the soldiers fall away from the smoke, coughing, Henry throws himself forward. He crashes into one of the redcoats—knocking him into two others—rights himself, and runs down the hall, away from the billowing smoke and the coughing, flailing soldiers, to the far door, and out.

He sprints through the dark for the safety of woods, shouts rising behind him. A musket shot follows—the round slaps earth on Henry's left. But no more follow, and as he gains the trees, he feels the beating of joy, and he laughs.

He circles to the other side of the fields and lingers to watch the house burn—in a few minutes it is wrapped by an enormous coruscation. A river of rising heat wavers the stars. The redcoats laugh, sing—and try to throw a pig carcass near enough to cook.

Henry is near the barn, and the redcoats are watching the fire, so Henry slips inside and finds a cart, well crafted, with two spoked wheels rimmed with iron and a open box large enough to hold Mother. The shafts might be harnessed to a small pony or a large dog. Henry pulls it into the night.

Dragging the cart through the woods he watches for Hollis and Charles, vaguely hoping that he might convince them to help him. To return to the cabin while avoiding the open field he takes a circuitous route, yanking the cart over roots and rocks, through mud and bushes, driven by fuming stubbornness.

He arrives exhausted and dispirited, and after so much effort to pull the empty cart such a short distance, it seems it will be impossible to haul Mother to the sea. In a fit he runs to grab the shovel. But Mother shouts, No no no! Not the dirt! Henry! Please!

Henry says, "Damn damn damn!" and beats the ground with the shovel.

She says, Don't use that word that way.

He sits on the ground, tears coming. "Mother, I wish you were alive."

She says, I know.

He says, "I wish Father were not in prison."

She says, Your poor father.

He says, "I don't want to be like Father."

She says, Hush.

He says, "I'm tired. I hate this. I only want things to be as they were, when we were all together. Why is our luck so bad? Must I go on?"

She says with immense gentleness, Yes, but not until you are ready.

He sags, rolls onto his side. Sleep comes as he lies on the bare earth.

Later he wakes in the dark, lifts up, crawls into the house and onto the bed, beside her. She's cold, stiff, murmuring. He sleeps.

In the first ruddy morning light she's still murmuring, which is pleasant, until he remembers that she is dead. He jumps from the bed. She has a terrible pallor, which is greening. A smell. He runs outside.

He sits on the tree stump where they slaughter chickens, watches the day gather light. The empty sky mingles orange, pink, and blue into some color that Henry cannot name. Snakes of mist, a couple of feet high, writhe over the rows of the garden, and the beanpoles jut out like spears. On one side of the garden hunches the trellis where scuppernongs grow and will be ripening soon. Mother always gave the first ripe ones to Henry.

The shovel lies nearby, and when he looks at it, he hears her say, at some distance, Not here, Henry, not in the swamp dirt. Take me with you.

He says, "I can't—"

The cart will move fine on the roads, she says. Don't be ungrateful.

He shouts, "You'll stink and—"

He stops himself. He doesn't want the black spirit to take her. In truth he wants her with him.

He stomps over to the barn, fetches out the pickle barrel. His great-great-grandfather—the last in the family to possess any noteworthy skill in crafting useful objects—had the idea that he would pickle large quantities of cabbage and eggs and take them to town to sell. He sealed a tobacco hogshead watertight and made the barrel's special lid himself. The lid edge is beveled and held in place by six rotating iron latches. These latches can be cranked down to create a watertight seal. Henry opens the lid, tosses out the cucumbers and eggs and onions in a gleaming pile in the dirt, and rolls the barrel into the house. Mother has stiffened terribly, and the barrel is scarcely large enough—Henry begins gently, but as he grows angry he wrenches her limbs, cracking joints, tearing muscles. Shoving and twisting he works Mother into the barrel with the brine. During this activity she mutters. He twists the latches to close the lid, listens.

To Baltimore, she says.

"During the last year, our financial condition has become a little discomposing," Father said the last time Henry saw him. "But the Phippses' luck will turn now, sure enough."

When Father's debts mounted in Alexandria, then Washington, then Annapolis, and he could not enter those cities for fear of arrest, he began gambling in Baltimore, a two- or three-day journey by foot.

When Father lost money in Baltimore, too, he sold the wheelbarrow and a musket for a small stake and departed for Baltimore to win back what he owed. Mother fell into bed with the black spirit, staring at the granite wall. But after only a couple of days she rose, and she began to work day and night with furious agitation. She told Franklin, who was now seventeen years old, that he had reached the age of manhood, and he ought to find a way to earn money to pay off Father's debts, so that Father could stay home, and they could all be together.

She was surely aware that she was stoking Franklin's notions of honor. Franklin avoided drink and games, debts and lassitude. He refrained from talking overmuch and would never, ever, break his word. Henry understood without pausing to contemplate it that Franklin did these things in reaction to Father's fecklessness, in the same way he understood that only Mother's efforts held the family together and after straining at this task for years the unity of the family had become her absolute preoccupation.

When Father returned from Baltimore he had lost even his hat and bore upon his head a sort of floppy mat that he had woven out of cattail leaves. He had been home for a couple of days and was whittling himself a pipe stem and talking about a horse that he would bet on, if only he had money, when Franklin entered the cabin, halted in the center of the room, and announced that he had joined the army. "I have here the fifty dollars bounty that I have been paid," he said, "and I will be paid eight dollars monthly, and I will receive one hundred sixty acres on discharge at war's end."

Then he stood regarding his feet.

Henry saw Mother blanch and feared that she would immediately lie down sick.

"But," she said, "we need this family together. I have always said so."

"We need money," Franklin said.

"I've said we need money, but, Franklin, not like this! Do you understand how much your father owes? You'll be in the army for years on years paying his debts. And all that time you'll be away from us!"

Franklin cleared his throat. "And, also, there is the national honor," he said.

"The what? What? What is that? Did you say national honor?" Mother leaned toward Franklin with her tiny body, and he bent backward as if wasps swarmed before him. "The national honor? Did the national honor give birth to your very enormous self? Will the national honor tend your hurts? Will the national honor be there when you are in a position of need? National honor! As useless as a rock in a field. You will leave us here, and possibly you will be killed, which perhaps you deserve, but we, your family, will be without you, and do you think we deserve that?"

She talked like this for a while. Franklin peered at his feet, said nothing.

Then Mother said, "And, what of Miss Mary?"

Franklin seemed dismayed that his feet lay so far down below. "She's gone," he said, "to live in Alexandria. She left a note. She says she doesn't care to see me again."

Mother said, "Oh no."

Everyone gazed at Franklin. Franklin did not move.

"Ah, Franklin," Father said at last. "I am sorry. Of all the aches, heartache is the most terrible ache."

Mother said, "But this is no reason to go to the army!"

Henry watched Father. Father, an avowed Federalist, often argued against the Republicans, Madison, and the war. "The Republicans decided to start this war! It's on their account!" he had cried. "They said Canada would welcome our liberating army! The Southern Republican poltroons who've never in their lives met a Canadian. So we marched into Canada, and lo the Canadians smashed us and slaughtered us and threw us out on our ears, and for good measure took our forts along the Lakes and roused the Indians against us, so that we have spent the last two years scrabbling to get back to even, never-you-mind conquering Canada. Because we're led by Madison's steaming idiocy and the Republican rabble, promoting incompetent allies in the army, enriching their friends, spending the nation into fathomless debt, propelling our boys into a hell of death and illness and amputations. The papers say that in the encampments around Sacketts Harbor the streets run with human excrement and every hour the bells toll another death. You've seen the soldiers who come home from the north— starved, wearing rags, half-mad, begging along the roads, sleeping in mud . . . "

Father could go on this way at considerable length. But now—now Father only rubbed his jowls. He, too, studied Franklin's boots. Mother turned in place, throwing ugly glances between Father and Franklin. Finally she shrieked with frustration.

"Dear," Father said, "please." He held up a hand. "The military duty is, after all, perhaps a thing only a man can understand."

Mother's eyes opened wide, and she looked as if she might pounce on Father and eat him.

Father hurried on. "Franklin, you are a good son. You are, in inarguable fact, a better son than I deserve. You have a strong sense of duty, as befits a Phipps." He blinked rapidly, as if thinking of the duty-mindedness of the Phippses made him sentimental. "Your mother raises worthy considerations," he said, "but another aspect that must be considered is the science of luck. As we all know, I have had a horrible string of bad fortune. But a thing going up must eventually go down, and our luck has gotten as bad as it possibly could."

"A thing going up," Henry said, puzzled, "must return down, but won't a thing going down stay down?"

"Ah," Father said, "yes, it's an imperfect metaphor, perhaps—well, the science of luck, which I have spent all of my life examining, in one way or another, doesn't fit any exact analogy. But perhaps, to give it a metaphor that your mother will understand very well, I should say that it is like the tide: what goes out, must come in. Pascal and Fermat and, most importantly, Bernoulli, were in the Phipps family library, before debts forced us to sell the books, and those logicians showed via inviolable reasoning that if you flip a coin many, many times the heads and the tails will balance out. Well, we've flipped tails so many times that we're due for a great long run of heads, and it certainly would be foolish to turn aside when such incredible fortune is due. I'll take to Baltimore the bounty money paid to Franklin and discharge my debts. It will mark a turning. The Phipps family will rise from this point, and you, Franklin, have created the moment from which we will rise."

"No no no," Mother said. "Not like this. You've said yourself, the war is the design of buffoons."

But Father smiled as if to himself, swung his arms out wide—he nearly hit Henry in the face—and cried, "Good fortune is before us!"

Mother collapsed a little, and Henry watched her with dread. But a moment later she lifted and said, "Well, I suppose it must turn, finally. Nothing can go downward forever, can it?" And so on she muttered, which, Henry noted, at least meant that she hadn't taken sick. Then he slipped out to walk awhile in the night-dark woods.

Franklin packed a bag and set out the next day to fulfill the terms of his enlistment. Shortly afterward, Father departed for Baltimore to pay his debts.

In a letter that arrived a week later, Father explained that he had had solemn intentions. But the thirst for drink was a kind of devil in him, and he thought surely it was harmless to stop along the way to purchase a hat and a dram of whiskey. That very afternoon a wind blew his hat away down a fast-moving creek, and nothing went right afterward. He gambled away Franklin's bounty money, borrowed more with which to win back what he had lost, gambled away what he had borrowed, tried to slip out of Baltimore at night in a cartload of manure, but fell asleep and was betrayed by his own snores. The sheriff pulled him out by one foot and locked him in the debtor's prison. With this letter came a second letter from a lawyer representing Father's various creditors, explaining that Father would be held until nine hundred twenty-five dollars of debt and interest were paid.

The sum was so large as to be absurd, yet Mother did not take sick. "Not like the tide," she said. "It is like your father is a nail. But no one hammers a nail forever, and fate won't do it to your father."

The weeks ground on through spring into summer. Franklin wrote that he trooped here and there to fight British raiders, arriving every time to news that the redcoats had already departed. Father wrote from prison to say that he had befriended an amiable mouse. "We'll keep our spirits," Mother said to Henry, "and all will come out right." She worked relentlessly, in the garden and the field, cleaning, cooking, into the night at the table making embroidery to sell, all the time muttering.

Until one day when Suthers, who spent most of his time at his office in Alexandria, came to the big house to visit with his daughters. On a gleaming morning near the end of June, Henry was engaged in his own private peregrinations when he came to Suthers's fields and saw Mother and Suthers standing in the long double track from the road to the house, talking. Henry stepped back to watch. He couldn't hear what they said, but Mother clasped her hands and leaned forward as she spoke, plainly pleading.

Suthers shook his head.

As Mother turned away, she clutched her right temple. Henry moaned. For the rest of the day he cursed and ran around kicking mushrooms, throwing rocks at frogs, smashing flowers, unwilling to return to the cabin. When he drifted back at twilight, exhausted, he found her as he feared: silent, elbows on the table, face in her hands. She whispered of a pain on one side of her head like a hole through her skull, and a scraping on the other side like a spoon inside a melon. Soon she lay abed, her right thumb in her opposite hand, her left eye open, her face to the granite wall. She asked Henry to snuff the lantern. The light, she whispered, plunged spikes into her eyes.

Henry feared—as he did every time—that this time she might never rise again. The sickness had always passed before, but when, how, and why were mysteries. Once, when Mother lay abed with her black mood, Father had come with a shovel and tried to pry her out. "Am I not master in my home!" he roared. Mother moaned piteously. But, when Father nearly had her tipped out of the bed, she sprang up and punched him in the neck. Father dropped to the floor in a faint. Mother lay down and did not rise again for a week.

The days dragged, on and on. Henry fed Mother a little, when she would eat. Otherwise, he had no guidance beyond his own impulses. He worked the garden and fields haphazardly, ate wrinkled dry little potatoes from the cellar, caught catfish and frogs from the river. At times he grew suddenly, terribly vexed, his entire body hot in an instant, as if a musket charge had gone off, and he threw down his work and ran away to a narrow limestone cave he knew.

Well hidden by brambles on the steep bank of a muddy creek, the cave was like a big open mouth, tapering to a blocked throat at the back, where a crack in the stone rose to make a natural chimney. He brought in hay to lie on, and sometimes he made a fire and spent a night. He liked lying in the complete dark at night, listening to the slop of the creek and the scuffle of the brambles working against one another when the air moved. Henry had never told anyone about the cave, but Radnor and his brothers knew—the slaves seemed to know about every kind of place like this. "You can't tell Mother about the secret cave," Henry would say. Radnor pursed his lips as if irritated to have to state the obvious and said, "Of course. It's a *secret* cave."

Through July Henry spent several nights in the cave. Returning to the cabin he felt guilty for leaving Mother. But she said nothing, lay in the same place she always did, face to the wall. August came in like the hot breath of a dog, and day followed day, and the best part was sitting in the cooling of first dark to watch the fireflies rise from the fields, as if the earth were burning with cold fire. Except for his worries about Mother, Henry's days were rather fine. Sometimes he went to the edge of Suthers's fields to watch the slaves work and the comings and goings at the house. He laid rabbit snares of a

design that Franklin had taught him, with considerable success, except the foxes often found the rabbits before he could
recover them, leaving a scatter of fur and one snared foot. He
passed entire afternoons by the creeks fishing with a string and
hook. He saw how Suthers's pigs evaded the heat and mosquitoes and biting flies by covering themselves with mud, and he
undressed and did the same.

He came home one day to find the cabin door open, rags
and broken things thrown into the yard. Mother appeared in
the doorway with a pot under one arm, chiseling the char with
a hatchet. "Henry! Look at you!" He looked down. He had
attempted to rinse off the mud, but he had missed some places.
"And what have you been doing with this pot while I rested?"
She struck it with the hatchet. "You couldn't keep a slab of
soap clean!"

Henry had such mixed feelings of relief and anger that he
could only stare and hold himself still, waiting for the anger to
fall. He didn't realize that he was crying until she reached and
touched his face. "Oh dear," she said. "My temper." She put
down the pot, hugged him, stood him at arm's length, nar-
rowed an eye. "I know it's been a hardship of late, but think of
your father. He's in a prison with rats and terrible miasmas and
the worst sorts of men. How much worse is it for him? I've
decided we must go to Baltimore." She returned to striking the
inside of the pot with the hatchet, still talking, almost shouting.
"Go get everything you can from the garden! As much as we
can carry!"

He set to pulling a row of carrots. The year's second plant-
ing, they weren't much bigger than his littlest finger. Sweating
in the endless heat, he began to seethe. Mother lay abed for
two months, no help at all, then she rises up and tells him he's
done a poor job of cleaning and sends him to work the garden!
He reared back and kicked his pile of carrots. Then he turned
for the woods and ran.

He lazed in the cool damp dark of the cave, daydreaming of Baltimore, where he had never been. He imagined a city of clamorous dazzlement. As evening fell he feared that when he returned Mother would be angry and tell him that he was as bad as all the other Phipps men. Which would be unfair, and thinking of it he became upset, and he resolved to pass the night here in the cave.

In the morning he slept until the sun had gotten well up. The sound of the whippoorwill woke him. It was a signal he shared with Radnor.

Radnor stood outside the cave quiet and grave and would not speak until Henry grew cross and began stamping his feet. Radnor said that Franklin had deserted, had been caught, had been sentenced to the firing squad, and by now Franklin was already dead.

Henry greases the axle of the handcart, pushes it to the cabin door, rolls the pickle barrel over, loads the pickle barrel. Mother mutters, Baltimore. She mutters, Your father, your father, your father.

Henry says, "But, Franklin."

Mother says, If they did shoot him, heaven forfend, you will need a second barrel. A big one.

In the yard Henry dumps a huge pile of feed for the chickens, then he gathers from off the ground several pickled cucumbers, carrots, beets, eggs. He scuffs off the dirt, drops them into a bag. He adds some of the bread and salted meat that Mother set aside for the trip to Baltimore. He spits on his hands, rubs them, lifts the cart handles, starts for the road.

Baltimore. It will be fine to go to Baltimore. But what he really wants is to help Father out of prison. To do that he will need money.

CHAPTER 2

Franklin Phipps sees three, sometimes four, stars. They twitch and shiver as he gasps. Ordered to keep his arms at his sides, he grinds his fingernails into his palms. His thoughts chase round and round. He'd tried to explain—what he'd done, what was right in the circumstances. But a fat-lipped officer in a smoky office in Alexandria said that he'd deserted, simple as that.

He had wanted to help his father, his brother, his mother, Mary Suthers. He'd helped none of them. To Mary—Miss Mary, little Mary Suthers—he had only brought shame and dishonor.

The Phipps family land had been lost by Franklin's father on cards staked by Mary's father—Mr. Jeremiah Suthers. When Franklin was born, the Phippses still owned their land and the house, although the house had become tumbledown and mossy. Franklin has a faint memory of peering out a second floor window at the fields where Father startled flocks of crows with a gravel-loaded blunderbuss.

At that time the cabin in the hillside was abandoned, but the Suthers family had been its last tenants. When Father was a boy, he lived in the house, and the Sutherses lived in the cabin, and Father and Jeremiah knew each other well. But Jeremiah's mother died of phthisis, and Jeremiah's father was a violent drunk, and at twelve Jeremiah ran away to Alexandria. Not long after, Jeremiah's father was trying to shoot a rat, hit himself in the foot, and died of septic. Jeremiah Suthers, now orphaned, worked as a laborer on the Alexandria docks and within a few years had made a place for himself as a small-time merchant and general opportunist. Everyone called him Suthers, and as time went on he grew his wealth and reach to become one of the city's most powerful men.

After Father had gambled away the Phippses' estate, Suthers took ownership. He allowed the Phippses to live in the same cabin where he had grown up, and to work as tenant farmers on the same field where he had sweated as a boy.

Why Suthers did this, Franklin was never sure. Father said it was because they had been friends as children, but Suthers didn't seem very friendly, and it passed Franklin's mind that the friendship between Father and Suthers might be somewhat imaginary on Father's side.

Suthers had the estate house fixed up, loaded it with cherry-wood furniture, glass-fronted bookcases, blue and white china, and French silverware, then moved in his family. They had no house slaves because Mrs. Suthers—who was several years older than Suthers and known for her practicality—didn't want blacks in the house, and anyway said she preferred to do her own chores, perhaps to distract herself from whatever thoughts she might have if she were not doing chores. Suthers, who at heart was rather miserly, approved.

Suthers had no sons but four daughters. Mrs. Suthers died in childbirth with the fourth, Mary, who came some six years after the next youngest daughter. Mary was nearly the same age as Franklin, and she was often out carrying around a frog or a baby squirrel or gosling. Franklin had once watched her climb an oak into the high, thin, swayingest branches, higher than even he himself would have dared, because she wanted to peek into a jay's nest. The eggs, she told Franklin, were the color of sky.

She had dark hair and narrow-set eyes in a face that tapered forward in an unusual way, somewhat like a badger. This was not pretty in any kind of usual way, yet Franklin was not sure that she was not pretty, or perhaps the question was somehow set aside by the force of her presence. She didn't seem to care about whether she was pretty, as the other girls did. Often her hair got loose and wild and her clothes dirty while she hunted turtles or caught tadpoles or dug worms to feed a baby bird she had found.

Franklin wooed her in secret. They met nights beneath the old walnuts. Sometimes that fall as Franklin talked with her, a nut dropped straight onto his head. He didn't notice. Franklin Phipps had always been big—big head and big shoulders and big hands and big belly and big thighs and big feet. If he were made of clay, he might have been divided and made into three of Mary.

The time with her was dizzying and marvelous, and when he received her note he felt as if an axe had struck his heart. She wrote that she was sorry, but she had realized that it could never be right between them, because her family had money, and his did not—he had worried about this, and they had talked about this, and she had said it didn't matter. Evidently she had changed her mind. It was the most terrible thing that had ever happened to him, and he went the next day to the army office.

For six months the army marched him, sent him to sleep in the mud, dressed him in old boots and too small clothes, fed him badly, didn't pay him—none of it mattered to Franklin, because he noticed only his heart's misery.

Then a letter reached him, from Mary.

She wrote that shortly before he had enlisted she had noticed a change in herself of a feminine nature. She did not understand it, and, to her regret, she had spoken to her sisters about it. Her sisters told her it was nothing, and then they wrote to Suthers. So it was that Mary's father appeared at the house, and he was the one who informed her that she was with child. When she admitted that Franklin was the father, Suthers had a note forged and delivered to Franklin. He had Mary bundled away to Alexandria where she was locked in a house with a nurse. He wanted to keep the matter quiet.

In the months since then Mary had attempted to flee without success, and she wasn't sure whether she would ever be able to transmit this letter to Franklin, for the nurse was like an owl watching a rabbit den.

The young man who delivered the letter told Franklin the end of the story. He had been in the street at night when he heard a hiss overhead. There, a girl was leaning out a window. She threw down to him a silver candelabrum and a letter. He was to deliver the letter; the candelabrum—which she had torn out of the wall—was his payment. The young man confessed to Franklin that he ordinarily might have kept the silver and thrown away the letter, except that he could not stop thinking of the remarkable vision of Mary's anguished face bearing down on him in the moonlight.

That night Franklin put on civilian clothing and set out. He walked without rest and arrived in Alexandria in the deep dark of the next night. However, when he located the house that Mary described in her letter, the door hung open, and when he searched the rooms, he found no one.

Confused and distraught, he returned to the street. Wandering on the cobbles, he'd not gone far when Mary herself appeared beside him and tugged him into a side alley.

Uncharacteristically—Mary said—the nurse had gone out in the night, leaving her alone. Perhaps she believed Mary was asleep. Regardless, Mary took the opportunity to slip away. She had hoped that Franklin would arrive soon and stayed nearby to watch.

Then she kissed Franklin, took his hand, and led him on through the night. The kiss made Franklin stupendously happy, and he told Mary they must be married. At the edge of the city they crept into a stable to pass the night.

They had been, however, followed. In the dawn twilight a sergeant and five soldiers arrived to claim Franklin. The soldiers caught Franklin unawares or he might have beaten them off. As it was he fractured one man's clavicle with a downward blow and threw another man into the neighboring stall where a mule kicked him before the sergeant leveled a loaded pistol in Franklin's face.

Into the barn came a cadaverous man in civilian garb, taller even than Franklin. This was Lodowicke, Suthers's principal associate. The soldiers fell back, and Lodowicke crouched before Franklin and Mary. With one hand he removed his hat, showing his bald head, while with the other hand he pulled a knife just far enough from the lapel of his jacket to ensure Franklin and Mary could see it. He spoke in whispers. Suthers himself had alerted the army to Franklin's presence in Alexandria, Lodowicke said, and Suthers had the connections to ensure that a firing squad was ordered. Once Mary was widowed, Suthers intended to buy the interest and compliance of a young man of proper station to make a respectable husband and claim the baby as his own. Then Lodowicke seized Mary by the arm and pulled her away.

Franklin leaped after them, but the sergeant put a foot out and tripped him flat onto his face. He was tied and taken to the army office in Washington. After a night locked up, he was set atop a donkey and returned to his regiment. That had been the day before.

This morning the regimental doctor gave Franklin a white cap and a white robe with a square of red stitched over the heart. Franklin's unit sergeant winked at him—this gesture seemed strange and cruel to Franklin—and waved for Franklin to follow. He led Franklin into a field where a grave had been dug beside an open coffin. The sergeant told

Franklin to kneel with the grave on his right and the coffin on his left. He pulled down the white cap to cover Franklin's eyes. "Keep your hands to your sides," he said. "Or we'll tie them back."

Now silence and stillness lie on the field, as if it is enclosed in amber. Until the clatter of a click beetle startles Franklin, and he nearly topples into the grave.

"Open pan!" the colonel calls. "Handle cartridge!" The weapons rasp and rattle. The men spit cartridge paper. "Prime! Shut pan! Charge with cartridge! Draw rammers! Ram cartridge!" Franklin has followed these steps hundreds of times, but now he hears them anew, with dreadful suspense. "Return rammers! Make ready! Take aim!" The men let out long, loud breaths, like sighs. "Fire!"

Muskets explode.

Franklin pitches backward between coffin and grave, convulsing, screaming Mary's name. His muscles clench; the breath goes from him. The white cap comes off, and he gazes at the sky. He cannot breathe. The sky darkens, comes down with a furious rushing noise that must be the beating of angels to bear him away.

Thinking of Mary he cries, "I'm sorry!"

But it seems he's not yet died. The hurt in his gut relaxes slightly. Everything appears to have detached from everything else. A warm wet place in his undergarments spreads.

This feeling snags his attention. It comes to him that he's fully alive. They missed! He breathes shallowly, trying to be quiet, play dead. Will they try to put him in front of the firing squad again, or finish him with a pistol? Hearing the sergeant approach, he holds his breath, but his heart is trying to throw itself out of his chest.

"Phipps," the sergeant says. "You're fine, Phipps."

All of Franklin is tingling and needles, but he doesn't want to be killed lying down. He flails a little, nearly rolls into the grave, finally sits up. Should he run? He's not sure that his legs will carry him.

"A reprieve, Phipps!" the colonel calls. "No lead in the muskets! We're going to need your rifle!"

Franklin looks around, sees afresh the scalding bright green of the world, the depthless sky. The ranked soldiers laugh or smirk or stare at the ground. The sergeant is standing in the coffin, grinning down at Franklin. "Up," he says. "Let's change your trousers."

Franklin moves his hands weakly against the earth.

The sergeant takes him under the shoulder, pulls him up, helps him stumble toward the camp. "Bit a of a shock?" he asks. "Colonel had strict orders from the army office in Washington to put you before the firing squad. He says to me, 'That Phipps, how old is he?' I tell him you're a big one, but only seventeen. I tell him you follow orders well, and you never give no trouble, but this one thing, which was because you had a girl, and she's in a womanly way. Not like some of these men we've dragged back from their homes three or four times. Then I tell him you're as good a shot with a rifle as I ever saw. Colonel says, 'By God!' And he thinks a little. Then he says, 'Someone at the army office doesn't like this man, but I can't understand it. The order says to put him before the firing squad, and so we will. But we'll do it like this—' He's a lawyer, you know. And you see how he did it. Clever, wasn't he? How did you like it?"

No answer rises to mind.

An hour later the colonel assembles the regiment, Franklin among them. The colonel climbs onto a rail fence, looks down, wavers, steps down a rail. The colonel served in the War of Independence, but he has been writing property contracts for thirty years, and he has grown bald, fat, and nearsighted. His most impressive feature is his educated tone. He tells the men that the British have landed a force of several thousand men at

Benedict. They are marching on Baltimore. Or maybe Washington. No one knows yet.

"You men," he says, then stops, takes a piece of paper from his pocket, peers at it. "You men," he says again, reading, "will need all of your strength and conviction. These British troops are experienced, hardened soldiers. These are the same troops who fought under Wellington at Badajoz, and at Salamanca. They have defeated the finest who carried Napoleon's eagles, and they are by legend the finest soldiers in the world." He pauses, and the men look at one another, wondering, perhaps, how far the colonel plans to go down this rhetorical pathway.

"But," the colonel says. "Be not afraid. For we have the advantage of knowledge of the land. We have the support of our families, friends, and neighbors on all sides. And, most important, we possess the advantages of American courage and fortitude, shaped in the colonies, tempered on the frontier. These British have never encountered American soldiers on American soil, and when they do, if we fight as we can, then I assure you, they will rue the day they set foot on this continent."

The words seem well considered and fine enough, yet the colonel delivers them flat. He puts away the piece of paper, takes out a handkerchief, blows his nose. Everyone is silent. He seems to be done speaking. A few of the men cheer, perhaps sardonically. Dismissed, they break up and scatter. Except Franklin, who stands trying to think of what to think, of whether to think, terror still warm in his veins. The instant when he had been dead yet not dead, and the rush of wings, returns to him with awful disorientation.

Henry walks between the shafts of the cart. Sometimes grief squeezes his throat, and he can scarcely breathe. Mother says things, but he isn't listening just now.

In time he becomes aware of footsteps behind him. He

scowls, pulls harder. He doesn't care to address questions about his situation. But the steps draw up and then keep pace with him, and finally with a feeling of loathing, he glances over.

He's surprised to see a girl. She's perhaps two or three years older than himself, with skin the color of mushrooms and bruises under her eyes. She gazes at him.

Henry says, "What?"

"Do you have any money?"

"No."

"You're pretty small to be dragging barrels around like a donkey."

"I'm not small. And it's just one barrel."

She laughs. "The big donkey is all alone and has no money. It's too bad."

"I'm fine!" he says. "I don't need help!"

"*I don't need help!*" she mocks. She walks with speed, easily outpacing him. Soon she disappears around a bend.

As the day advances, he sees others on the road: a group of a half-dozen men in fine black frock coats trotting their horses, a whistling slave leading an enormous pig, a fast-moving carriage with shrouded windows, a wagon loaded with beehives. None of the travelers speak to Henry. Wet all over with sweat, occasionally raising a shoulder to brush at the mosquitoes on his neck and face, Henry trudges past fields of corn and tobacco in long curving rows, past the deep old forest, past a cabin with a half-dozen barking dogs, past a long pond that ripples with the movements of water striders. Mother whispers, "Baltimore. Baltimore."

When he sees the girl again she is sitting in the shade of a tree, sipping water from a leather bottle. Neither speaks as he passes.

A minute later he hears her coming up behind him, again. She strolls alongside him for several minutes. "Where're you taking it?"

"Baltimore."

She laughs. "If you can drag that all the way to Baltimore, I can be the Queen of Maryland. How old are you?"

Henry resents the question, but somehow he doesn't want her to go away again. Mother says, She may be dangerous. Henry laughs, though laughing takes his breath and leaves him wheezing. Mother says, Well, she may be.

Forgetting what the girl asked, Henry says, "Mother died." His eyes tear up. "Father's in the debtor's jail, in Baltimore."

The girl angles her head. "That seems a poor sort of a joke."

"It's not a joke."

"Too bad about that," she says. "Too bad. Could be worse. Could be you never knew your mother, or your father."

Henry grunts, regrets saying anything. "Bad luck always turns, Father says."

"Ha," the girl says. "I hardly know anything about anything, but I know that's not true. I've known girls with so much bad luck you could drown in it."

"Well, Father doesn't need luck anyway. I'm going to get him out."

The girl walks in silence a minute, then asks, "You haven't any other family?"

"My brother is away with the Maryland regiment. I'm told he's dead, but I don't believe it."

"You should go to family, or a friend of your family."

"The Sutherses' house burned. The Suthers women were never friendly to us anyway, except Mary, and she's been gone. There's no one else, because everyone has grown angry with Father over money."

"Go to your brother's regiment. They'll take you as a cook or drummer boy or let you roll around the cannonballs or some such thing."

"Army pay for a soldier is bad; for a boy they will pay less or nothing. And Father owes a great deal of money."

"Too bad about that."

They walk for a while.

"Too bad," she says, in a softer tone, "that someone won't show you where the war is. At a war, there're soldiers with money and nowhere to spend it, and there're all sorts of things just lying around. A war is like a rich man dancing with a hole in his pocket."

"Do you know where the war will be?" he asks.

"Good thing you don't need any help."

"Oh, go away," he says.

She moves ahead for a few minutes, but then stops to work something out of her shoe, until Henry catches up again. "What's in the barrel?"

"Mother."

"What?"

Henry stops, opens the barrel, shows her. The girl looks at Mother, at Henry, at Mother. She says, "Oh."

He closes the barrel, starts off again. He hears Mother humming. He says, "She wants to be sent out to sea."

"It's foolish to go all the way to Baltimore to go to the sea."

"She wants her family together. Then the sea."

"A sensible person might hide the barrel somewhere and return for it later, with the family."

Henry had never considered this. He stops a moment, then starts forward again. "It's difficult to hear her when she's far away."

"You're a funny boy. Are you sure you haven't any money at all?"

"I have a half-dollar, is all."

When they come to a hill, she helps with the cart.

They have traveled a mile or so when a bearded man on horseback catches up alongside them, slows to their pace, stares at the girl, says, "You're too goddamn pretty to be clumping along in the dirt. I've room here." He pats his saddle.

The girl doesn't look up. "Leave me be," she says, "or my brother will box your ears."

Henry startles—brother?—catches himself, sets his shoulders back. The man looks him over and laughs. But he spurs his horse ahead. "Enjoy your trudge, filthy bitch."

Henry stops and stares, quivering with fury. "Come on," the girl says, moving ahead. "By the way, that's what good you can be to me," she calls back. "If you were wondering."

They strike now a larger road. To the right lies Baltimore; to the left lies Bladensburg. From Bladensburg, the road continues to Washington.

Henry sets down the cart. His shoulders burn, dust grits his tongue, and the shafts of the cart have shaped blisters into his palms.

The girl starts left.

Henry looks after her. Mother will be angry if he turns from Baltimore. Already she mutters ominously. He calls after the girl, "Are you going to the war?"

"Too bad you can't pay anyone to show you where the war is," she calls back. "But you might take a chance. Might be where I'm going."

He watches her walking away, feels desolate, feels angry with Mother for making him feel guilty, feels she has no right to do so, being dead. He grabs the cart shafts, starts after the girl.

From the barrel Mother cries, No no! Henry! Where are you going? Go to Baltimore. To your father. Baltimore.

Henry pulls the cart after the girl.

Mother cries, Your father is in Baltimore! Go to him! Take me to him! Ungrateful child!

"I need money to buy Father out!" Henry yells. "I can't do him any good with no money."

Mother cries, Your father will know what to do, you're only a boy, and we're all scattered. Turn around! Turn around!

The girl stares back at him.

Henry puts his tongue out at her. He plods grimly.

"If you're bound to tail after me," the girl says, "you might as well know my name is Abigail."

Henry tells the girl his name.

Mother shouts at him for nearly a mile, then falls to mumbling.

The fires of the army bivouac glimmer a half mile ahead, below the town of Bladensburg.

But nearer to hand is a tobacco field beaten down by a chaos of tents and canopies, campfires, wagons, horses, carriages, livestock, dogs, cats, screaming babies, a preacher preaching from a wagon, barrels of whiskey, rum, and wine, crated fighting cocks, and all kinds of people—Abigail says they are hangers-on, soldiers' wives and children, sutlers, farriers, gamblers, whiskey dealers, tobacconists, seamstresses, butchers, spies, curiosity seekers, ne'er-do-wells, and opportunists.

"And," Abigail says, "ladies of modesty such as myself." But Henry already understood that she was a prostitute. He had traveled with Father to Washington and Alexandria and had seen the harlots about, at the taverns and gambling places. He understood they were looked down upon, but he had a notion of prostitutes as a kind of a practical service, like gravediggers or providers of stud dogs. Once Henry had been with Mother when she went to try to sell some lace to the Suthers sisters. Father at the time was away in Annapolis, and the eldest sister said, "Don't you worry about the city women?" Mother replied serenely, "Oh no. His apparatus doesn't work that way anymore."

As they enter the encampment, a man with a face craggy as a walnut glares at Henry. "What's in the barrel?"

"My mother," Henry says.

Three small boys crowd in and jeer, "Show it! Liar! Show it!"

Mother says, Leave me be. "Better to let everyone see," Henry says. "If they know there's nothing of value in the barrel, no one will steal it." Well, Mother says, for goodness sake, preserve my dignity. Henry opens the barrel, adjusts her limbs, stands aside.

The boys fall back, screeching with delight. "His mother! He pickled his mother!"

People gather. Henry stands on the cart. "Clear room! Make space! Everyone can look, but give her room!"

Mother murmurs, It is a light affliction, which is for but a moment.

A woman says, clucking, "Ought to be a Christian burial."

"I'm taking her to my father, and then to be buried at sea," Henry says. "She says that's what she wants." He doesn't mind the attention. He tells the story of how she died. He tells it in a way that makes the crowd laugh.

"You seem awfully cheerful," a man calls, "for a boy whose mother is freshly pickled."

"Well, of course I still hear her," Henrys says. "So it hardly matters about the cow."

They laugh again. One by one they come to the open barrel. People go and bring back others. He's asked to tell the story again, and by the time crowd thins, they're calling him the mad boy.

Abigail has vanished; the sun has dropped away; the stars make shining holes in the sky. A warty, kettle-shaped woman lifts onto her toes, looks into the barrel, asks, "Georgina? Is that her? It looks like Georgina."

"That's not Georgina!" Henry cries, offended. "That's Francine Phipps!"

"Such a wonderful lady, Georgina. She could make a custard the angels envy." The woman wanders off, but returns a few minutes later and hands Henry a warm pig's foot. "I did love that Georgina," she says.

Henry closes the barrel, rolls underneath the cart, chews on the greasy pig's foot. Mother mutters, They saw me, but seeing is nothing, and they saw only flesh and learned nothing, nothing.

Darkness expands the noises of the camp—the whooping of the drunks, the whinny of horses, the rattle of dice and bottles, the singing of tavern songs. Mother natters, hums. Someone shouts strange insults: "Gundiguts! Sapscull! Nigmenog!" A baby cries and jabbers. Cats screech. Henry rests his head on his elbow, counts breaths to a hundred, and sleeps.

Someone rolls up, presses against him warmly. Henry, startling awake, instinctively raises a knee, and it lands in soft flesh.

Abigail curses. "Don't be beastly," she says. They cannot both fit under the little cart. Her stringy hair is in his face. Her boney length bumps him. Mother says, Immoderate.

Henry wriggles backward and is cuffed in the head by a boot. "Little girl?" says a man's voice. "Little whore? Come out. Aren't done yet."

Henry squirms as the man kicks again. Barking his shin on the cart, the man yelps. "Damn it, that will come back to you." He sounds drunk.

"Who's that?" Henry whispers.

"Tell him to go," Abigail says.

The man grunts as he tries to roll the cart, but he's only pushing the shafts into the ground. He throws his body into the cart, shaking it. "This is all coming due, whore!"

Henry says, "Go away—" Abigail punches him in the ribs. "Ow!" Henry yelps.

"Sound big," she whispers.

"Go away, you!" Henry shouts in his deepest voice.

The man guffaws. "You find a croaky squirrel? A mouse with a cold?"

"Well, he's bigger than he sounds!" Abigail says.

One oughtn't tell falsehoods, Mother notes.

The man delivers a kick that catches the top of Henry's head. Henry cries out, reaches, grabs the man's ankle. This doesn't help much—Henry is kicked again. Abigail meanwhile slides out from the other side of the cart. The man kicks yet again, and Henry wonders furiously why he is holding this ankle. But then Abigail shoves the cart backward, slamming it into the man's knee. He howls. She jerks the shafts upward, bringing the cart down on the man's shin. He roars and bends to grab Henry, but she drops the shafts, and the back of the cart swings up into his chin.

The man falls on the ground, moaning. "My teeth," he slurs. He spits into the dirt. Henry stands and sets to kicking the man. Abigail yanks him away. "Boys," she says, "always hitting this, kicking that. It's nonsense. He'll be up as soon as he finishes spitting teeth. We should go."

They drag the cart to the opposite side of the encampment. Henry crawls under it again. Abigail follows. "I'm sorry," she says, "but you're not of any use to me if you can't act bigger than that."

Embarrassed, annoyed, Henry says, "I'm trying to sleep."

"Good," she says. She rolls onto her side, away from Henry.

"I don't know why you led him to me," Henry says.

"No one ever needs any help, I suppose you think," she says.

"You have helped me," Henry admits.

"Too bad you're a fool," Abigail says, "or you might be something else."

She yawns. Soon she's asleep.

But Henry lies awake, listening to Mother mumble.

Finally he climbs out. In the distance the fires of the army bivouac still burn. Henry starts walking.

He follows the road until he finds a soldier standing picket at the perimeter of the army camp. Mouth open, eyes half-closed, he doesn't notice Henry until Henry tugs his sleeve. Yawning, he tells Henry that this is an encampment of the Virginia militia, and he doesn't know a Phipps, and he doesn't know anything about a firing squad, nor the whereabouts of the 5th Maryland, Franklin's regiment, nor anything else, since all he does is march in circles the day long like a demented idiot.

Henry returns to the cart, lies down beside Abigail. Silvery moonlight comes and goes off the edges of the cart wheels as clouds pass.

When Henry wakes, Abigail is gone. He climbs up and sits with an arm around the barrel. The sky has only a little light in it. A breeze lifts and drops. A rooster starts going.

A moment later a rider comes pounding out of the army bivouac, toward the civilian encampment. He doesn't slow as he comes but gallops right in among the rough rows of tents and wagons, spilling buckets and barrels, scattering pigs and chickens, bellowing, "It's Washington! Washington! The redcoats have turned to Washington! We'll meet them at Bladensburg!"

The camp heaves to life with shouts, cries, curses.

Men mount horses and spur them. Several sheep have gotten loose and dogs chase pell-mell. The sutlers yank down their tents. The whiskey dealers throw empty bottles into their wagons with terrific clattering noises. Mother says quietly, Well. I don't know what you think you'll do now. We might as well go to Baltimore.

"I'm going to the battle," Henry says.

That isn't wise, Mother says. People are killed in these events. That's their purpose.

Already the army drums roll and tap, the noise reaching

Henry faintly. A column starts from the army bivouac. Henry looks at the barrel. His hands and shoulders burn from yesterday's walk. "I can't take you. The British will be there any minute. I'll be too slow."

You will not leave me, Henry, Mother says.

"Too bad—" a voice says.

Henry yelps, jumps, turns—Abigail is only inches away.

"Too bad," she says, "you've no money, and you're going to miss the war while you stand bickering with a pickle barrel."

Grimacing, Henry looks at the distant army on the road, at the barrel, at Abigail.

"I'm going," she says, her face flushed, backing away. "Are you, or not?"

Mother says nothing at all, which alarms Henry terribly.

"I'm going, and I'm bringing the barrel," Henry says.

"Not today. Too slow. I'm not going to miss the war for a barrel of pickled lady." Abigail lifts her skirt and runs.

Henry takes up the shafts of the cart, yanks, lurches the cart ahead with the force of resentment. He follows in the trail of all the others hurrying on. "If there're musket shots," he says, "I'm going to drop you and run."

But Mother chatters happily now, and he is glad she is not silent.

He does not, after all, need to go far. In less than a mile he is on the dirt track through Bladensburg—two rows of small houses and shops and a church with a narrow, leaning, weathered steeple. To his left, between the buildings, he can see the water of the East Branch and beyond that willows and elderberry, and beyond these he can see American troops forming. There are thousands of men assembling in lines, many more soldiers than he saw in the bivouac last night. Drum taps, a fife, and high cries quaver over the river to him. But the buildings around him lie still and silent, with the exception of a speckled hen wandering the street, pecking and glaring. It screeches and runs before Henry. He nears it again; again it screeches and runs ahead.

Bless the chickens. However stupid I ever felt, Mother says, I could be sure the chickens were considerably more so.

He passes the last house, and the road turns to meet the East Branch, about forty corn rows wide, flowing unhurriedly south. Splintered wheel ruts mark a narrow log and slat bridge. On the far side the road bends through a meadow, and there in the middle of the road stand two cannon, their maws open toward Henry.

Stretched across the meadow behind the cannon is a line of American troops in triple ranks. Behind them the land gently rises, bearing the road with it, to a second line of troops, some half-mile away. And far behind the second line, visible as specks on the crest of the slope, is a third line. Sections of these lines are in upheaval while mounted officers trot here and there, shouting. There are thousands of militiamen and soldiers altogether, rather motley looking. Only a fraction are dressed in the army's uniform, a blue jacket with white cross belts on the chest. The others wear black jackets, or common shooting jackets, or old-fashioned frock coats. Many wear breeches tight on the legs, puffing their posteriors. Some stand stiffly, while others are slumped or swaybacked, muskets set on the ground as crutches or chin rests. Away to the right the meadow ends at an apple orchard, and past that the forest begins. On the left runs the river. Behind the second line of troops is a large, disorderly group of horses and carriages and men and women in civilian clothes.

Henry crosses the bridge, swings around the cannon, and leaves the road, dragging his cart across the meadow before the serried ranks of soldiers, grasshoppers boiling from the weeds ahead of his boots.

He comes to the apple trees and weaves through until he

reaches the edge of the deep forest. "I have to leave you here," he says.

Everyone abandons me, Mother says quietly.

"I can't drag you uphill through an army when the battle might start any minute!" he says. He pulls the cart further on, taking a rough path into the trees, then turns into the shadows and brush. "I'll hide you here. No one will find you, and I won't be far away, and I'll come back soon."

Go on. Why not? she says mournfully. No one ever gives any regard to me anyhow.

He shoves the cart deep into a chokecherry patch. Mother's gingham dress is under the barrel, and he adjusts it to better hide it. "I'll be back quickly! With money!" he shouts, turning away. He devoutly intends to return the moment the fighting ends and he has in hand money, items of value, *something*.

Nearing the army's second line, Henry studies the soldiers. If Franklin's big form is among them, Henry doesn't see it. Doubt touches him like a cold finger: the thought that Franklin may in fact be dead.

Amid the triple ranked first line are two clusters of small cannon, several cannoneers seated in the shade of their caissons, and a few officers with fancy hats and shiny accoutrements surveying the field. The civilians are in a messy sprawl of groups and clusters above the second line—there are men in finery and men in tatters, men on sleek horses and men with no shoes, women in dresses and petticoats and sun hats and bonnets, and women with cook soot on their faces. Among them are a number of boys and girls Henry's own age and younger, with their families, chattering, eating lunches from baskets like folk gathered for a horse show or a hunting dog demonstration. Other children roam in gangs or hawk apples, or corn cakes, or dippers of water from a canvas bucket.

He discovers Abigail deep in conversation with a man with

purple, pox-scarred cheeks and an ear trumpet—she flicks Henry away with her fingers. He doesn't mind, goes onward. The sky is clear; the sun throws a dazzling light on the lines of troops. Laughter rises high and sharp. A man clutches his son, points to a rider amid a half-dozen men in fine black jackets, says, "Madison!"

Henry knows of the president mostly through Father's vulgar complaints about his appalling Republican warmongering politics. It scarcely surprises Henry that Madison is an unimpressive, small, sweating, fat man, straddled on horseback like a toad.

A cannon, sighting its distance to the bridge, erupts—the ball skips through the meadow and neatly leaps the bridge. Cheers rise. Henry circles back to a position not far from the orchard, wondering, when will the redcoats come?

Mother grumbles faintly. More American units march in, a few score from the east, then several hundred from the Georgetown road. Sweat-black horses come in at a trot, pulling cannon that slew and sway, raising streams of dust. The soldiers in the field never stand in place long before someone in fancy dress gallops up and orders them to slightly different locations. It's growing hot.

Then a few dozen American soldiers appear on the other side of the river, running hard through Bladensburg. They turn onto the bridge with shouts and sprint across.

Finally now the officers cease trotting about. Everyone stills.

For what seems a long while nothing happens. Even the birds are quiet, and the cloudless sky is like a bell of blue glass.

A voice cries, "Hush!"

Which, in the perfect quiet—except for Mother's distant natter—seems to Henry a silly thing to say. But then he hears, from away over the river to the right, the wafting rattle of drums. A minute later, a bugle's warble.

No—it is several bugles. And now the British come out of the trees into sight on the Bladensburg road, redcoated, bayonets glinting, a single, long, long column that comes on and on from the trees, in hundreds, then thousands. In the red column there are also streaks of blue, and some of the soldiers are black-skinned, although they are much too far away to see if Radnor is among them. There are also men dragging small cannon, carts, and tumbrils. A few men ride on stolen farm nags, with improvised blanket saddles and rope reins.

The head of the column halts a hundred yards short of Bladensburg. A few dozen redcoats depart the ranks and move forward. They break into several houses. After a minute they return to the street and wave.

A command is shouted. The thousands of British bayonets lift, and a flash of light travels down the length of the column, like an enormous animal rising to hunt.

The drums roll, the bugles sound, and the red column starts forward.

As the leading troops reach the center of Bladensburg, the two American cannon in the meadow road explode. The trails kick back gouging the dirt and roily smoke rises. The balls strike the Bladensburg street and bounce into the redcoats— one soldier is caught in the stomach and rises upward, arms outflung like a preacher. The British break ranks and scatter, and the civilians on the ridge cheer and laugh, and Henry with them.

Subsequent cannon shots, however, uselessly knock holes into the town roofs, while the redcoats scuttle from house to house, and soon hundreds are crowded behind the buildings and trees nearest the river.

An officer rides forward, shouting, and raises a shining sword.

The redcoats hurrah and surge as if a sluice gate had opened. Many stream for the bridge, but others run to the river, raise their muskets overhead, and splash into the water looking for fords. The cannon on the road open fire and sweep a dozen redcoats off the bridge—flying and tumbling, spun like toys, limbs torn from torsos. The men behind fall back briefly, then push forward, stepping over and upon the bodies.

The first line of American muskets fires raggedly as the redcoats enter the meadow, and it doesn't slow them much. Henry notices certain rough-looking civilians, one by one, slouching into the orchard and drifting downslope. Henry joins them. As he sidles from one apple tree to the next, a man leers with the yellow teeth of scurvy and gums the color of swamp mud. "Going to get you some, boy?" he says. "Just keep yourself well out of my way. There'll be plenty to go around."

The British troops split left and right, some toward the orchard, others toward the first American line. The line gives way almost immediately, breaking ranks and fleeing as the redcoats surge forward to seize the two cannon in the road. Henry, fearing that the battle is already over, nearly runs out of the orchard to chase down some American troops and yell at them. But the second American line stays in place, and some of the men from the first line begin attaching themselves there.

Redcoats behind a warehouse in town ignite a series of rockets that fly over the river spewing fire and sparks and making a sound like enormous shears tearing through cloth. They seem horrible and glorious to Henry. But they only land in the grass and scuttle around, and then the American cannon begin hitting the warehouse, and the rockets stop.

The second line starts downhill, toward the British, marching with muskets at shoulder, officers yelling where the wide triple rank bulges ahead or sinks behind, drummer boys beating the march, while overhead the red and white and blue flags and the regimental banners ripple and snap. Some of the redcoats are forming ranks in the meadow to meet the Americans, while others continue to flit into the orchard. Henry runs alongside the march of the second line. The scurvied man trots nearby, his body bent as if he were in a cellar.

When the American line halts on the hillside Henry can see red jackets only a couple hundred feet downhill, spread across the meadow and all among the apple trees. The Americans spend a few minutes straightening their formation, and meanwhile the redcoats in the orchard pot several of them. Then the American officers shriek, and all the long line of American muskets discharge flame and a sudden billow of smoke with the sound of a great wave smashing a stony beach.

A few of the redcoats in the ranks at the foot of the meadow drop, and others break and run. But the redcoats in the orchard continue loading and firing at the Americans standing in ranks. The Americans begin shooting as fast as each man can load. Some aim at the troops ahead; some aim at the orchard, making pale wounds in the trunks of the trees.

It is a strange, reversed scene—Father told Henry how the rebels won the War of Independence by sniping from the woods at rigid British formations, and he and Franklin played it that way when littler. The American troops are going about it incorrectly, and Henry dances on his feet in irritation. Meantime, there are still many redcoats across the river, and they have found a ford upstream of the bridge and pour into the orchard, so more and more redcoats are firing from the trees, and the American line grows crooked and broken as men scream and curse, working to reload or turning to the wounded. A man casts his musket aside and runs: others follow. The British burst from the woods, running with bayonets.

The smoke swells so that Henry cannot follow the scene, although he glimpses figures silhouetted by the haze and hears the muskets banging, and the cannon booming—these fewer and fewer as the Americans begin hauling the artillery away. Bayonets clash and men scream and horses scream. The air stinks of burned powder, and the dead lie here and there in humps in the haze. Jutting from the banked smoke is an American flag, but then it teeters and falls, and the redcoats in the meadow huzzah and press ahead.

Henry lurches to one direction and another, trying to see. The sloping meadow directly before him has begun to empty as the Americans retreat, the redcoats chasing, but bullets still fly nearby with short, sharp noises of keening and thwacking when the scurvied man springs up, and, with prancing steps and startling recklessness, shouting "Lord Lord Lord!" runs into the meadow. He falls on the nearest body, an American, tears opens the blue jacket, begins to rummage.

Henry's surprised to discover how many civilians are peering from behind trees and through the bushes, rough-looking men and narrow-eyed women, frozen, bated, leaning to watch the scurvied man work amid the flying bullets.

The scurvied man lifts up a chain that gleams gold. He puts it in his teeth, grins, cackles, whoops.

The others rush forward, Henry with them.

He bolts past a couple of men who seem to have actually hidden themselves in the landscape, for they appear as if out of the ground to bend over the dead and wounded. He passes a wild-eyed old man cursing and clouting on the neck a crone already working over the body of a bespangled officer. As the British swept out of the trees into the meadow, Henry noticed one gut-shot redcoat who doubled over, then straightened and fell backward out of sight amid tall weeds. He sprints the last distance, crouches. The fallen redcoat is a young man scarcely old enough to scrape hair off his face, staring skyward with surprise and consternation, as if a shopkeep had just quoted an outrageous price. A hole in his belly emits a red ooze.

Henry sets the soldier's gleaming musket to one side, lifts his warm, heavy hand, drops it. He says, frowning, "Maybe you're the one that loosed the cow."

A musket ball crackles through the weeds: Henry looks after it absently, then again at the soldier. He squirms his feet, cracks his knuckles. He feels shy. Why? The feeling angers him. The man is dead. No one is watching.

Faintly, faintly, Mother shouts across the distance, Henry, after all, it's nigh impossible for a rich man to enter the kingdom of heaven!

"He doesn't look very rich," Henry says doubtfully, but supposes he might examine the dead soldier's possessions before deciding what's to be done with them, so works the jacket's shining buttons, reaches in—

Hands seize Henry from behind.

Henry squeaks, flails. He is lifted like a sack of flour: his view gyres from earth to sky and back. In a rush of air, Henry flies.

The landing crushes the breath from him. He opens his mouth wide but, fishlike, cannot breathe, while darkness and stars crowd in.

Then air comes in a wild gasp. Coughing and wheezing he scrambles to his feet. Bending over the body of the redcoat is a tall stout man, bald and brown as leather on the top of his head, and hairy everywhere else with tufts of wiry stuff sprouting from face, hands, neck, ears.

Henry jumps at the man's back—the big man grunts and ignores him, even as Henry pounds him. It is like punching the ribs of a draft horse. Henry slides down the man's back, but as he drops he catches hold of something on the man's belt, pulls it free—a knife.

Henry raises his gaze from the knife in time to witness a remarkable event: the redcoat sits up.

Henry and the hairy bald man stumble back. The newly animate soldier blinks, smacks dry lips, furrows his brow, looks at the wound in his gut. "Hurk?" he says. "Hurk? Hurk."

He coughs blood onto his trousers; then reaches forward as if to wipe at it, but the gesture loses momentum; his hand falls.

The hairy bald man regains his footing and steps toward the redcoat, feeling at his hip. Finding nothing there, he feels to his other hip, his stomach, his back. He peers at his belt. He turns. Henry laughs and waggles the knife.

"That's mine," the hairy bald man says.

"You're going to knife him!" Henry cries.

"You stole my knife. This is robbery."

"You can't knife him," Henry says. "Go find a dead one."

They both glance around. Where, Henry wonders, did all of these people come from? Dozens of looters have spread across the meadow, up and down the slope, bending to the bodies, running from one to the next, like ants on a sugar spill.

"That's my good knife." The man scratches in his tangled beard. "I need that knife. I can't afford to lose things, like a good knife."

"Hurk!" says the redcoat.

Damned is the man to whom too much is offered, Mother shouts.

"That doesn't make sense," Henry says, irritably.

"Weevils ate our crop," the hairy bald man says. "We are starving. My wife has boils on her eyelids. I have six daughters, and how many have the ague? Six. We have nothing. Nothing but illness."

Henry says, "A cow fell on my mother and killed her."

"I am sorry for your misfortune. But I need that knife. It is my good knife. Also, I need the dead man's things."

"He's not dead!" Henry says.

"Hurk!" says the redcoat.

"Well, he ought to be. Isn't he a redcoat, invading our republic?" the hairy man says, face pinkening. "Aren't we Americans? Isn't he an assailant on our national sovereignty? Is this not a war?" His eyes glisten, and he rubs a hand in the sweat on his head. "Our well? Dry. Our horse? Sores in the mouth. Cow? Gives no milk. The knife, please."

Tell him to go away, Mother shouts.

"Go to hell," Henry says.

Language, Henry! Mother shouts.

The bald hairy man roars and lunges with a quickness that startles Henry. He catches Henry's knife hand by the wrist, squeezes, and lifts straight up, so that Henry's feet come off the ground. For a moment he holds Henry at eye level, his wooly, filthy face inches from Henry, stinking of rancid grease. He says, "Sorry boy," and joggles him violently, as if to see what will happen first, a snapped neck or an arm torn out of joint.

Something explodes, and a crimson rag seems to drop onto the hairy bald man's head—he lets go of Henry to touch his head, and his fingers come away dripping blood from a wound slashed there.

"Hurk!" The redcoat lowers his musket, smoke seeping from the barrel.

Henry looks at his hand—the knife is still there, in his fist. He flourishes it.

The hairy bald man gazes at the knife, then whimpering and burbling he turns and retreats with his head in his hands.

The redcoat slumps back to the ground, goggles the sky, smacks his lips. Henry leans closer. "Hello?" he says. "Hello?" He shouts: "Hello?"

The redcoat's eyes jump, then still, jump, then still.

Oh no, Mother says.

"Please breathe, sir," Henry says. "After all, you're probably not the one who let the cow loose."

Mother says, Who the Lord loves he chastises, and scourges every son he receives . . .

Henry says, "Won't you stop? You don't believe in any of that."

Mother says, But maybe this boy does.

Henry sits in the grass, takes the soldier's hand. The flesh has cooled alarmingly. Henry says, "It's too much of everyone dying."

The redcoat doesn't appear to hear. Mother says, It is a war, Henry, and you see you need family, now especially.

The redcoat shudders. A cicada noise comes from his throat. The color falls from his face. His gaze looks nowhere. Sadness and loneliness swell in Henry. He squeezes the redcoat's fingers.

He sits for a while. Uphill, where the armies still clash, the American second line is gone, and most of the third line is too, except for two hundred or so Americans at the high point of the Washington Road, working several cannon and loading and firing long rifles at the redcoats who venture into the open on the slopes below.

The smoke covers much of what is happening, and Henry only watches vaguely until a breeze rolls the smoke aside, and although the Americans are thousands of feet away, one of them is plainly much bigger than the others.

Henry jumps up. He starts running. Soon he can see the big soldier—tall, bull-necked, a man who fills his uniform like a sausage fills its skin.

"Franklin!" Henry shouts, leaping along, "Franklin! Franklin! Franklin Franklin Franklin!"

Smoke drifts in and hides the Americans. Henry runs on. He can see redcoats working around to the backside of the hill. They have nearly surrounded the position when the American officers start screaming and waving. Their troops abandon the cannon and break down the road toward Washington.

Henry moves as fast as he can, but he is winded and wet with sweat. On the slope above him, everyone is running—the American troops stream westward, the redcoats following like wolves after sheep.

Henry passes wounded making awful noises and looters stooping to their work. As he crests the hill, he stops to regain his breath. The British officers are calling their men, reforming a column in the road. Henry can't see Franklin anywhere.

He hesitates. He took nothing from the battlefield. He looks back down the hill—he can see hats, muskets, knapsacks, and jackets lying all about. There must be valuables to be found. But a few of the redcoats are turning to chase off the looters. An officer fires a pistol toward a group of men gathered at a broken caisson, and they scatter. It upsets Henry that he's gained nothing here.

Presently the British bugle and drum strike up. The column's rear is still collecting men and forming up as the front end sets into motion toward Washington.

Do not go without me do not go do not go do not go do not go do not go do not go do not go do not go! Mother's shouting comes faint as a whisper on the air.

But the sight of Franklin, alive, has set Henry's nerves afire: he must go after Franklin. He cannot go back now, or he will lose his mind, will die. He raises onto his toes and moves with sneaky steps, silently, away from Mother crying, Come back come back come back come back come back.

Fainter and fainter her voice reaches him, and then he puts his head down to run.

CHAPTER 3

Mary contemplates forgiveness. Who can she forgive, and who can she not? Can she forgive the nurse beside her? Mary thinks no. Her father? Certainly not. Her sisters? She thinks of her eldest sister, who never forgives anyone, though she is a devout woman and knows as well as anyone that Christ urges forgiveness, for everyone. But can any mortal woman find such depths of generosity in herself?

They proceed in a silence broken only by the drop of the lash and the thrum of a million insects, a churning, almost mystical sound so continuous that Mary no longer hears it. She sweats in streams, and all her body aches. Her enormous belly cannot be positioned in any way that feels natural. Franklin is dead, her father said, and he put her on this wagon to Baltimore. She has drifted through a fog of nausea and horror for hours upon hours, the hired nurse stiff beside her, and the hired man hunched before her, lethargically putting the lash to one and then the other of two harnessed mules. The nurse has patchy scraps of white hair and one of her cheekbones is collapsed and scarred, as if staved in with a table leg. She keeps a sharp-edged thimble on one finger, and she has a trick for flicking her hand to land the thimble like a whip's end-knot—on Mary's cheek are two small half-moon bruises.

Mary is miserable, but she is also minding the scene going by. In Baltimore she will be locked into another of her father's houses, to give birth alone, far from anyone she knows. Her best chance for escape is in this journey. She needs only to slip a little distance away, then hide. The driver is old and limps. The nurse, while cunning, is a townsperson who knows nothing of woods or swamp.

They move on oozing black ruts, marsh plants simmering greenly on either side, issuing a moist smell of decay. Flies ring the mules' eyes. The continual lurch of the wagon shoots flame into Mary's back. She fades in and out of a doze and finds scores of mosquitoes on her face. The black tracks extend forever ahead. She has been and will be here forever. Franklin is lost to her. The baby will be born while they still creep through this swamp.

She admonishes herself for her despair, sits up, attempts to sharpen her mind.

It doesn't last. She's slumped and dazed when a violent pitch and jerk of the wagon startles her up again. She sees the mules leaning in the harness. The hired man curses and lashes; the mules stamps and shake their heads. The wagon is pitched to an angle and stuck.

The driver climbs down to examine the right rear wheel. It has slid off the track and down to the hub in a hole filled with molasses-colored muck. The driver sets both hands on the wheel and strains to lift it. The wagon doesn't budge. He looks up. "Everything out."

The nurse assists Mary to the ground with a pinching grip to her elbow, and Mary stands in the soggy track while the nurse and the driver unload the baggage—two heavy chests, sacks of provisions, a rocking cradle. The nurse climbs up to lash the mules while the hired man pushes the wheel. Mary moves a step backward.

The driver shouts, "Hit them! Hit them, damn it!" The nurse beats with the lash. The driver puffs, sweats, turns red.

Mary turns, runs. There's swamp to either side, but just ahead the road bends into high, tangled growth. She despairs, however, at how slowly she moves. She was always fleet—faster than the boys in a foot race, not that any would admit it, except for sweet Franklin, his duty to honesty overriding his embarrassment. But now she plods heavily.

She glances back. The nurse and the hired man do not notice yet, and ahead is the bend. If she can make the bend, then hide in the willow and reeds—

"Mary!" the nurse cries. "Reprehensible child!"

Mary swings her feet fast as she can—the mud of the road seems to clutch her shoes and grab the hem of her dress. Her heart goes as hard as it ever has. She leans forward, ready to leap to the willows, ready to ball herself around her belly and roll like an egg.

But the nurse comes up with startling speed. She seizes Mary's arm and spins her back toward the wagon. "Where will you go?" the nurse demands, her face near. "You have nowhere to go."

This is true. Mary weeps as she climbs back into the wagon. Mary's sisters—eleven, eight, and six years older than Mary— told her, again and again, how their mother died giving birth to Mary amid an extraordinary hemorrhage of blood that overspilled the bed, leaving a stain that could not be scrubbed away, so that finally the floorboards had to be torn out and replaced. Mary had been given suck by a black nursemaid, and Mary's sisters said that the milk had transmitted to Mary the nursemaid's debased negro character. Abandoned amid sisters who regard her an intruder and a species of murderer, Mary has, at moments, wondered if her own motherhood will kill her and balance matters, if it might be as well if it did. It's a thought she shakes off, but it seems to cling a little more after Franklin was taken away to the firing squad.

The wagon goes on, the nurse gripping Mary's wrist with boney, sweating fingers. "You're a fool to run. Your father will find you a rich husband," she says, "or he will make your husband rich. You'll tell servants and slaves what they must do.

They'll wash your clothes and make your meals and empty your chamber pot and mind your children. You'll be like a queen."

"My father will marry me to some horrible, simpering man who will do whatever my father tells him."

"What could be wrong with that? Your father is a great success."

Mary shakes her head miserably.

An hour later they come into the shade of the forest, and Mary rouses herself, says, "After all, Franklin promised to marry me, and I can have my own baby."

"You're, at best, a kind of widow," the nurse says.

Tears come again to Mary's eyes. "There's no reason I should be forced to behave as if I am ashamed."

The nurse snorts. "It will be easier for your father to find you some proper husband if the matter is kept quiet. You can simply say that your new husband is the father."

"I'll never do that."

"If you insist on that attitude, and if that baby is a boy, I do believe your father will take him from you."

Mary feels savagely that no one will ever be forgiven for this.

Her father would not forgive his daughters first for not being sons, and then for not marrying and having sons. Her sisters would not forgive the world for disappointing them. Mary could see plainly how grief came from the knots of unforgiving. But taking her child from her: how could she forgive it? She would hate her father, her sisters, her mother, every person alive and dead. She would live only with animals, who never needed forgiveness.

"I want Tuesday," Mary says.

"Pardon?"

"Tuesday."

"An indulgence, a creature like that."

"So that I can have the one thing that's nice. I'm sure I'll feel better if I have Tuesday."

The nurse pinches her lips and twists the thimble. After a moment she relents. "If the cat will make you less difficult, I will mention it in my letter to your father. Perhaps he will grant it. I don't know."

Mary tries to straighten her back against the pain there. She cannot understand how she can sweat so much without bodily seeping through the wagon's floorboards and mixing into the wet all around. It is Franklin's fault, poor Franklin, she would punch him if he were here, not that he would notice much. "He said this wouldn't happen," she said, "if I was on top."

The nurse glares. The driver guffaws.

"I don't know why I believed him," Mary says. "But I'm sure he really believed it."

Washington lies only a few miles from Bladensburg. By the time Henry has walked halfway there, the sun sulks low in the west and the road is swarming with people fleeing the city with possessions and provisions piled in wagons and carts with slaves and livestock trailing behind, while soldiers from various American regiments and militias trudge the other way, looking for their army. Henry talks to a soldier with a star-shaped wound on his forehead, a cobbler with a sack full of shoes, a pigkeep with piglets in a box—they all tell Henry that the army will go to Washington to stop the redcoats.

A painted sign advertises the Fiddlestick's End, an inn that appears to have been constructed and amended using loose scraps of wood by men largely ignorant of the techniques of carpentry. The door has come off the hinges and lies on the ground, revealing a rowdy crowd demanding space for the night. Nearer to the road, a group of men stand round a fire passing a jug. They are old men, or men who look old, laborers with savaged hands and creased faces. All watch the jug, except one harelipped man who shakes a panful of dried corn over the fire. It passes Henry's mind that he's hungry, and that he left his food with Mother, but he rushes on.

Presently he comes to an American soldier walking the other way—toward Bladensburg. "Where are you going?" Henry says. "The redcoats are headed to Washington."

The soldier shrugs. "General Winder says we're going to Baltimore."

Soon Henry meets another soldier, and another, more and more, headed toward Bladensburg, bandaged men, empty-handed men, walking in ones and twos, slumped, quiet. They form a rough line, and near the end a large shape appears out of the sunset and dust—Franklin.

Henry runs, crying, "Franklin! Franklin!"

Franklin blinks, blinks, grins—he sweeps up Henry and holds him high. "Pest!" he says. "Vexation! You're here!" He crushes Henry in an embrace, sets him down, smiles, smiles, frowns, squints. "Henry. Why're you here?"

Franklin has Henry by the hand, and he pulls Henry along the road toward Bladensburg while Henry jabbers—he saw Franklin and his regiment at Bladensburg, fighting, the last Americans on the field.

"That wasn't my regiment," Franklin says. "The captain ordered a retreat, which seemed disgraceful to me, when others were fighting yet, so I slid over to stand with Barney's marines. But that's not the point." He considers, recalling the point. "Why aren't you home?"

"Franklin," Henry says. "Mother's dead."

"Mother?" Franklin halts, gapes, shakes his head, peers at Henry. "Dead? No. Mother?"

Henry opens his mouth, but his throat closes.

Franklin bends backward, looks to the sky, lifts his thick arms, and roars—a terrible, animal sound of pain.

When it stops, Henry hears it whisper back off the trees.

Or, no, it is Mother's voice, far off, shouting something he cannot make out.

Franklin drops his arms, stands slumped, stares at his boots. Then he clumps forward. "This way. Tell me."

Henry casts a glance back toward Washington, but Franklin has taken his arm again and drags him along. Henry tells about Mother, the redcoats, the cow. "But," he says, "she still talks to me."

"You said she's dead."

"Yes."

"Which is it, she's dead, or she talks to you?"

"Both."

"That is considerable strange." Franklin ponders for several paces. "I don't see how it can be."

"When she is close, I can hear her as clearly as I can hear you."

"What does she say?"

"Oh, you know how she talks. She wants to go to sea. Can't hear her very well now, though. I think she's too far away."

"Too far away? I don't understand it. Maybe you're touched in the head."

"She says we're all to be there—Father, too—and send her to sea."

"That does seem the kind of thing she would say. But Father, too?" Franklin says nothing for a distance. They tail behind the line of soldiers. Before them a man staggers and groans. The dying sun throws wine-colored light onto the clouds. "No," Franklin says finally. "No. It's not possible. You know I tried. I gave him my bounty, and I am duty-bound to the army now because I tried. You know how he spent the money."

"If Washington has been abandoned, there'll be things for the taking."

"You mean—" Franklin squints, thinking. "Theft?"

"We need money. Father—"

"That's a mean, dishonorable idea," Franklin says.

"Things people have left behind," Henry says, "can't be needed very much, really."

"No. That's not right."

"But—"

"Don't thieve things, Henry. I have to tell you about Mary. Mary is going to have a baby. You will be an uncle." Franklin looks down at Henry with a great smile and claps his shoulder. "But Suthers's men took her away. I have to find her. For now, you'll join my regiment. You can help the cooks. You'll have food and a place to sleep. They may even pay you something."

"It will take a hundred years to buy out Father that way!"

Franklin says nothing. Henry assumes he is thinking, but then realizes that the angle of Franklin's head is not his thinking angle. Franklin is listening.

"Washington's that way! Over there! Behind you!" It is the men by the fire at the Fiddlestick's End.

A soldier says, "We go to defend Baltimore."

The harelipped man with the pan of popping corn has abandoned it and now stands at the edge of the roadway. He has bloodshot eyes. His harelip gives his words a lisp that sounds like mockery. "Ah! Baltimore! Right! But Johnny Bull hasn't even gotten to Washington yet, has he? Odd. And I hear there were races today at Bladensburg. Say, who won the races at Bladensburg? Maybe that skinny one there? He looks quick! Surely it wasn't that fat one, or that bandy-legged one. Who won the Bladensburg races? You? Or you?" Behind the harelip, his friends grin.

Franklin slows. As if it were a happenstance of the mechanics of his slackening pace, he reaches a stop before the harelip. He still has a grip on Henry. "I didn't see any races," he says.

"You finished well back, I suppose. Not your fault, you're

so big. But you beat those redcoats, I guess, showed them how sprightly an American can be, even a great big one."

"There were—" Franklin appears confused, works a finger in one ear. "—no races."

The harelip smiles and his gums show high. "Coward."

Franklin lets go of Henry and reaches with a fast, reflexive movement, as if grabbing a cup that someone has elbowed off a table, except that this movement ends with Franklin's fist meeting the harelip's nose.

The harelip stumbles, twitches once, then drops straight down. In a heap, he lies unmoving, except for the blood that flows from his nostrils.

The other men look at the harelip, look at Franklin, then turn from Franklin, to the fire and the jug.

Franklin reaches for Henry, but Henry has danced backward several steps. Franklin says, "Come here, you."

"I'm going to Washington," Henry says.

Franklin shakes his head. "I forbid it." He steps and reaches. "Come with me."

Henry ducks the big arm, spins, runs. He hears Franklin's heavy step follow, but he knows he is lighter and faster than his brother. Soon the footsteps stop.

"Henry!" Franklin calls. "Father's a wastrel! You cannot redeem him by debasing yourself!"

But Henry has no care about wastreling or redeeming or debasing. He knows the words—from Father's rants—but is indifferent to them. He only wants money, his father free, his mother to sea. He runs on.

An enormous draft horse has died in its traces, backing up several wagons coming out of Washington. A carriage attempting to detour through an adjacent field has broken an axle in a ditch. Henry skirts by. He passes a man carrying a framed painting on his back, two traders leading a chain of slaves in sackcloth, a woman with rabbits in a barrow. A man leads what appears to be second man on a leash, naked, moving on all fours. But then Henry sees that the leashed creature is not a man but a sickly thin bear with mange.

A red-haired boy Henry's own age is coming the other way, and Henry asks him for news. The redcoats are putting the government buildings to the torch, the boy says. "Soon you'll be in eyeshot of the fire."

It is true—minutes later, a blushing orange glows over the horizon.

Henry alternates trotting and walking, thrilled in his heart—ahead stands an entire city, abandoned. He feels drawn like an animal to bait, and wonders if this is how Father feels pulled to drink. He doesn't care for that idea, and begins to run.

The horizon glows brighter and brighter, then throws up a flare. Out of the distance rolls a crack, a boom, then another, followed by an uncanny rumble of the earth underfoot. Henry goes on, seeing in his mind great brick houses full to the ceilings with silver platters, gold jewelry, ivory snuff boxes, emerald studded spittoons, gilded clocks, Spanish leather wallpaper, silk carpets, tables laden with suckling pigs and stuffed pheasants, kitchens packed with tubs of sugar, barrels of molasses, slabs of chocolate, maybe even oranges.

But when he enters the city, he finds himself in narrow streets lined with filthy and flimsy wooden structures, built of warped and rotting boards, sinking into the mud, windowless, most of them sorrier-looking than his own cabin. Explosions continue breaking from southeast of the city; great fireballs rise there in a flickering false dawn. Henry runs down a curving alley, becomes turned around amid the small leaning hovels and vast piles of garbage, retraces his path, and finally enters a straight, wide street that rises and offers a vista of buildings near and far. Several are aflame, churning up thick rising columns of smoke and flurries of debris that spiral and flutter on the heat like bats. A quick hunched figure scuttles by with an armful of china. Close behind comes a waddling man bearing a pile of coats and handfuls of tallow candles.

Henry runs past the wooden houses to the first brick house—he associates brick with city finery—and circles to the rear. He tugs the door, and to his surprise it flies open. In the doorway stands a small, well-dressed man holding a cabbage. He draws the cabbage back and hurls it.

The vegetable hits Henry's forehead, snaps his head back, nearly knocks him off his feet. "Thief! Thief!" the man shrieks. "Horrible boy! Thief!"

Henry flees back to the street, feeling his forehead, fearing it may be split open. It seems only bruised. But it makes him so angry that snot bubbles from his nose. Why should a man beat his face with a cabbage for opening an unlocked door? It should be locked if he didn't want anyone to open it. Why— Henry thinks bitterly—I might have been attempting to warn of a fire on the roof or a thief in the window. He casts around, and his attention settles on the largest house in sight, a wide brick house with a whitewashed frame around the front door, a row of first floor windows in the brick, and another window eyeing out of the steep roof. Henry circles around trying windows, doors, but nothing gives. Finally he lifts a rock, puts it through a window, turns the latch, clambers in.

He detects the scent of fresh flowers, and it stretches his hopefulness toward happy greed. The fires throw quick, freakish slants of light through the window, showing handsome pieces of furniture. Henry laughs with pleasure, a little quiet hiccup laugh, in deference to the quiet of the house. He drops into an enormous wicker rocking chair with a down-filled cushion on the seat, and he thrusts himself forward, back, forward, back, an indulgent motion that raises in him, as if by the working of a crank, the feeling of a king contemplating the extent and wealth of his realm. He's never sat in a rocking chair before. Father said that chairs oughtn't move and anyway were not a proper field for new inventions, but this was probably because if he could get his hands on a rocking chair he would immediately sell it for gambling money. Forward, back, forward, back, Henry's noble feeling cranks higher and higher. As he rocks, he listens for Mother—maybe that is her voice? Ever so faintly?

The crack of an especially impressive explosion interrupts his thoughts. He goes to the nearest cabinet, swings the carved doors, ready to take wonderful things from their places.

Nothing. He feels along the empty dark shelves, finds only a single shard of broken crockery. He rushes on, to a tall chest of drawers, to a massive oaken desk, to the cupboards, to a wardrobe large enough to make a spacious henhouse—all empty. In the kitchen there are no pots, no pans, no silverware, no cups. Nothing on the mantle, nothing on the table, only heaps of cold ash on the hearth, and something underfoot— Henry bends to feel. Cut roses, dumped wet onto the floor, they prick Henry's hand. He stomps them.

He runs upstairs, opens a door, finds a long, dark room. He draws a curtain from the single, small window: the objects of the room disappoint. The furniture is rough cut, and there's a filthy rug, a bed with greasy bedding in a heap, some scattered bits of food crust, many stains, tobacco shards, and insects that scuttle away from the light. On the wall hangs an oval mirror, its silver blackening as if diseased. A set of drawers beneath the mirror hold patched trousers and shirts, a fieldworker's smock, a brown hat shaped like the cap of a mushroom. In the corner he finds a horsehair trunk, throws it open, finds neatly folded fabrics. He pulls these out by fistfuls: trimmed with silks, stiffened with starch, heavy with small buttons and knotted lacings, they are women's things, nicer than anything Mother ever wore. A laced velvet vest, a silk taffeta gown, a whalebone stay, a bright yellow linen dress, a white silk chemise. Why are they here? The dress is a marvelous fine linen. "Mother," he says, holding it up, "do you like it?" He cannot hear her, but perhaps that is due to all of the noise in the streets. Somewhere a horse is screaming. The dress is cut for someone a little larger than himself—it slides easily over his head and his clothes. He looks in the splotchy mirror, turns left, turns right, reaches behind to fit the waist, straightens his back, sets his shoulders, rolls his eyes. Certainly it is too long, but if it were hemmed—

"Hello, my lady!"

Henry tries to jump, turn, and pull off the dress all at the same time. He briefly glimpses an extraordinarily ugly redcoat leering from the stairs before he becomes hopelessly tangled in the dress. Fumbling, blind, he cries "I'm no girl!" He twists, yanks, drags the length of the dress overhead, casts it aside.

The redcoat stands gazing at Henry with fleshy lips pinched into a bud of disgust. His ugliness is so complete, so magnificent, it makes Henry gape—a large purpling nose, cavernous pox scars in his cheeks, a weak chin that recedes to nothing, hair snowy with dander, small uneven eyes, teeth snaggled to all angles like bits of burnt wood. It is as if someone had composed a face out of butcher's scraps.

The redcoat snorts. "You do make a miserable sort of maiden. A disappointment, aren't you?"

"Go away," Henry says.

"No bosom, no bottom, no girl at all. Quite disillusioning. Are you finding some charming things? All emptied out downstairs. Did you empty it? Doubtful. That way when you arrived, was it?"

"I live here," Henry says sourly.

The redcoat laughs. "Aye. And my arse lives in a bowl full of daisies."

"I live here!" Henry cries. It seems true enough, since he arrived first.

"That's the reason you put a rock through a window."

"Never liked that window," Henry mumbles.

"So, playing dress up? What're these nice things doing in a corner of the servants' quarters, you suppose? Dead girl, likely. Couldn't bear to be rid of them, put them here to be out of sight."

"Dead girl?" Henry looks at the yellow dress on the filthy floor. Already a cockroach is exploring it.

"What's your age? Nine?"

"I'm sixteen."

The redcoat grins, showing his horrifying teeth. "If you're sixteen, then I'm already dead. Which I don't think I am, although I did think I might die yesterday, when General Ross had us quickstepping for mile after mile through your forsaken countryside." While he talks, the redcoat examines the chest of clothes that Henry has already explored. "Mosquitoes, flies, miserable heat. Man beside me staggered and dropped right there, dead as a spiked twelve pounder." The redcoat pulls the drawers and spills their contents to the floor. "This after weeks on weeks inside the holds of swaying vile ships, everyone vomiting. Put us on land and away we go, marching, trotting, bodies falling dead, no pause to help them, no decent burial." He riffles the bedding. "Meantime, General Ross on his horse like Alexander traipsing over the mountains on an elephant." He opens the mattress tick with a knife and shakes out the straw stuffing. "Worthless," he says, scowling. "People here live like savages." He looks at Henry. "Now where?"

Henry, who has been watching for an opportunity to dash for the stairway, glares. "Where?"

"Yes, where next?"

"I live here," Henry says. "This is my house."

"Dedication to a lie is laudable only to a point, my boy. We have a city before us, spreading her legs. There's far more to be had than any one of us can carry. Better the two of us together than each alone, am I right? You know the country, and I know what I'm doing. We'll make a fair split, seventy-thirty, since I am bigger. Yes?" He peers at Henry with his small, misaligned eyes.

Henry looks at the shambles on the floor. Musket shots sound in the distance. He listens for Mother—he hears something, so faint, he can't be sure . . . Urged by an instinct or feeling—mostly the feeling that dislikes loneliness—he says, "Seventy-thirty?"

"Sixty-five and thirty-five, then!" The redcoat swings around and starts down the stairs. "I like a man who drives his bargains hard!"

Henry grabs up the yellow dress, shakes out the roaches, folds it tight, hides it under his shirt, follows the redcoat down.

The redcoat says his name is Morley, an artillery man. "I didn't like my orders. So, I gave myself my own orders: go plundering! A man has to know when to seize the initiative, and no man has many chances in life like this one."

The first house they break into is also emptied, nothing left but the dirt on the floorboards and pig bones on the table. As they push through the back door of a second house, a musket blasts, and Morley and Henry turn and flee. In the street men hurry by with saddles, buckets of nails, an elephant tusk, entire windows. "Soon everything will be gone!" Morley says with anguish. They move in the shadows at the edge of the street under a sky flaring with marigold colors. They pass a corner where a dozen or more black men—freedmen or slaves left behind—stand watching balls of flame shoot into the southeastern sky. British soldiers pass by, and the black men say hello and the soldiers say hello, all polite, all smiling. Morley cowers behind a corner until the British have gone. He and

Henry start to bicker about which houses to try—Henry wants only brick houses, but Morley says the brick has served them ill because brick indicates the sort of family with the resources to guard or evacuate their things. He drags Henry to a large wooden house, goes straight through the back door with his shoulder.

They grope forward in the dark, slowly, slowly, until their eyes adjust, and they can see a little, can see flat, empty surfaces. Morley stomps about, pulling out drawers. He finds a single small silver dish, which he shows to Henry, then shoves into the front of his trousers. He pulls a mirror off the wall, drops it to smash. He stops at a door, peers at the gap at the bottom. A trace of light shows there. The door is locked. "What, ho!" Morley cries, bangs on the door. "Come out! Come out!"

Henry comes up as Morley, again, drops his shoulder and crashes through the door, with the skill of a man who has done this many times.

A woman screams—she is crouched on the floor of a small bedroom, shielding a candle with her hands. "A pretty lady!" cries Morley. "Come, share the light. Come, talk with us."

The woman, heavy, plain, red-faced, recovers her composure and scowls at Morley, saying nothing.

"Such a discourteous reception!" Morley says. "But it is understandable. My entrance was a trifle vigorous." He moves a half-step nearer, smiling. "Let's start over, more sociably. You would scarcely believe how long I have been denied any feminine society."

Henry edges backward. "We might as well go. There's nothing here."

"But she wants to get to know us first, yes, my lady?" Morley extends a hand, trembling, very slow, as if she were a skittish animal.

With her right hand the woman lifts something from the floor—a broom. Then she blows on the candle.

The plunge of darkness is followed by the noise of a blow, like a hard struck muskmelon—Henry supposes it is the broom on Morley's skull. Morley shrieks. Amid the shrieking comes a second, more fleshy thwack. "Damn! Damn woman!" Morley shouts.

Scuffles, grunts, curses, a yelp.

"Bit me!" yells Morley. "Like a mad dog!"

They've struggled into the parlor, and by the scant light from the windows Henry can see Morley's arm around the woman's neck. With his other hand Morley is trying, with incomplete success, to restrain her arms. "Rope," Morley calls to Henry, breathing hard. "Find rope."

"I'll kill you," the woman says oddly calm, even as she struggles. "I'll kill you. I'll kill you."

"Where am I going to find rope?" Henry says. "We might as well leave."

"The lady is a fascinating conversationalist," Morley says, pushing her hand from his face. "We should all get familiar with one another."

"I'll have your eyeballs from their sockets," she says.

Henry says, "We're gaining nothing here."

"I'll break your neck and send you to hell," she says and strains to turn her head back, teeth gleaming.

"It seems everyone's nerves are a little fraught," Morley says. "Henry, get me a sheet, a curtain, a pair of trousers, anything will do for rope."

Henry stomps a foot. "Leave her!"

"I'll take your heart out of your chest with my own hands."

"Oh, hush! Hush!" Morley begins to force her toward the floor, but she swings a foot up, hard, and Morley screams. He throws her into the wall, and she falls, but stands again.

Morley snuffles. "She kicked my pego."

"We'll be on our way," Henry says.

"Sinners," she says. She crosses to the fireplace and lifts an iron poker.

"We're departing," Henrys says, pulling Morley—who is bent and groaning—toward the door. "This isn't the house we thought it was," Henry says. "We apologize."

"You are an absurd liar," she says.

In a fit of dread Henry jerks Morley outside and drags him to the street, not looking back. She calls, "You'll blaze like torches in hell."

"What a bitch," Morley says to the ground, still bent, hands on crotch, moving with fast shuffling steps. "And you were no help at all."

"I need money. I don't need to waste time with women."

Morley sighs. "It is a weakness of mine," he says. "I have a poverty of will against the tender sex."

Henry says nothing.

"A tuberous, mean, ill-bred thing, that one," Morley starts to straighten a little. "Bah. Do you know that I'm a married man? Aye, that woman is as the dirt on my boot when compared to my wife. But, alas, I was forced to leave my poor, dimpled Spanish love at the docks when we finished off Napoleon's mollies in Iberia." They stand at the edge of a wide dirt street, flames eating buildings in either direction. Morley takes in the view with disgust. "A muddy, malarial village dressed up with a couple of fancy government offices. The fire is a spectacle, but it is nothing compared to when we put St. Sebastian to the torch." They start down the street, keeping close to the houses. "Burned the city entire. And we had all the women we wanted." Morley looks around as he walks. "If an officer objected, we turned our muskets on him. We had fires and pillaging and women night and day for a week. Say—" Morley stops. "What is that building? Is that the Patent Office?"

"Patent Office?" Henry halts, bewildered.

"The houses are no good. We've seen that. Let's gather some useful inventions out of the Patent Office." Morley's little eyes shine. "A good invention will make us a lifetime of treasure. We'll take the best and burn the place. Then who's to say they aren't our inventions?"

Henry says, "That's the strangest idea of plundering I ever heard."

"We'll be scientists and businessmen, like true Yankees. It's not the usual way, but great men must think extraordinary thoughts and take unusual action. Why, it may be the finest idea I ever had," Morley says, growing rapturous. He hurries on, leading Henry around a row of shops. Henry is doubtful. But he also feels reluctant to try another house; the houses have turned out so poorly. In the light of a lantern held by a redcoat in the middle of the street, a British officer stands in discussion with a civilian. Several more redcoats have gathered to watch. "They'll burn it soon. We must hurry. You go over there on the left," Morley whispers, "and I'll be over there to the right. You make a little noise, to draw their attention, and I'll slip across."

Radnor holds close his red-painted musket—last night he held it even while he slept. On Capitol Hill, the Capitol burns. Nearby, the White House burns. Down the street, the Treasury burns. Around the corner, the War Department burns. Here and there other smaller buildings burn, shops and houses set afire by looters or by sparks blown in shining streaks overhead. The heat raises gossamer purls of steam from the muddy streets, and the air stinks of burned wood, burned paint, burned corn, burned leather, burned gunpowder. There is also, Radnor notes, a faint dewy scent of rain. Clouds cover the stars and reflect back the city's fires with a dim infernal light.

A disheveled white man is pleading with the lieutenant to spare the Patent Office. His argument runs like so: the British have said they will only burn government property; the paper-work and models inside the Patent Office are the property of the private citizens who own the patents; ergo, the contents of the Patent Office must be spared.

The lieutenant listens with his head cocked, as if bent by oblique reasoning.

Radnor likes the lieutenant all right. "A free man," he said to Radnor the day before, "with all the rights and obligations of a subject of His Royal Majesty King George III, and the full honors of a Colonial Marine in His Majesty's Navy." As he spoke the lieutenant stood in more or less the same spot where Radnor had come every day, year after year, to toss the dinner leavings to the pigs. He handed Radnor a musket. "Now let's humiliate some Americans, so that we can leave this dreadful, immoral continent." Donning his redcoat, Radnor silently pledged that he would never again feed another man's pigs. The uniform fitted poorly, but he hardly cared. For years he had worn nothing but a rough linsey-woolsey smock.

His unit had dragged their forage carts through Bladensburg behind the fighting—the air still stank of burned powder when they came into the long, sloped meadow, but the looters had already stripped the corpses nude and the flies moved on them like agitations of black lace. The regiments that had led the fighting were sent to the rear, and Radnor marched among the first men to enter Washington's streets. He gritted his teeth, watching the dark windows on either side, expecting shots. But the streets lay quiet, except for the crackle and tumble of the timbers of a single house that a scouting party had set ablaze. The only souls to be seen were a few blacks watching the British. Several approached and pleaded for a musket and a uniform. "No time, alas, no time," the offi-cers yelled, shooing the men away. "We have urgent business." Radnor, tangled inside with guilt and grief and delight, kept his eyes forward when he felt the onlookers' gaze.

Capitol Hill was taken with no fighting at all, almost a disappointment, the cartridges in his cartouche box heavy on his hip, the musket in his hands longing for use. In the weeds around the hulking Capitol building they formed ranks, and a dozen of the Colonial Marines, Radnor among them, were pulled out and dispatched to the White House. Radnor helped to rope a flagpole and pull it down. They used it to smash the White House windows, while others threw in pots of burning oil. Then they were sent to torch the Treasury.

At first it pleased Radnor to play a role in the arson, and he felt considerable pleasure in watching the White House and other buildings burn. But then it struck him that the British were parading himself and the other black marines to these places for a reason: to taunt the Americans with the image of freed slaves torching the nation's symbols. Radnor didn't know that he cared to escape slavery only to be made a token of someone else's purposes. The other black marines didn't seem to care, but Radnor brooded on it.

Some eight years ago, Suthers had taken Radnor and his two brothers as debt service from a Virginian tobacco farmer. Radnor's mother had been a house slave and taught them a little of how to read and write and behave in a civilized manner, but then she was sold away to Alabama and vanished forever; Radnor never knew his father. Radnor, Hollis, and Charles were young, strong children when they came to Suthers's estate, but the Virginian farmer likely believed he'd gained a measure on Suthers, for Hollis's eyesight was failing, and Charles had a lump hidden in his throat. Within the year Hollis was blind, and Charles's lump had to be excised, after which Charles could not speak. That autumn the Virginian farmer's tobacco harvest burned in the barns, and while he was fighting the fires, his house caught and burned, too. It was considered perfectly obvious that this was Suthers's doing. The Virginian farmer went the next day to Suthers—not to complain, but to ask forgiveness.

Suthers had no interest in farming; he held the estate only as a marker of prestige. He told Radnor and his brothers that if they would work hard, he would not bring in an overseer to drive them. He also said that if Hollis or Charles attempted to run off, he would kill them. "And if you run off," he said to Radnor, "I will catch you, sell you away, and kill your worthless brothers."

A couple of times a year, Radnor slipped off in the night and journeyed to see Frisbee, his mother's cousin, and the only remaining blood relation of himself and his brothers that he knew of on the Chesapeake. To journey to Frisbee's plantation, spend an hour there, and return, while staying off the roads monitored by the slave patrols, took the entirety of a night, sunset to sunrise. The last time Radnor had been there, in March, Frisbee told Radnor that he would soon be gone. Working at night with a stolen adze, he had fashioned a one-man canoe in the swamp, and as soon as he had a reliable report of the position of the British ships in the bay, he would paddle to join them. Frisbee said that if he could, he would bring the British to Suthers's plantation to claim Radnor, too.

Radnor might have begun at that time to worry for his brothers' fate, except that he allowed no hope Frisbee would be able to fulfill his promise. Hope existed in Radnor's experience as a sufferance, a thing with tiny talons for tearing at the flesh, to which he gave as little attention as possible. Surely it was more likely that Frisbee's makeshift canoe would founder and vanish in the open water.

Then one day Radnor stood up from rooting potatoes and saw, unlikely as a dream, faded red jackets coming through the corn, Frisbee himself in the fore. A fist seized Radnor's heart, tears welled in his eyes.

When he talked to Charles and Hollis they told him he

must go, but by then, secretly, Radnor had already decided. He would go. And it troubles him deeply, now, standing here in the uniform of the British Crown in the street of an infernal Washington, that he didn't think for an instant that he actually might stay with his brothers, that he abandoned them without hesitation, Hollis and Charles, as much family as he possesses in this world. Before him lies an abyss of loneliness.

The lilt of a bird—a strange, misplaced sound—scrapes Radnor's attention. It sounds again, and again. Then he realizes—it's the boy's whippoorwill call. He certainly wouldn't have expected it here.

He makes no sign that he has heard while he considers. Now he's a free man, there's no need or requirement for him to associate with lower sorts like the Phippses.

The whippoorwill call continues, growing loud and shrill, less like a bird and more like an anxious dog.

Radnor sighs, moves into the shadows down the street. Against common sense, he is not entirely without fondness for the child, always running about, laughing or fuming. Also, he feels he bears a debt to Mrs. Phipps. When he and his brothers were brought to Suthers's estate, Suthers intended to keep Hollis and Charles and sell Radnor to a trader in Arkansas, but—Radnor witnessed this himself—Mrs. Phipps, muttering, marched across the fields, and, standing barefoot in the dirt, told Suthers that he simply mustn't split a family, even a slave family, that he must keep the brothers together, since to one another they were the only family they had. Suthers looked over Mrs. Phipps with a strange look and said nothing. And maybe Suthers had had his own reasons, but the sale never happened. Radnor tried once to thank Mrs. Phipps. She waved him away. "It's simple enough," she said, "family being all we have in this world, really."

An ox lies dead at the edge of the street, its hulk sunk into a black pool of its own blood, throat cut, perhaps to prevent use of the creature by the redcoats. Two eyes and a top of filthy hair peek from behind its flank. "Henry," Radnor says. "How did you come here?" Henry says nothing, only grins—dirty, thin, jittering. "You arduous boy," Radnor says. Henry laughs. It is remarkable, how that sound causes memories to stir.

"You've turned redcoat," Henry says.

"Fight this war, and I'm free. Or so I've been assured."

"Suthers didn't treat you so bad." Henry looks doubtful. "We lived nearly as poor as you."

Radnor laughs. "Whatever amount of truth is in that, it is on account of the Phippses' blood disinclination toward hard work."

"Father's luck will turn," Henry says, patiently. "And Mother works hard, when the sickness hasn't got her—"

"Henry." Radnor cuts him off. "We labored for another man. I saw my mother sold away in chains, screaming, beating her own head bloody. And for you there comes a day when you can strike out and make your own life, but for a slave that day will never come. That's a heavy weight on the soul."

Henry whispers, "What's happened to your brothers?"

"The British wouldn't take them, because of their afflictions." Radnor glances back—the lieutenant is still in discussion with the patent official. "They've gone to hide."

"How long can they hide?"

"A long time," Radnor says, looking up and down the street, determined that he will not weep before the boy.

"I'm going to get money to buy out Father."

"I could name a whole lot more useful purposes for such money."

"Radnor," Henry says, solemn. "Mother's dead."

That's unexpected. "I'm sorry." Radnor touches Henry's shoulder. "A fine lady, your mother. Talked a great deal, and considerably variable in her mood, but a fine lady."

Henry says, "I still hear her."

"Well," Radnor says, "of course you do."

"She wants to go to sea. I put her into the pickle barrel, for now. And you were wrong about Franklin being dead. I saw Franklin, alive."

"Really?" The mother dead in a pickle barrel, but talking; the brother executed, but alive. Possibly the boy has lost his mind. But, Radnor notes, I am leaving all this behind. "Well, I'm glad." Radnor takes out of his jacket pocket a little stick that he has carved with notches. "If you see my brothers, will you give this to them?"

Henry turns it in his fingers. "What is it?"

"It's a message."

Henry tucks it into his pocket, nodding. He seems to be thinking about something else. "The thing of it is—" Henry, so thin and small, seems scarcely there in the flickering firelight. "Well, you're with the redcoats. What if you're supposed to shoot Franklin?"

"Then I'll shoot him."

"He can hit a snake in the head at fifty paces." Henry peers solemnly at Radnor. "He'll shoot you first."

It occurs to Radnor that Henry isn't worried about Franklin; Henry is worried about Radnor.

Radnor chuckles. Then flinches as a wetness strikes his cheek. Rain.

"You!" Someone in the dark shouts. "You! You there!"

A scuffle erupts, and several soldiers rush to join in— grunts, inarticulate cries, sounds of fists landing, fabric ripping.

They haul into the lantern light the ugliest man Radnor has ever seen. He wears an unbuttoned redcoat, a shirt torn open, no hat, no weapon, trousers high with strange bulge below the waist.

Henry says, "Morley." All this time he's been hidden behind the ox, but now he steps into the street.

"Looter! Looter!" the men call, jabbing the ugly fellow with their muskets.

"No! No!" Morley shouts. "A misunderstanding! Operating under strict orders! Conveying a message to Colonel Brooke! You'd best unhand me!"

A redcoat swings a musket at Morley's groin, and the blow clangs. Something drops from Morley's trouser leg. The lieutenant picks it up, turns it in his hands—a silver saucer.

"Looting is three hundred lashes," the lieutenant says. The rain begins falling faster. It seems everyone has forgotten or given up about burning the Patent Office. The lieutenant waves toward the bivouac. "Bring him along," he says.

"The hell you doing, boy?" Morley shouts to Henry as he passes. "By God! I waited and waited on you!"

"No one said you should try to pass so close to them!" Henry yells, quivering.

"Friend of yours?" Radnor asks.

Henry only gazes after the prisoner and seems to fall a little into himself.

Radnor nods goodbye to Henry, follows after the others. The rain slops down in torrents. He glances back once, expecting to see Henry alone in the street beside the ox. But he's gone.

Once when Henry was five or six Father woke him with giddy whispers and led him outside. "Look," Father said. "Watch the stars."

Henry, groggy, watched.

A barred owl raised its usual questions: *Hoo cooks for yoo? Hoo cooks for yoo all?*

But nothing happened overhead, and Henry, feeling cold and irritable, scuffled his feet. "Watch," Father said.

"My neck hurts," Henry said.

A star slid fast over the sky.

"See," Father said.

"I've seen a shooting star before," Henry said, still cross and muddled with sleep.

Another slipped by. Another. Another.

"Oh," Henry said.

"See!" Father cried. "Look at them, a-going it."

Some went long and slow, others fast, short, scarcely present before vanishing. A bright one grew brighter as it fell, blinked out an instant before colliding with horizon. Father hooted and cheered for it.

"Will the sky run out of stars?" Henry asked.

"Naw," Father said. "They're just showing off for one another, like boys jumping into a swim hole."

Henry loves Father. Curled inside an abandoned chicken hutch, he thinks of Father, of stars, of swim holes. He feels bad: he has done Father no good yet.

He has been snugged in here for hours, and although he shoved the yellow dress under his head for a pillow he is sore of shoulders, back, neck, one arm asleep. Hearing the rain finally stop he wriggles from the hutch, sits in the opening, rubs his head—feathers spring aloft and spiral down. He locates peas on the vine and several small hard green apples and crunches on these, squatting in the mud, contemplating the irregular fall of water off the leaves of a cottonwood and a little box turtle that moves laboriously toward a low place filled with debris and sewage. Although the rain has ceased, the light is oddly dim, the sky filled with roping dark clouds. The air sits on Henry with a cool wet weight, unmoving.

Finally he rises and makes his way through deserted streets littered with trash, finds the British bivouac on Capitol Hill and joins a few civilians watching nearby.

The hulk of the burned Capitol looms like a foundered wreck, surrounded by fire-browned grass and stinkweed where dozens of sparrows hop to and fro. The British troops stand in formation. A tripod of halberds has been driven into the earth. A shirtless man, arms out, is roped to a fourth halberd tied across the tripod. Nearby slouches Morley, also shirtless.

A drummer boy beats a slow cadence and calls the count—twenty-three, twenty-four, twenty-five. The soldier with the cat-o'-nine-tails appears little older than the drummer boy. On each beat of the drum he raises the cat and brings it down.

A wind gusts, stutters, dies, and comes again.

Blood slimes down and drenches the back of the man at the halberds, soaks the length of his trousers, drips to the ground.

Henry, in guilt and helpless discomfort, shifts on his feet and gives his attention to the uncommon weather—the clouds have turned blacker and blacker, and they writhe and weave, trending, strangely, east to west.

The count has reached one hundred thirty-seven when the man under the lash groans and collapses, pulling down the halberds. Two redcoats drag him away. The drummer resets the halberds. Morley with his face bent down lifts his arms to be tied.

An expectoration of rain sprays everyone, then stops.

The drum sounds, the cat rises and strikes. Morley moans.

The count passes twenty, thirty, and there's no more rain—until at the count of forty-four the wind punches with startling power into the face of the regiment.

Everyone flinches.

An instant later the rain comes down in a collapsing wave.

The wind screams and drives the rain so that it stings. The officers flail their hands and shout. The regiment fragments and flies to all directions. Henry stares after them, squinting into the wind and rain. Then he sees that Morley has been abandoned at the halberds.

Bent low to grip the weeds, Henry fights through the wind. Morley has pulled the halberds down, but they are still bound to his wrists—Henry unties them.

Together they lie flat while the wind grows more and more wild, an unbelievable force. A tree tilts to the ground, raising a tangle of roots from the earth. Tents sky overhead. A wooden sledge spins past.

It is a hurricane. Morley has crawled away. He shouts something. Henry pulls himself along the ground toward the dark shape that seems to be Morley, a journey that takes several minutes. He finds only a low shrub. He calls and casts around. He drags himself blindly on, shouting though he scarcely can hear himself. Finally he rolls into a ditch.

Here he surrenders and waits while the stormwater flows around him in torrents. The sky grows so dark that he can only see by the lightning that scars the sky. The thunder crashes monstrously in his ears, and the weather rages an hour and then another, or perhaps it is many, many hours, Henry cannot tell as the storm seems to have broken time's usual passage, leaving him in a chasm of soaking violence.

Yet there's nothing to be done. He even dozes a little.

Finally he notices that the wind is faltering. Slowly, the rain thins.

He wrenches his limbs from the mud and crawls from the ditch, into a world of mire and battered things. The rain dwindles. Through the clouds the sun smolders—it is late afternoon.

He wanders about, looking for Morley. He pulls flattened greens and carrots and radishes from a drowned garden and watches a party of redcoats work to right a wagon upside down in the street. Chewing a radish, he lingers near a half-dozen blacks talking on a street corner. One of the men has arrived from Alexandria. The British fleet has captured Fort Washington, giving them an open path up the Potomac, he says, and everyone who can is fleeing Alexandria. He glances at Henry. "Seems," he says, "like the redcoats might roll up the whole American nation, easy as anything, like one of those nice Turkey rugs." Gazing at Henry, he tilts his head.

The others turn to Henry.

Henry looks around. "What?"

"Sir," the one from Alexandria says, "if I may speak rather boldly, intending no insult, you are so dirt-covered that someone almost might not know if your skin were black or white."

"Oh," Henry says. "I'm white."

The little group chuckles, a thin vibration, nearly not a sound. The one from Alexandria says, "Yes sir, personally, I had no doubt." He dips his head in a grave nod. Then, as if on a signal unknown to Henry, they turn and move down the street.

Alexandria. Henry has been in Alexandria before, with Father, when Father had a little money. He remembers the wonderful cobblestone streets and the craftmen's shops—baker, tailor, harnessmaker, cordwainer, sailmaker, locksmith, china mender, glover, barber, perukemaker, cobbler—and the docks and the tall sails, and the taverns where Father drank, and the warehouse space where Suthers ran his card game.

It grows dark while Henry lingers near the British camp, watching for Morley. A redcoat tells him to go home, gesturing vaguely with his musket. Henry finds a place where he can sit hidden by bushes. The redcoats are hauling timbers from the Capitol and nearby buildings to build large fires. Henry rests his forehead on his knees.

When he wakes at dawn, the British army has vanished.

People are already scouring the abandoned encampment for valuables, but there is only garbage. Henry watches and contemplates his prospects briefly, then turns and sets out for the Potomac, to cross to Alexandria.

The bridge has been burned to black sticks extending from either bank, skeleton hands reaching but unable to grasp each other. Several watermen with skiffs and shallops tied at the foot of the bridge offer to ferry passengers. Henry pays his only half-dollar.

As they cross, the current sweeps them well downstream. Setting Henry ashore, the waterman says he is less than five miles from Alexandria.

Is Mother angry? Henry can only hear her so terribly faintly that it's impossible to say. But he's glad to hear her.

It strikes him suddenly that he has forgotten the yellow dress, in the chicken hutch. He stops in the road, and he thinks of going back for it. But he hasn't any money for the ferry. He sighs and goes on.

Again he encounters refugees, loaded carts and wagons, strings of livestock. The rain begins again, softly. But a sparkle of sun catches his eye: on his left, the sun shines in clear sky.

"A rainbow," he whispers. "Make a rainbow."

Soon it's there, dim colors in the shining rain against dark clouds.

"Brighter," he says. "Brighter, brighter, brighter."

To his delight the clouds open around the sun, and the rainbow glows brighter, and yet brighter. Soon it is complete from end to end. It spans the sky like an immense and solid thing, and very nearby, so that he might run to the foot of it in a minute or two. But he has tried this before; he knows it will move away from him exactly as he moves toward it. Still, it makes him happy.

CHAPTER 4

Morley moans, rolls, spits, beats his head once on the ground, rises. He's only rested ten minutes, but if he lies here any longer he will fall asleep, and miss his chance.

The soldiers of the British army lie on the road, the grass, and an adjoining rye field—thousands of redcoats sprawled out as if ruthlessly slaughtered. Morley threads a path between them, toward a wood at the rear of the column.

None of them have slept since the hurricane yesterday. Morley helped to build the campfires high at twilight, to give the impression of an occupied camp for as long as possible. Then, shortly after nightfall, the army formed a column and marched away in silence—horses muzzled, ironwork wrapped with rags. A curfew had been announced, enforceable by death, and the dark streets lay deserted.

They marched to Bladensburg and halted in the meadow only to collect such wounded and belongings as they could locate by torchlight in fifteen minutes. The officers rallied the men into column again, and they crossed the river and passed through the town and continued on, returning as they had come two days earlier. Blacks appeared out of the night and begged to join them, but the officers were twitchy and anxious at the prospect of becoming trapped inland, and all were sent away. They quick marched for hours, and the effect of this after the marching and battling and commotion of the last days pressed the limits of endurance. When they halted briefly to await the report of scouts, men dropped to the ground and had to be kicked awake again. Morley marched in a wretched daze, exhaustion like a fat man hanging from his shoulders. Sweat soaked his hair under his cap and ran down his neck to burn in the wounds from the whip. The chafe of the straps of his knapsack gradually turned into a cold, prickly sensation. At times he seemed to doze even as he marched. He fell to his knees, rose, stumbled on.

They marched onward as dawn came. The sun added heat to the awful humidity; the insects swarmed to life. When they finally stopped, men collapsed where they stood or stumbled a dozen feet to find shade. The drummer boys came through with canvas buckets of water, and the men put their faces in to drink like goats. "At noon," the officers said, "we march again."

Morley steps over a soldier sleeping with his face in the mud. Morley's back is pierced by dozens of splinters of pain. He can recall every one of the forty-four lashes he took. The colonel won't forget the count. After this rest they will complete their march to the ships, sail to the outpost on Tangier Island, and go straight back to flogging. Morley figures he will have to suffer another hundred or hundred and fifty to satisfy the colonel. He doesn't intend to be available to suffer it.

He passes the Colonial Marines, and among them the black American that the boy dallied with the night previous in Washington—the black, curiously, sits awake and watches Morley as he comes up the road. Morley supposes that the man recognizes him. Morley grins. The black man gazes back with no reaction.

He reaches the trees, starts wending through. In a moment he is out of sight in the dense wood. Pleased, he whistles a few notes, his mood only constrained by the trafficking of mosquitoes on his face and hands. He supposes he will join the American army. He knows of others who have walked away to offer their services. The Americans pay twice as much as the King.

He reaches the far corner of the field that borders the road, and from cover he watches the column rise, assemble, set into motion. A pair of drummers trail behind; the crack of the beat reaches him a little delayed behind the flash of the drumsticks. The column vanishes around a bend. Presently the sound of the drums disappears, too.

Morley sets out northward, not sure where he is headed, but sure that he will find something, something to lead him to the next thing, and on.

But as the day passes he begins to doubt himself. He walks wreathed in biting flies and mosquitoes and God knows what other dreadful tiny monsters. Every direction brings him to fetid swamp. He sweats so much that he is as sodden as if he had just finished a swim in the sea.

But—he tells himself—the cork is pulled, and he must drink the wine. He takes off his jacket, casts it aside. He soaks his forage cap in a trickle of water and sets it on his head.

He comes to another reedy, stagnant marsh. He doubles back.

Perhaps he should have stayed nearer the road, but there would have been British troops straggling along it to avoid. He assures himself that he will find it again eventually. Anyway, things certainly will be better here in America. There are opportunities all about for one who sees them. Money flows in great rivers to those who earn it. He's tired of serving under officers who bought their positions and sneer at the commoners they command. American officers, he's heard, treat soldiers with more respect and less of the lash, due to all men being equal—excepting, Morley notes, the slaves.

The bird calls here are strange, harsh splinters of sound. He worries about snakes. He trudges through a meadow full of little golden flowers, strikes swamp again, curses, turns aside.

A human sound reaches him, so faint that he considers the possibility that he's imagining it. He tracks toward it as best he can—a woman's voice, singing, away somewhere through the trees. He hears also a chuckling of water.

A young woman in a bonnet stands in a creek, the hem of her dress pulled to her waist. She's been washing—laundry is piled in a basket—but just now something has distracted her. She stops singing and digs with her hands in the mud. She's roundly formed, wet legs gleaming smooth and delicious.

Indeed, this is a land of happy chances, Morley thinks, as he tiptoes along the creek bank.

She pulls from the earth a series of small white shapes—turtle eggs.

Morley reaches a place opposite her. The moving water covers any small noise he makes, and he feels quite fortunate indeed—until a man appears on the other side of the creek and calls, "Hello!" He carries a musket. He says something to the woman, and she turns to look at Morley.

Morley straightens. "Forgive my interruption!" Morley smiles big, waves both hands. "I have departed King George's Royal Foot Artillery, and I want to join the freemen of the American army! Can you help?"

Morley crosses over and approaches to shake the man's hand. He has a scarred hole in one cheek, big enough to put a thumb in. It whistles as he breathes, and he looks suspicious, but Morley talks fast about sneaking from the British column and wandering lost with the insects and the snakes. "Why," he says, "I've traveled the earth and fought Napoleon's armies, but seeing one of your colossal frogs, well, I thought it some unholy devil spawn. I nearly swooned."

The man barks a laugh. He relaxes. He and his wife lead Morley to their encampment—they are peddlers, with a horse and a peddler's wagon with many drawers built into the sides, like an enormous piece of furniture on wheels. Some of the drawers are missing. The peddler explains that his wagon over-turned in a rain-swollen river, sweeping away nearly all of his merchandise. His words sibilate through the hole in his cheek. He has hardly a thing to peddle, he says, except his wagon and his horse, and if he sells those, then what is he? A peddler with nothing to sell is not even a peddler.

While they talk, the wife cooks rice, greens, and turtle eggs. They eat, and Morley praises the food lavishly, kisses the lady's hand to watch the color rise in her neck, offers elaborate grat-itude for the hospitality, asks again the direction to the road to Baltimore, which is where, the peddler says, the American army will be.

Morley sets out with regret in his heart. During the Peninsular War, his wife Mercedes had traveled behind the army with the other women and children and sutlers and such. Every woman he sees reminds him of his sweet Mercedes in Spain—marvelous Mercedes of the dark eyes, delightful dim-ples, and—well, he's more or less forgotten the other features of her face, and due to the problem of language they could only exchange a few words, but he remembers her high, loud, long laugh, which, granted, wasn't so different from her shriek of fury when she was angry, usually when she felt he was with-holding money from her. But her laugh was glorious. He saun-ters on the road, full of belly and free.

A half mile outside Alexandria a dozen redcoats stand around two wagons positioned crosswise in the road. Henry slips into a cornfield, circles the checkpoint, and enters the city through the beaten earth yards of small whitewashed houses. He peeks into a window, and a stern-faced man stares out. Henry smiles. The man stares. Henry thumbs his nose and flees. He starts toward another house, but someone he cannot see shouts, "Go away! Go on!"

Wandering the city streets, he begins to feel downhearted:

it is not like it was in Washington. Here men watch from windows, sit in open doorways. When Henry spies a house that seems promising, someone across the street yells at him. He comes to a row of shops, but there are people here, too—men at the door of the chandler's, in the windows of the silversmith, at the rail of the notions shop, gazing at Henry with mistrust. This mistrust makes him cross. He has done nothing to them, and it is unfair and an aggravation.

He stomps downhill to the warehouses and docks, and here is some noise—the British are emptying the warehouses of bolts of cloth, crates of glassware and crockery, barrels of tobacco, tea, coffee, and black pepper, casks of molasses, whale oil, and whiskey, bales of cotton, piles of beaver pelts and uncut leather, and dropping these load by load into boats and rowing them to tall ships flying the Union Jack.

Henry comes to a place he recognizes—Suthers's four-story warehouse, stone-walled on the first floor and brick above, with an office in the corner. Henry backs into the shadows across the street. He feels a kind of relief, as if, perhaps, he traveled here not for looting after all, but to come to this warehouse, to Suthers.

What Henry knows of Suthers is what Father has told him, that Suthers ran away at twelve years old—away from the hillside cabin where he and his father lived in poverty—and came to Alexandria. He started as a laborer on the docks, but soon became involved in buying and selling goods and running card games. "Now," Father said, "he also runs horse races, cockfights, boxing matches, and God knows how many other things." When Henry was at the warehouse with Father, he watched how the men came to whisper with Suthers where he sat beside the card games. Suthers was a small, wiry man with thick uncombed hair and the intense gaze of a weasel surveilling a henhouse. At Suthers's side sat a tall bald man with hollow cheeks and deep-set eyes—Henry found the bald man staring at him, and then he saw that the bald man settled his gaze this way on everyone in the room, one by one, excepting Suthers. Father said that the bald man's name was Lodowicke, and according to popular estimation, Lodowicke had killed enough men to fill a potter's field.

While Father played faro, Suthers seemed to ignore Henry, but late in the evening Suthers left the room for a while, and when he returned, he handed Henry an orange.

The faro players stopped in surprise. It surprised Henry especially; he had never held an orange before. Everyone was looking at him, so he raised the orange to his mouth and bit into it like an apple—the bitterness of the rind made his eyes bulge and sucked his lips around his teeth.

The faro players risked falling from their chairs laughing. Suthers smiled a little and returned to his seat. Henry nearly cast the orange to the ground, but the novelty of it stopped him, and soon he was glad—when he worked out how to peel the rind from the meat, the orange seemed the most delicious thing he had ever tasted.

A bucktoothed man on a little, tottering mule comes up the street, stops, ties the mule, opens a door, disappears into Suthers's warehouse.

Henry steps into the street, toward the door, thinking that when the man comes out he might gain a glimpse inside, or possibly even somehow slip through the door to take what he wants—if the redcoats haven't already taken everything of value.

He stops beside the doorway and waits. In a moment the door opens. The bucktooth comes out carrying a wooden box drilled with holes big enough to push plums in. Henry stands off to the side, but the bucktooth sees him immediately.

So Henry steps forward, right into the man, knocking the box to the ground.

As the box crashes, something inside yowls. A cat. The bucktooth yells, "Goddamn you, boy!" He's blocking Henry's view of the doorway, and then he shoves Henry back and bends to pick up the box. Painted on the lid is "*402 Ann.*"

Henry retreats to watch the bucktooth tie the box to the back of his mule, mount, and go. Then he returns to the office door, but it is locked.

Between Suthers's warehouse and the next warehouse runs a weedy alley; the far end opens toward the harbor, and two horses are there, harnessed to a wagon. Henry enters the alley looking for another door, a window. There are none. So he continues to the horses, then creeps around the horses to peer over the wagon.

Three redcoats stand along the wharf beside the water. They hold muskets with bayonets and seem to be waiting. They mutter among themselves, and the two taller soldiers twist to stare around. The third soldier seems familiar, and then Henry recognizes the way he stands small and still with an intense gaze—Suthers. Did Suthers join the British? It seems strange. Then Henry realizes that one of the other redcoats is the tall bald man, Lodowicke, his baldness disguised by a British shako, face pale and gaunt.

For a time nothing happens. Redcoats at work looting the warehouses call and shout on the docks and from the boats in the water, but Suthers, Lodowicke, and the third man stand silent. Henry's attention wanders—to the hovering specks of the gulls over the harbor, to thin clouds like gatherings of cottonwood seed, to an eye-shaped knot in the wood of the wagon before him. He hears, it seems, a trace of Mother's voice, thin and stretched as smoke on a wind. As if she were shouting far, far away. She seems perhaps alarmed.

The three on the wharf turn to look at something away to their left, where Henry can't see. He slithers into the wagon—

it's empty and smells of goat piss—to peer through a gap in the boards. He wants to see Suthers more clearly.

"Help with that?" Suthers asks.

Two redcoats, sweating, come along the wharf carrying a chest between them. "No," one says. Behind these two come three more redcoats, muskets hung at their shoulders, walking at ease, laughing about something.

Suthers attends to their passing, glances up and down the wharf.

Clicks his tongue.

Then things happen quickly, things that Henry can only watch in horror.

Suthers and the two with him step forward and drive their bayonets into the backs of the three guards. The two that Suthers and Lodowicke strike startle and crumple like shreds of paper in a flame. But the third cries out, wrenches himself off the bayonet, falls to one knee. He gropes for his musket on the planks of the wharf. Ahead of him, the two with the chest drop it and turn. One backs away, lifting his hands. The other pulls a pistol from his belt and raises it, shaking.

A musket blasts, and the one with the pistol is knocked forward as if someone had swung a log into his back.

Lodowicke slips his bayonet between the ribs of the man on one knee: he falls with a sigh.

Two more men in redcoats emerge from the adjacent warehouse. One holds a smoking musket. Suthers says to him, with disgust, "I told you to hold your fire."

The one with his hands raised leaps—he lands in the water with a great splash.

"Let him go," Suthers says. "The chest. In the wagon."

The wagon—Henry can't climb out without being seen, so he rolls and tucks himself under the driver's bench.

From somewhere further down the wharf come shouts,

pounding steps, metal clattering. Henry glimpses Suthers running to untie the horses. The chest crashes into the wagon. In a mad, noisy scramble Suthers climbs onto the driver's bench above Henry and lashes the horses while the other men swing into the wagon, yelling. A musket fires, and another. Someone screams, and the lash snaps on the horses. Another musket shot. Hooves strike rock. One last body crashes into the wagon, right in front of Henry—it is Lodowicke, holding his head with both hands, bleating. Henry cringes. He's blocked under the bench, against Lodowicke's back. He can't see Lodowicke's face, but there's some terrible wound there. Another musket blast, away behind them now. The wagon moves faster, faster, crashes off a wall, leans around a corner. Lodowicke's bleats stretch into screams.

They race onward. Suthers bellows, "Quiet, damn it!"

But Lodowicke still screams. The other men are shouting at Lodowicke to shut up, while Lodowicke flails, his back writhing before Henry.

Suthers calls, "Be rid of him."

Hands seize Lodowicke, lift him, tumble him over the side of the wagon.

Henry hears a moist snap, like a rat under a boot.

"Aye, his leg," the man nearest Henry says.

Suthers is working the horses, Lodowicke is gone, and two men remain in the back of the wagon with Henry. The fifth member of the group must have been left behind or killed at the wharf. The man nearest Henry turns. He has a wide, bearded face that reminds Henry of the hideous door-knockers on fancy houses. His glistening, bulging eyes settle their gaze straight onto Henry.

Slowly, bracing himself against the lurching of the wagon, he bends, gets Henry by the hair, yanks him out, holds him up, squints. "Who in the blessed hell are you?"

Henry can barely breathe, much less answer.

"Suthers," the door-knocker calls. "Do I throw this one right out, or do I carve him up first?"

Suthers glances back. "Henry? Henry Phipps?" Suthers looks at Henry for an instant with widened eyes, then some new feeling compresses his gaze. What that feeling is, Henry isn't sure. He is fairly surprised that Suthers knows his name. "Set the boy down," Suthers says, returning his attention to the horses. "*In* the wagon."

The door-knocker drops Henry. He and the other redcoat imposter look down at him. The second man has the dangling jowls and wilted look of a fat man who came on hard times and lost his fleshiness. He gives Henry a narrow, mean glance, then, turning away, knocks Henry in the ribs in a way that could almost seem unintentional. Even with Lodowicke gone, the box of the wagon is crowded with the three of them, the muskets, the chest. Suthers keeps the horses at a trot, and the wagon sways and jars violently. Henry glares at the back of the jowly man's head.

"Henry," Suthers calls. "Up here."

Henry hardens his astonishment into a frown, swings up onto the bench, sits tall. Suthers, holding the reins with both hands, leans into Henry. "Why are you here? Why aren't you with your mother?"

"She died," Henry says. "She's dead."

Suthers straightens and does not speak. He rides the jouncing wagon as if nailed to it; only his hands with the reins move. Perhaps he lifts his head a little. "I'd like you to ride with us," he says. "All right?"

Henry weighs this for only a second. He is reluctant to set out alone again and feels a willingness to trust Suthers—perhaps because of the orange. But, mostly, he is profoundly curious about the chest in the back of the wagon. He says, "All right."

They have come out of the center of the city and pass smaller and smaller houses. The man with the door-knocker face and the man with the jowls reload their muskets. They emerge from the last of the buildings and pass between cornfields, toward the British checkpoint.

A couple of redcoats sit in the wagons set across the road; the others idle nearby or rest on their haunches amid trampled corn.

Suthers slows, stops, smiles.

"The admiral wants roast pig for supper," he announces, in an imitation of English tone that startles Henry. "This boy—" Suthers claps Henry on the shoulder. "—has volunteered to show us a well-stocked sty."

"That right?" An officer comes to Henry's side of the wagon. "What about wine?"

Suthers winks at Henry.

"Maybe we can find wine," Henry says. "Whiskey's more likely, though."

"Sorry, can't let you back in without wine. Whiskey hereabouts tastes of sawdust and horsemeat."

One of the men in the back of the wagon makes a little hiss. Henry, glancing round, sees figures in the distance coming up the road.

"I understand that's exactly what it's made from," Suthers says.

"No reentry without wine!" the officer repeats, pleased with his joke. "Hear me, boy?"

Henry nods. He doesn't dare look back again, but a commotion can be faintly heard.

Neither does Suthers look back, but his smile drops. "All right," he says. "We'll get your wine. Let us through."

"Good wine!" The officer laughs. "None of that American vinegar and bile. You only get through with good wine!" He slaps one of the wagons in the road. "Make way!"

Two of the redcoats set to shoving the wagons apart to open a path. They do not move quickly. The noise behind them comes nearer. Shouts carry faintly over the distance.

The officer turns and squints.

"Don't!" comes a cry, thin but clear. "Don't let them pass!"

A musket shot explodes behind Henry—one of Suthers's men. A redcoat in the road sits down and looks curiously at the hole in his chest. Suthers snaps the reins, but it hardly matters, the horses are in a panic and bolt forward, knocking men aside. The redcoats yell and fumble to level their muskets and blast the wagon, shots that splinter the sideboards and whistle the air. Suthers bellows insults at the horses, and they buck and scrape between the two roadblock wagons.

In a moment they are free, but Henry, bent low, watching backward, sees one more shot pop off with smoke, flame, and the sound of a hammer hitting mud as the ball strikes the shoulder of the man with the door-knocker face.

"Bah," he says. He sits to look at the wound. "That there is horseshit. That's a damnable injustice."

In a minute they have run clear out of sight of the checkpoint, but Suthers continues to lash the horses. The door-knocker blanches, holding his shoulder. A considerable amount of blood slops on the floorboards.

Finally Suthers whoas the horses. They are sweat lathered, frothing. Suthers says, "Losing Lodowicke is a heavy price." He looks round. "But it's ours now. The redcoats won't come this far into the countryside. Take off the uniforms. For God's sake, bind that wound."

He doesn't wait but a moment before he sets the horses to a trot again.

The moon rises three-quarters full in the twilight, and the road glows whitely. Suthers keeps driving the horses on. The door-knocker lolls in the back and gasps.

"Hm," the jowly man says. "Mr. Suthers? Say, why're we taking this boy? He will slow us."

"The boy is fine."

"He seems indeed a fine enough boy, as boys go, as you say. It's only that I don't recall planning for any boy."

"If I tell you the boy comes, he's coming."

"I only mean that it doesn't seem like a stone-hard plan if it changes every time a boy pops up. See what I mean? Who is he? Just want to know the plan."

"Bite your tongue," Suthers says, "or I'll cut it out for you."

The jowly man scowls and cuts nasty glances toward Suthers's back, but he says no more.

A little later they come to the black skeleton of the bridge at the Potomac, deserted and quiet but for the trill of crickets and the plash of the river. Suthers jumps down, stalks to a small boat pulled onto the riverbank, kicks it.

A man rises out, grumbling.

Suthers talks low to him. The man stops grumbling.

Suthers returns to the wagon, leans in, opens the chest, removes two heavy sacks. He turns away, leaving the empty chest in the wagon. The boatman unharnesses the horses and leads them into the darkness. A few minutes later he returns. Suthers, his men, and Henry climb into the boat. The ferryman pushes the boat into the water, climbs in. He works the oars. Suthers sits in the prow with the two sacks at his feet. The air on the river lies still, muddy smelling. The river surface gleams with all the stars overhead.

"Where're we going?" Henry asks.

Suthers says, "Shh."

Henry looks to the shore ahead, a black fringe on the shimmering dark water. He eyes the two sacks. Suthers has a firm grip on them.

When they reach shore the burned bridge lies somewhere away in the darkness upriver. Suthers pays the boatman from his pocket, puts one sack on his shoulder, gives the other to Jowls. In file they walk a trail along the bank of the river, stumbling, tripping. At one point, Jowls falls, and the sack he carries clinks.

Door-knocker struggles and lags.

"Faster," Suthers says. "Faster."

This goes on a long while.

Finally they reach the burned bridge. They turn onto the road into Washington and soon come to a tavern, windows dark. Suthers says, "Wait," opens the door, goes inside. Jowls drops his sack to the ground and stares at it. After a minute Suthers returns with a fat boy with a lantern who takes them around the tavern to a barn. The fat boy saddles and brings out three horses. Suthers lashes the two sacks behind the saddle of one, mounts, motions for Henry to climb up behind him. Jowls and Door-knocker mount the other two horses. They start into the dark streets of Washington.

No one is about. The moon has gone down, and a suggestion of dawn twilight seeps into the blackness between the stars. Henry sways with the movement of the horse. Why is Suthers taking him? Where?

Henry doesn't know.

He thinks of the orange Suthers gave him. He remembers Lodowicke pitched over the side of the wagon, the crack of his leg. He is curious, uneasy, and uncommonly tired—he tries to stay awake, but his head hangs until it touches the broadcloth of Suthers's coat, and a moment later he sleeps, with his hands at Suthers's waist and his cheek on Suthers's back.

Mother stands beside the road, barefoot in her gingham dress. "Henry?" she says. "Henry?"

Henry tries to answer but somehow cannot: all that comes from his throat is a tiny grunt. Suthers doesn't notice, and their horse carries them onward. Henry attempts to grab Suthers by the shoulder, to point, but he cannot move. To his immense vexation, as they pass Mother he cannot even turn to look. "Henry!" she cries, sounding already far away. "Bring him to see me. Make him stop. Bring him."

Henry makes an anguished effort to cry out, to turn, to topple himself from the horse. Finally he succeeds in leaning a little, and he feels gravity rolling him sideways—

He wakes in a spasm as Suthers throws an arm back to grab him. He shoves Henry back onto the horse. "Ease up, son."

Henry blinks, his ability to see in the morning-bright world returning by degrees, even as he hears Mother calling, Bring him to me. Bring him to me.

They are well down the road from Washington, nearly to Bladensburg. Henry looks back—in the distance behind them huddles the Fiddlestick's End, where Franklin punched the harelip. He and Suthers ride alone; there's no sign of Suthers's two underlings. Below Henry's legs, black streaks of sweat mark the bay flanks of the horse. The two sacks from the chest on the docks are tied behind Henry.

Henry says, "Where are we going?"

"You're awake," Suthers says. "Now tell me what happened. What happened to Francine?"

Henry tells about the cow, while at the same time he hears Mother shouting, Bring him, Henry! This once, you must do as you're told!

As Henry talks Suthers is quiet and his back is straight and tense, until the end, when Henry has fallen silent, and Suthers says, "Awful," and he bends over the reins.

Henry bursts into tears.

Suthers, brooding, says nothing. Henry quits crying as soon as he can.

Mother calls, Henry!

Henry says, "Halt the horse, please."

"Not here," Suthers says.

"She wants to see you."

"Who?"

"Stop!"

"I said, not here."

Henry throws himself sideways off the horse, hits grass hard with one shoulder, tumbles, sits up.

Suthers turns the horse, looks at him. "You're daft."

Henry says, "Let me show you."

"Show me what?"

Henry doesn't answer. He starts away. Presently he hears Suthers dismount and follow, leading the horse.

They wend through the orchard and come into the brush and the chokecherry patch. Here is the cart and pickle barrel.

"What's this?" Suthers says.

Henry opens the barrel.

"What is that?" Suthers asks.

Mother looks dreadful. It startles Henry; he had a different image in his mind. Her skin is puckered and sallow, except where dark stains of coagulated blood show through. But it is her. "Mother," he says.

"Good Lord!" Suthers jumps back, casts around, then creeps forward to peer into the barrel. "Francine," he says. He rubs his face. "Henry," he whispers, not looking at him, "why did you do this?"

Henry listens for Mother amid the fume of his mind, but she only hums now, happy. "She's happy," he says.

"Please," Suthers says. "Elaborate."

"She says she doesn't want to be buried. She wants to be sent to sea with her family around."

"Says?"

"She says it now. Well, not just now. Now she's humming."

"I don't hear any humming."

Henry shrugs. "I do."

Suthers listens. Then he shakes himself, turns, puts his hands on Henry's shoulders, bends, and watches Henry's eyes with unnerving intensity. He says, "She's dead."

"She told me to bring you here," Henry says. "Just a moment ago. She shouted as we rode."

Suthers blinks as if Henry had puffed air in his eyes. He nods, stands up straight. "Shut the barrel."

"Why did she want me to bring you here?"

"She's dead," Suthers says. "We should bury her. But I am in a hurry, and I expect she'll keep until we return."

Mother says, her voice achy, Take me with you.

Henry says, "She wants to come with us."

"No!" Suthers grimaces. "That's madness." He touches the side of the barrel, says, "Goodbye, Francine." He turns away. "She'll be fine here." He leaves Henry to tighten the lid.

Henry expects Mother will complain, but she says, The two sacks, Henry, and then return.

As they walk the horse back through the orchard, Suthers hands Henry a water flask, and a piece of salted pork. Henry asks, "Where are the other two?"

"I paid them and sent them on." Suthers looks around as if thinking of something else. "Henry," he says, "how does a man measure himself?"

Henry instinctively dislikes this question, its tone. He says, irritably, "Probably with some sort of a stick with marks on it."

"Yes, a measuring stick. But of what kind?" Henry says nothing, but Suthers bears on. "I believe the measures of a man's success are two. One is worldly success, measured in money. The other is eternal success, measured in family. I began with little of either, and I have built them up by my own efforts. Everything I do, I do for one of those two ends. Money and family. And of course we attend to the love of family by the mechanism of money, and we extend both measures of success by passing money to our heirs. Such is how we recognize great families. Generally they have been royal born, but it is possible now for any man to raise himself up and make a great family. Family over all others. Family before oneself, even. This was my father's abject failure. I've had to start all anew."

Henry squirms.

"A thing I have learned with dire certitude," Suthers says, "is to never be in debt to another. A debt offers great power over a man. It has a spiritual force. If we measure a man with money, what is a man worth if he is in debt to another? He is worth less than nothing. And what has such a man done to his family?"

Henry, trailing a little behind, can see only Suthers's back and the hair on his head, speaking mouthlessly. He hates it. "I'm going to get the money to buy Father out," Henry says. "It's what Mother wants."

"I will not help you with that," Suthers says. "I never give away unearned money, and although I do make loans under certain terms it is better that you stay out of debt with me. Neither will anyone else give you money for Phipps. Phipps's character is clear enough and cannot be changed. If you raise the funds to free Phipps, he will only put himself back into the debtor's prison. You might as well ask a grain weevil to stay out of the grain."

Henry shakes his head. "His luck has to turn."

"If there was ever a matter that had nothing to do with luck, Phipps's condition is it. But I do believe you are different from him, Henry."

Although he has often thought that he does not wish to be like his father, at the moment Henry feels he would rather spend a lifetime in prison than agree with anything Suthers says. Henry says, "I am a Phipps."

"I think you have more of your mother in you."

"I am a Phipps."

"I know you are alone in the world," Suthers says. "Phipps in prison. Brother in the army. I have an opportunity for you. I would like for you to work for me. Errands. Messages. Some labor. Certain small tasks. You will be paid fairly. How you spend your money is your own matter, naturally."

"Could I buy out Father's debts, then?"

"It would take time. You may develop other ideas for your money."

"Time," Henry says, feeling as if they are speaking of several eternities.

"What do you think?"

"All right, yes, I will work for you," he says, with no intention of working for Suthers, thinking that with the first chance to grab the sacks and run, he will do it.

Suthers nods. "You're not a good liar, Henry. But I believe you will work for me. You'll see."

They have come out of the orchard, and the scent of moist earth baking rises off the meadow. The dead of the battle at Bladensburg are gone; everything of value is gone; all that remains are damp cartridge papers, cannonball divots, and the black marks where the rockets sputtered around.

"You'll be wondering what's in the sacks," Suthers says. "It's money. Silver and gold. It belonged to a merchant and thief and ingrate with a face warty as a toad's named Delmore. I've had intelligence as to the location of Delmore's funds for some time, but no clean opportunity to access it until the British presented themselves. Delmore foolishly believed his hiding place was secure and did not evacuate the money. I arranged for the location to be mentioned to the British, and they raided Delmore's little stronghold. My intention was to take the money from the British discreetly, so that Delmore would not connect me with the incident. It was to have been a quieter exit. Delmore is not entirely a fool. He may guess what has happened. He may already have someone tracking us. He'll likely send someone to watch for us at the estate."

"Your house burned," Henry says.

"I know." Suthers glances at him. "How did that happen? Do you know?"

Henry shrugs. "And Radnor joined the British."

"Yes," Suthers says. "His brothers have also run off, but we'll find them. The house is of no matter. It had the Phipps smell in it, and I often thought of burning it down myself. Still, if Delmore has men looking for us, that's where they will go. I have a place where we can spend a day or two, let them exhaust their searching and grow lax."

The East Branch chuckles as they pass over the bridge.

Suthers stops at the tavern in Bladensburg, dismounts, pulls Henry off, ties the horse, says, "Watch the horse."

The instant Suthers passes through the doorway, Henry starts on the sacks. He doesn't have a great deal of experience with horses, and he doesn't trust this one. He wants to leave the horse. But the sacks are tied to a loop on the saddle with an unusually complicated waterman's knot, and it takes him a moment to unravel it. Then he heaves the sacks to his shoulder, starts running up the street.

He's not crossed thirty feet before Suthers steps from behind the corner of the tavern. In his hand is a rake, which he swings into Henry's shin, sending him facedown into the mud. Suthers sets a knee in Henry's back, produces a length of rope, and there in the street binds Henry's hands behind his back. "You ought to give matters a little more forethought," he says to Henry, cheerily. "Restrain your impulses a moment." Suthers pushes his face into the mud, and then it's all Henry can do to tongue the muck off his teeth and breathe.

"Believe me," Suthers adds, yanking Henry to his feet, "I am in fact working to advance your interests."

He produces an sack of linsey-woolsey and pulls it over Henry's head.

Henry loses any notion of location. It's exhausting to keep balance on the horse while blind, hands bound. At one point, they enter a wide stream—Henry hears the flow and swirl of the water and the splashing of the hooves, feels droplets thrown up onto his legs. Something causes the horse to buck in the water, and for a moment his blind world tilts far backward. He only stays on the horse because Suthers again reaches back to grab him.

Eventually they enter a narrow trail—Henry feels leaves and branches on his legs, his shoulders. The horse snorts and sidesteps. By glimpses of light through the weave of the hood Henry guesses that the day is closing.

Finally they stop.

Suthers dismounts, pulls Henry off the horse, sets him on his feet, pushes him ahead. Henry's shoulder jars off a door frame. The light here is very dim. A door closes behind. Suthers takes the bag off Henry's head, unties his hands.

They are inside a small log cabin, light admitted by two openings chiseled high in the wall. It is a single room, rank with scents of mildew, moss, and mouse droppings. The only furnishings are a shabby corn tick mattress, a stone bench set into one wall, and a small charred hearth under a stone chimney. Suthers nods to the mattress. "You can have the bed."

Then Suthers goes out. Henry hears a bar slide into place across the door.

Intensely aggravated, Henry immediately resolves to burn every structure Suthers owns if necessary, and he begins searching in a frenzy for a flint. Soon he finds in the chinking between logs the sharp half of a broken nail, which he tucks in his trouser waist at the back.

He finds nothing more between the logs, along the rafters, or at the corners of the floor. The logs are set directly on hard earth, and he might dig out, but it would take a considerable while. He hits the door, but it seems solid. He feels through the mattress. He searches the hearth, then peers up the chimney, built of river rock and daub.

The chimney is narrow, and he is doubtful. He goes

around the cabin again, but he can find no other possibilities. He returns to the chimney, puts his arms into the chimney, shimmies his torso up, gets his feet underneath himself, pushes up, straightens his legs, lifts on his toes, moves worm-like upward.

After gaining a foot or so, his shoulders become jammed at a painful angle.

He tries to wriggle back down, but it seems he will tear his shoulder out of its joint. He attempts upward again and gains a few inches, but now he is only more completely trapped than before. He cannot force himself either way.

He writhes and squirms. But he is stuck fast.

Perhaps an hour passes. The door opens and closes. Henry is still in the chimney, arms numb.

Suthers laughs a long while, which makes Henry angry, and he kicks uselessly. Suthers grabs him, yanks him down.

"Sit," he says, gesturing to the mattress. Henry reluctantly sits, arms hanging at his sides like sausages. He cannot lift them, and as the blood returns spears of pain follow. Henry does notice that Suthers's sleeves are wet, as are the bottoms of his trousers. He's been in the water.

Suthers lifts a stone from the base of the chimney—underneath is a small space that holds candles and flints and a tin of dried meat. Henry scowls and feels bitter; he'd been dangling right above it.

It has grown dark. Suthers lights a candle. When Henry is able to work his arms again, Suthers hands him some meat. They eat. "You'll work for me," Suthers says.

"No," Henry says.

Suthers continues as if Henry had not spoken. "—but for now I'll keep to myself the privilege of knowing where we are, and where the money is located. I used to come here to hunt, sometimes, when I was younger. Raccoon, possum. No one knew of this place, and I could be alone. Eventually I acquired a deed to the land. Not that it matters really, since still no one comes here or cares."

When he finishes eating, Suthers takes a small leather-bound account book from his jacket pocket and bends over its pages to study the figures. He glances up, catches Henry watching. "Sleep," he says. "You had precious little last night."

Henry lies on the mattress. Something bites into his ribs. Searching with his fingers, he finds a small stick. When he searched the mattress before he didn't notice it, and now he nearly casts it aside before he finds a pattern of notches and scratches worked into it. For a moment he thinks it is the same stick that Radnor gave him in Washington—no, that's still in his pocket. He takes out Radnor's stick. The two are very similar. Could this new stick have been stuffed into the mattress before it was carried here? Or did Suthers lie when he said no one else had been here? Perhaps a slave didn't count, in Suthers's mind.

Henry closes his eyes, thinking he'll pretend to sleep. In the quiet, the noise of a stream can be faintly heard. He rubs his thumb back and forth over the notches on the stick, wondering what they mean. He'll pretend to sleep, and when Suthers sleeps, he can escape.

But with his eyes closed he quickly drops deep into sleep.

He wakes once in the night.

The candle is still burning. Slitting his eyes, Henry turns his head. Suthers sits with his book open in his lap but ignored. He is looking straight at Henry.

This frightens Henry, and he doesn't care to think on why Suthers would sit in the night looking at him. He tightens his eyes shut and presently sleep overwhelms him again.

"Henry," Suthers says.

Henry lurches up, looking round for Suthers, seeing no one.

Suthers is behind him—the bag comes down over Henry's head, and Suthers grabs his hands and binds them.

"Time to go," Suthers says.

He pulls Henry along by his shoulder, lifts him, sets him onto the horse, climbs up in front. He spurs the horse into a trot.

Hungry, furious, sore—Henry sets to work freeing the piece of nail from the waist of his trousers without at first any clear idea of what he will do with it.

It's snagged in the cloth, and fearing to drop it he works slowly. By the time it comes free, they have exited a narrow trail of brushing leaves and branches and are moving on some open road. He tries to scrape the nail through the rope on his wrists, but finds that he cannot bend his fingers far enough. He sits a while in despair, until another idea strikes him. It also passes his mind that perhaps it is not exactly a good idea. But he has no other.

Awkwardly, leaning until he feels he may tumble backward onto the crown of his head, he works the nail under the saddle, point downward. He raises his weight off the saddle, then sits down, hard.

The horse, for a moment, only shudders. Then it screams and rears so violently that Henry is flung as if from a catapult. He crosses the air with his clothes flapping, and he supposes, indignantly, that he will die now.

He strikes soft earth, however, on his side. The breath goes out of him, but after a moment he is able to sit up. He feels very pleased with himself.

Still, however, the sack is on his head: he cannot see. The horse is well away, the sound of its gallop vanishing into the distance. Nearer, Suthers groans.

Henry works at getting his feet under him, to stand and

flee, though blind and bound. He can find a tree, he thinks, and scrape the rope off.

"Stay there," Suthers says. "I'll untie you."

Henry saws himself forward and back until he is standing. "I'm going."

"Really? You're going to run? Like that?"

"I think so," Henry says, feeling around himself with a toe.

"Wait there, God damn you. I need your help. My leg is broken. I'll untie you."

Henry hears Suthers drag over the ground, groaning as he goes. He feels fingers working the knot. It slips open. Henry pulls the bag off.

Suthers sits with his legs stretched. "Look." He pulls up the left trouser leg—between knee and ankle, bone bulges against the skin. "You're going to have to help me."

Henry backs away.

Wincing, Suthers says, "You can't leave me here, Henry."

"I can't leave Father in prison," Henry says.

Suthers shakes his head. "Henry, you have to understand something. You're not a Phipps."

Henry laughs at this absurdity.

"You're not."

Henry considers kicking Suthers in the nose. But curiosity restrains him. "What else would I be?"

"You can't leave me here with this leg."

"I can, I think."

"You can't leave your blood, Henry. You can't escape it."

Henry stares. "Blood."

"Son," Suthers says.

Henry slowly, slowly, steps backward.

Suthers shakes his head. "Can't ever escape your own blood."

"You're not my father," Henry says, backing away more quickly now.

Suthers nods. "Henry—"

Henry turns, runs hard.

"Henry!"

He is on a narrow road, running, with no notion of where he is or where he is going, shouting, "Mother? Mother?"

She's silent, however, or he cannot hear her over his breath and the sound in his ears of his blood beating.

CHAPTER 5

Henry sits at the sandy edge of a pond, watching a half-dozen newts sun themselves in a few inches of water. When Henry shifts, the newts dart and vanish: a mist of silt rises where they were. A minute or two later they glide back, small, eerie creatures. When he was littler Henry would catch them with his bare hand. But now he only watches. The water lies still and smooth, and the trees open above the pond and funnel the sky down to be held on the water's surface. A crawfish extends two claws from a hole, then retreats. A few minnows move by languidly.

Henry is hungry, and he doesn't know where he is, but he sits, wanting only to watch, to be absorbed somehow into this place. He's tired and feels useless and unworthy.

He lifts his head. "Mother!" he shouts. "Is it true?"

Across the pond a frog splashes into the water.

Suddenly, he can't bear the quiet. He jumps up and sets out.

Suthers is far behind now. Henry continues on the narrow road, and he knows by the sun that it goes generally eastward. He runs wildly, making his lungs and limbs burn. From among all the dead bodies and abandoned buildings of Bladensburg, Washington, and Alexandria, he has gained not one thing.

Finally he slows. His legs are sore and he's limping a little when he comes to a swaybacked old horse and a peddler's wagon with drawers on both sides.

The peddler and his wife tend a fire, and above it simmers a supper of rice and fish. It smells marvelous. Henry stops and asks if he might have a plate in trade for gathering firewood or catching fish or some other service. The woman asks if he is alone. Henry says he is traveling to see his father in Baltimore. She says, "Sit with us."

She gives Henry a bowl of food, steaming and too hot, but Henry pushes handfuls into his mouth anyway, with a feeling of boundless gratitude. He lets her refill the bowl and watches her energetic waddle around the fire, listens to her bicker with her husband, the peddler. She's thick-waisted, smiles with her eyes. The peddler has a hole in his cheek as if a hot poker had been stuck through it.

"Eat more, eat more," the peddler says, the words whistling through his cheek. "I always wanted a boy myself, but we have had no children, despite bountiful efforts."

The peddler explains that he has recently lost his merchandise in a flooded river. He says they have been at this encampment for days. He doesn't know what to do. At least here they can catch fish and find turtle eggs, although the flavor of fish and turtle eggs is starting to make him feel ill. They press more fish on Henry.

Their names are Hy and Dosia. "It is a hardship," Hy says, "but it brings us closer to the Lord's command to live in poverty, to abandon worldly things."

Dosia rolls her eyes. "I'm sure it is all for the better," Dosia says. "But if circumstances take a turn for much better than this, I don't know what we'll do."

They tell Henry that he must sleep the night here, that he oughtn't be alone on the road at night. They give him a blanket, and he rolls up in it beside the fire while Hy and Dosia bed down under a piece of canvas that stretches from the back of the wagon.

The frogs and crickets and cicadas sound like the chattering of a loud, shrill crowd. Hy's breath whistles and catches in the hole in his cheek. Henry closes his eyes and tries to listen

through or between the noises for Mother's voice, but there's
nothing.

In the dark of the night, the peddler's horse shrieks, moans,
then a moment later falls over dead. Henry stands with Hy and
Dosia looking at it in candlelight. "She was old," Hy says.

"Worn heart, maybe," Dosia says.

"She was a good horse," Hy says, lip trembling, "but the
Lord's ways are not our ways."

"I'm sure this is a blessing, really," Dosia says, and attempts
to roll her eyes, but she is weeping.

"I've brought bad luck," Henry says, feeling dreadful.

"No," Dosia says, "we brought our own." She pulls Henry
into an embrace. She is warm and soft, and Henry too weeps a
little.

They do not sleep more that night, but build the fire high
and sit with their backs to the wagon, watching the darkness.
The conversation drifts. Sometime near dawn Hy says,
"Might have been the ugly look of that fellow that killed her,
slow." He describes to Henry the man he discovered moving
toward his wife in a manner that had alarmed him, although
after Hy flushed him out, the man said he was a redcoat
deserter and seemed neighborly enough. "But what a face the
man had," Hy says, "as if some hairless rat bred with a bowl
of porridge."

In the morning they eat a little cornbread and greens with
horse steaks. Dosia turns to Henry. "Stay with us a while."

Henry is stilled by this idea, pleased, the food swelling in
his stomach.

"Yes!" Hy says. "Stay until your brother is out of the army."

"You oughtn't to be wandering alone," Dosia says.

"You're but a boy," Hy says.

This last strikes Henry wrong. He shifts. He says, "I don't
know."

"Terrible things have happened," Hy says, "but surely it is for the best somehow, and maybe this is the how of it."

"You have to stay with us," Dosia says. "I am so sorry for a boy without a mother or father. We've always wanted a child."

They gaze avidly at Henry, and he squirms. When Dosia touches his knee, he jumps. "I have a father," he says. "And I have a mother."

"You told us your mother is dead," Dosia says, gently.

In truth, it has slipped his mind a moment. Reminded, the absence of Mother, and the absence of her voice puts a hole in Henry's chest. He backs away.

"Wait a moment," Dosia says. "Don't run off."

But Henry thinks of Mother waiting. He thinks of Father waiting. He says, "Thank you for the food and everything but now I have to go."

And he runs.

Henry discovers Morley asleep on his back in a ditch beside the road to Baltimore, no coat, his head cushioned on his folded cap. Henry contemplates him, breathing softly among grasses and the lacy flowers of wild carrots. He remembers how furious Morley was when the British captured him outside the Patent Office. But, after all, he did help Morley at the halberds.

Somehow it is a consolation to see a face that he knows, even such an unpleasant looking face.

Henry wavers under a soft crush of exhaustion. It is now late afternoon. Since leaving Hy and Dosia, he has eaten only unripe apples, and he hardly slept last night. He tried to nap around noon, but it rained. His clothes are damp.

Trying to think of what to do is like trying to balance on a greased tightrope.

He lies down to rest a moment.

"My favorite Yankee boy!"

Henry wakes, blinks, rolls, peers up: Morley's hideous face grins down.

Seizing Henry's hand, Morley shakes it with vigor, at the same time dragging Henry onto his feet. "Wonderful to see you! Why, I almost even recall your name! Gerald? Edmund?"

"Henry," Henry says grumpily, still sleep muddled.

"Exactly! Terrific name for an ambitious American boy. I admire you Americans so much, I've decided to turn American myself. I'm going to Baltimore, and you must go with me. Unless you don't want to. American boys named Henry go where they will! But I would miss your company, and my former countrymen will now certainly sail on Baltimore. Opportunities will be at every hand and under both feet."

"I'm going to Baltimore," Henry says.

"That's what I mean! And I'm going to Baltimore too! We'll travel together! I'm going to join the American army and take their bounty payment, of course, but I expect there will be a period of confusion during which I might slip away and join you in hunting opportunities."

Morley cheerfully shares a massive cut of ham, which he says he acquired from an unlocked smokehouse. Then they set out. Morley chatters on and on as they walk, and Henry feels happy.

The journey to Baltimore is three days by foot with bad roads and poor river crossings. They walk as long as there is light, and they glean food from fields and farms as they go. In the evening twilight they build a campfire with wet wood to smoke away the mosquitoes and sit pinching ticks off their ankles.

The first morning, when they return to the road, Henry stands a moment looking southward.

Morley says, "See something?"

"No."

"You are thinking of a girl."

"No!"

"What then?"

"Oh. I'm only thinking of home."

"My boy, you'll never make a liar. What is it?"

Henry scuffs his foot in the dirt. He hesitates, but it is too much to keep in. "There is a great deal of money back there. But there is no way of finding it." He tells of the chest, of the hooded rides with Suthers—the story he tells Morley excludes only the two notched sticks in his pocket. "I could see nothing, and we went for miles and miles across country that may have no track or trail."

Morley seizes Henry by the shoulder and makes him tell it all again, in absolute detail. "Dear God, boy!" he exclaims. "We'll find that horse that threw you, and it'll lead us back! We'll get hounds and sniff it out! We'll trick this Suthers into telling us where to go!"

It takes Henry an hour and more to calm Morley and convince him that the rain has washed away the scent, and any attempt to gain information from Suthers or even his horse will inevitably end with Suthers's terrible wrath landing on them.

Finally, groaning, Morley sets to trudging northward, toward Baltimore, although he often glances backward. Henry says, "Suthers's silver won't come trotting up behind us like a lost dog."

"You oughtn't even have told me of it," Morley says. "But it's not the first time that riches have brushed my fingertips." As they walk he tells of treasures and profits he almost had in Iberia—he once covertly acquired a dozen valuable casks of twenty-five-year-old Armagnac, only to be foiled by the inopportune death of a tumorous nag; at another time, he had information from a lover of a fortune in bullion hidden in the maze of stalls, storerooms, chambers, and tunnels under the bullring in Badajoz, but he became horribly lost in a series of forgotten caverns, and he survived only by eating rat meat.

That night, after they have been silent a while, staring at the quivering fire, Morley says, "Perhaps I have mentioned that I am married." He speaks in a reverential tone. "I do not speak of her often, for she deserves better than I can say with words. Her name is Mercedes."

Henry has never heard such a name before, and he asks Morley to repeat it.

"Mercedes. Her dimples! Her laugh!" Morley says. "I know that I am a poor thing to look on, but she never flinched from me." Morley sighs. "She is still in Spain. I could not bring her with me when the fighting ended. We had won the Penninsular War, you see, and the time came to leave the Continent. We sailed from Bordeaux, and it was a terrible scene, for she was not the only one. Every soldier's wife who had no papers to prove a legal marriage before the Crown was refused transport. Imagine the vast crowd of weeping and desperate women at the docks, Henry! We sailed away as they pulled their hair in bunches, beat their breasts, and held their tiny children aloft." Morley himself wipes a tear. "When I have my fortune," he says, "I will return to Spain and find her! I swear it! I will take her from the oak forests where she now herds pigs, and I will give her every luxury, my boy. I will lift her from squalor, nigh to the stars themselves!"

After this, as they travel Morley mentions Mercedes from time to time, always hopefully and with a kind of wonder. It reminds Henry of how Father speaks of the day his luck will turn.

The high sun dries the road, and the dust splashes like water. In the late afternoon the cicadas shrill, on and on. Then it rains again, and they rest under a plank bridge until the rain slows, and they walk in the drizzling wet.

When the clouds go, they leave the atmosphere rinsed

clean, and that night Henry traces the movements of bats by the flicker of the stars that they cross before. He wakes in the darkest hour to find the kind of light that takes the color out of the world, leaving only blacks and grays. He closes his eyes again, and in the morning he wakes with spiders in his hair. He stands, and where he had lain the grass is dry and holds his shape, as if he looks down at his own ghost.

Radnor leans at the rail, gazing on the restless iron-colored water. Around him the other Colonial Marines talk, shout, laugh. A lazy drizzle begins, no more than a falling mist. As the mists gather into larger and larger droplets, the captain orders the sails down, and presently it is raining, falling in drifting curtains, hissing on the waves. A sailor calls, "You ought to go belowdecks, get out of the wet." But Radnor stays at the rail, turning through thoughts of his mother long lost to Alabama, of his brothers cast into hiding. He wishes he could stop these weary thoughts at the same time that he fears if they stop he will lose them completely. When Hollis and Charles are caught, will Suthers kill them? Or, because Suthers holds a coin dear, will he try to sell them, separately, far apart? Which of these two alternatives would be worse? What will they do if they do not have even each other—Hollis to speak for both, Charles to see for both? Radnor doubts himself and his purposes and reasons. He should have stayed. The cold and wet seem nothing to what he deserves. Before him the indifferent sea chews and works itself.

They disembark on sandy Tangier Island, at the mouth of the Chesapeake—the British have a built a pair of redoubts with long walls of earth and logs and armed with cannon. It is called Fort Albion. Hundreds of liberated slaves are here. Many have become Colonial Marines, others have become sailors in the Royal Navy, and yet others work at reinforcing and provisioning the fort.

Some of the freedmen have brought wives, sisters, and children to live in a village of huts beside the fort. After days of military drills and labor, families splash in the sea at sunset. Men paint the faces of former masters onto pumpkins and take extra practice with muskets and bayonets. The British provide rations of whiskey and rum, and folks gather at fires to eat, to laugh, to sing.

Radnor sings with half his voice, on the dim edge of the scene. He is drawn to watch the others though it hurts to watch, and to sing with them though it hurts to sing. He shies from conversation, as if he will have to leave at any moment, and he cannot afford to make friends here.

He wonders if there would've been a way to bring along Hollis and Charles, if he'd only been smarter, if he'd tried harder. He watches the men with their families, and he thinks of things he wishes he had said to his brothers before he left. *I am sorry. I do not deserve to go. I wish you could go in my stead.* These would have been true things to say. But he had thought only of his own freedom.

He asks around, if there is any possibility that someone can take a message to Charles and Hollis. Some of the other marines say that they hope to convince the British to return to raid one plantation or another, where they can free family or friends. But no one cares to go to the swamps where Charles and Hollis hide. And as days pass, Radnor understands that the British have lost interest in making landings for loot or slaves. All preparation now is toward the invasion of Baltimore.

One evening a green-eyed British captain also stands at the edge of firelight, watching. He begins talking to Radnor. He regards Baltimore as a particularly despicable base of villainous, malicious pirates and indolent Republican resistance. He talks of slaughtering the bungling militia that guards the city, looting the place thoroughly, and burning it down into the mud.

Radnor asks permission to speak. He tells the captain about his brothers' debilities, their situation in hiding, the impossibility of merely conveying a message to them. "But," he asks, "when we win this war?"

"What we ought to do," the captain says, frowning, "is take and hold a city like Washington or Charleston, build fortifications, and spread word to the slaves all around that they may join us, and be free, and fight for their kin. We announce that we are assembling an army of freed black men, that we will march and conquer every American state and liberate every black man, woman, and child on this continent. Slaves would come from all directions, by the hundreds and the thousands. I am certain we could raise an army of ten or twenty thousand in a month. As we march and conquer territory, we free more slaves. Word of our purpose will spread as we go, and slaves will come across great distances. We could have America on its knees in a year. The New England states are already sympathetic; the Federalists trade freely with Canada and talk of secession. Meanwhile the southern states fear their slaves, their internal enemy. At the prospect of a vast slave army, they will demand the northern states send more soldiers, more matériel, more taxes. The New England states will revolt, secede, and make peace. With the nation cleaved in two, our job is half-finished. We end the matter with a march to New Orleans, under a banner of freedom carried by an army that grows larger, more ferocious, and more glorious every mile we move."

"Yes," Radnor says. "Yes." But he remains still, because of a sadness in the captain's tone.

"It's known here that this is what we should do, that this is how we can win the war, force terms, and end the abomination of slavery, at little cost to ourselves. Here, we know it. But in London the view is different. In London this is dismissed as a risky strategy. In London the American war is peripheral to the great conflagration on the Continent. In London's view, the purpose of the American war is not to conquer the states, nor to free black men. The purpose is merely to punish the Yankees who initiated hostilities, to punish the attempted invasion of Canada, to punish the burning of York. In London's view, the purpose of this war is humiliation. It is enough to pillage a few cities. London isn't interested in expending good men and arms on the governance of barbaric colonies that do not wish to be administered in a civil manner." The captain shrugs. "I'm sorry." He smiles a little. "But you, at least, are free, and that is invaluable."

"Maybe it's invaluable," Radnor says. "But then how can I ever pay the debt for it?"

"Surely," the captain says, "your brothers want you to be free and happy, not to squander your freedom in despair."

Radnor says nothing, lets the conversation end, feeling there is a chasm between himself and a man like this, who has never even noticed his own freedom, he takes it so much for granted.

Later, as he looks around, he notices a girl near the fire, watching him. She smiles. Her face is shaped by high cheekbones and great dark serene eyes.

Radnor turns away, feeling ashamed.

Now comes the familiar stream of refugees—men and women in flight with children and laden wagons, carts, horses, goats, and cattle. All morning they have plodded past Henry on the road out of Baltimore, in numbers that grow as the sun gains height.

"What news?" Morley calls to an oxen driver.

"British sails in the Patapsco!"

"Ah, good!" Morley says to Henry. "I feared we might arrive too late to join the fight!"

They circle past a great barricade of logs laid over the road. Hundreds of slaves shovel trenches and heap the earth onto long bulwarks. And now Baltimore lies before them, the largest city Henry has ever seen: a vast number of buildings extend in a sprawl below columns of smoke rising from chimneys and kilns; docks and ships spread into the water; and on a peninsula in the bay stands the stone-walled star of Fort McHenry.

Morley leads on, eager to claim his bounty. "I haven't even funds enough for a dram of rum," he complains. "And I don't want to miss the fighting. I enjoy a piece of cannon blasting. It's all the rest of army life that isn't worth a damn." They skirt the city toward the fort. Peering along streets as they pass, Henry sees people moving in flurries, gathering and dispersing, like fretful hens. From time to time the boom of an explosion rolls in from across the water—it is the sound of ships being scuttled to block the harbor.

At the fort entrance a drawbridge spans a muddy trench, and a blinking, sausage-faced young soldier stands guard. Morley strides up, more or less every inch of him filthy with the dust and mud of travel and sleeping in the open, so that he looks like a singularly ugly indigent or perhaps a mad prophet as he raises his arms and cries, "I am a soldier of the Royal Regiment of Artillery and a veteran of the Peninsular Campaign under Field Marshal Arthur Wellesley, the Duke of Wellington! I have left my position in the King's Army to join the freemen of the republic of the United States of America!"

"What?" The guard looks at Henry.

"He wants to enlist," Henry says. "He's good with a cannon."

"Oh, that's fine then. We need help with the cannon. Go in and ask for Captain Evans."

Henry imagined that the debtor's prison would be a large, forbidding gray structure of stone, but instead it is a pleasant brick house, someone's home not long ago. "You're the first visitor for that one," the jailer says, peering at Henry. Rheum glistens under his eyes and trails down into his beard, as if a pair of snails had gone that way.

He rummages in a box of keys on the floor. A commotion of wagon drivers yelling and horses shrieking beats through the window. "Will you take the prisoners away before the red-coats come?" Henry asks.

The jailer cackles. "No one's leaving here! You think Johnny Bull wants these shirkers more than we do?" He leads Henry into a narrow, dark hallway. Leaving the fort, Henry had been intent on finding the jail as quickly as possible, but now he drags his feet. He loves Father beyond measure, but Father's faults make him furious. And the usual anger is complicated by fresh uncertainty, sorrow, wretched guilt—as if what Suthers said were Henry's own fault.

The jailer stops at the end of the hall, turns a key, swings the door, steps away. Henry scuffs up to the doorframe.

Father sits on a small stool, a mouse in his hands. When he looks over, his eyes are bigger and more protruding than Henry remembers, while the rest of him seems smaller, lined and dry, with wild hair and a rough beard. His neck is long and corded. He wears a one-piece, coarse smock like the slaves wear.

Seeing Henry, his eyes grow bigger yet. The jailer swings the door of the cell shut behind Henry, and Father makes a sound like a puppy shriek of joy. He rises, drops the mouse— it hastens to a corner—and grabs up Henry, crushing him and swinging him so that Henry's legs whip back and forth. Though thin, Father is still big-framed with big joints that squeeze Henry the way Henry remembers. Henry tries not to cry, but it's hopeless, and he sobs against the familiar feeling of Father's beard on his face and Father's familiar fusty, uric smell. "My boy! My dearest boy!" Father says. "Why tears? Father is here!"

"Mother," Henry says. "Mother is dead."

"Dead?" Father sets him at arm's length, gapes. "What? What? Dead?"

Henry nods.

Father screams. Letting go of Henry he turns and crashes his head into the wall, again and again, until Henry drags him back. Father spreads his hands, and Henry chokingly explains, while Father grips and pulls on his beard. "You say she's dead?" Father says. He winces, grimaces, hugs himself. "I can't make it fit in my mind." He sits on the tiny stool, the only furnishing in the room, aside from a filthy flat mattress and a bucket of piss. Light enters by a small, barred window. Tears stand in the hollow places below Father's eyes, and he asks Henry to tell again how it happened, and Henry does.

Henry adds, fighting through another fit of grief, "I had to leave her behind."

Father peers at him, confused. "She's gone to a better place, I suppose, as she well deserves."

"Father," Henry says, "after she died, she kept talking to me."

"She did?" Any doubt seems to pass from Father in an instant. "That's no surprise, is it? She always had a great deal to say."

"She wants to be sent to sea, with her family around." Henry tells about the barrel, the cart, talking to her. "But she went quiet, and I had to leave the barrel at Bladensburg."

"You say she's inside the pickle barrel? She's inside the pickle barrel Great-Great-Grandfather made?"

Henry nods.

Father looks closely at Henry a moment. Henry looks back at him.

Father blinks. "Well," he says, shrugging. "The pickle barrel is a temporary condition for her, as you say."

"We'll send her to sea."

"Yes, yes. The dear woman," Father says. "I wonder why she stopped talking?"

Henry wants to tell Father what Suthers said and to hear Father pronounce it a lie. But looking at Father's eyes, where there is a fragile new tracery of blood vessels all through the whites, Henry's resolution fails him. What if what Suthers has said is true—and Father doesn't know it? What if Father discovers that Henry is not his son: what then?

"But her moods were never accountable," Father says. "Melancholia. An excess of bile. She needed some sort of physic, though I never could work out what sort exactly."

"She said all of us should be there, for the burial at sea."

"A dilemma, that. I'm in a situation of some irony: my freedom of movement is constrained by the same government that, in principle, has the task of safeguarding it."

"I'm going to buy you out, Father."

"You have money?"

Henry shakes his head. "I'll find some, soon."

Father bolts to his feet, waves his hands. "Don't!" He whirls and paces. "You're too young. How could you take on such a task? The amount of money in question is very, very considerable. No no no." Father sighs. "Better to leave your paterfamilias to his fate."

"But," Henry says, "I'll find the money!"

"Perhaps Suthers will mind you until Franklin is released from his service."

Henry stamps his feet. "A war is like a rich man dancing with a hole in his pocket! There's money all about! All I have to do is pick it up!"

Father shakes his head. "My boy."

"The British are on their way to Baltimore! All sorts of things will be left lying around. It'll be as easy as collecting feathers in a henhouse."

Father sits again on the little stool. Low and hunched, his

gaze twitches around, taking in the cell with dismay and self-pity. "Truly," he says, "it is a misery to abide in this hole, day after day."

The mouse comes to Father's feet. Father lifts it, strokes a thumb along its back. "Each of us here has his own mouse," Father says, cheering a little. "Sundays, we are allowed to race them in the hallway. We have to do something to exercise our spirits. No whiskey and nothing to do but race our mice and polish the bars with our eyebrows. This one's Speck. Alas, Speck has had some poor luck lately, but it will come around. Always does." Gray, quivering, the mouse looks at Henry with eyes like chips of wet black stone. "See how strong this one is?" Father says. "What a fighter?"

It appears, to Henry, an unexceptional mouse. "They must run to all directions."

"Oh, no. We plug up every hole along the hallway, and we set them going from one end with a cat behind. It is an old, lame cat, but we still lose a racer from time to time. This is the third Speck, actually. Yes, my luck is certainly due to turn."

"Father," Henry says, suddenly incensed. "You say that and say that, year after year, your luck will turn, your luck will turn. But: your luck never turns."

He halts. He has never said this before. He expects Father will seize him up and whip him.

Father opens his lips, but says nothing. Henry launches onward. "Think of Suthers," he says. "Suthers doesn't wait for his luck to turn. Luck doesn't mean anything to Suthers. He just goes and takes the thing he wants."

Father peers at Henry. Someone moans down the hall. A donkey brays in the street. Father seems to have shrunk. "There may be some truth in that," Father says.

Henry crouches, scratches a thumbnail in the black grime on the floor. "No," he says, regretful. "Suthers is mean of spirit and unscrupulous."

"He is rather close-fisted. But he has been a friend to me."
This statement is extremely aggravating. Feeling that, after all, he must know, Henry says, "I have sometimes thought that it almost seems as if I am related to Suthers."

"Really?" Father says, doubtful, but Henry can see the idea turning in his mind. "Well, I wish you were!" His tone, his shining look: it's clear that what Suthers spoke of has never entered Father's thoughts. "A remarkable man. You shouldn't say he is mean, unscrupulous. No. You are much too harsh. You ought to be more respectful."

"But surely," Henry says, and out of grief and love he summons the deepest apology he can find, "surely, your luck really is due to turn."

"That," Father says, "is as true a phrase as has ever been spoken."

They both watch a moment as the mouse gnaws Father's little finger.

"I heard Mother's voice," Henry says. "I really did. It went on and on."

Father straightens up. "Henry," he says, "you are right. I must think of the distress of you and your mother." He looks very solemn. "You have my permission to buy me free, if you are able. I do not know how you might do it, but you are industrious, and you have a way of setting your mind to a thing. And my luck is due to turn, as you say. Luck always turns in due time, Henry. It is a mathematical principle; Bernoulli proved it! One only needs to keep ready, so as to be able to grip the rising with both hands." The mouse suddenly leaps to the floor, darts, vanishes. "Look at that vigor! So fleet and sprightly! Sure to win on Sunday."

Henry's heart swells, but he cannot bear to cry again. He rushes to the door, hammers for the jailer.

"You might stay a little longer," Father says. "You'll need to collect a great deal of money, I fear." He looks at his empty hands doubtfully.

"I'll return soon!" Henry says. The door swings. He steps out.

"And, Henry," Father calls, "I am in direst need of whiskey! If you only find a little money, do you think you might fetch me a dram?"

Coming into the street, Henry's instinct is to run hard, away from the prison. So he does. He races as though hounds are upon him, through the streets, giving no attention to where he is headed, to make his legs burn, his lungs burn, his eyes tear. Sweat comes out all over.

When he cannot run anymore, he rests at the side of the street. People are emptying houses and shops into wagons. Others barricade windows and doors with scraps of wood, or they collect buckets, barrels, and troughs of water for fire-fighting. No one looks twice at Henry.

As afternoon wanes, he rises and drags on through the streets, unsure what to do. He wanders into a bakery, where the sweet odor almost makes him sick, and he hopes to snatch a bun, but the baker shoos him out and locks the door behind. Before him two dogs fight with furious noise. A half-dozen American soldiers walk down the street, and passersby cheer. A woman and man embrace, and she goes off in a cart, weeping, while the man sets away in the opposite direction. Passing a corner, Henry notices a sign: "Ann Street."

He remembers the cat, the box drilled with holes.

From somewhere up ahead comes a thready scream, but it seems scarcely exceptional amid the general tumult. Henry studies the numbers on the doors. Shoulder-to-shoulder on both sides of the street are narrow two-story brick houses. Number 402 is like the others, but on a corner. In the last dim daylight the windows are dark, except for an orange glow on the second-floor ceiling.

The scream sounds again. Henry stiffens—it comes from the house before him.

The door is locked. Henry peers in the window, at a nicely furnished room, empty of people.

Another awful scream ropes down. It seems to come from the window directly overhead.

Henry trots around the corner. Toward the rear of the house is a servants' door—not locked. He eases it open, moves along a dark empty hallway, through a kitchen, into a parlor, finds a staircase. The screams have eased to moans, a grunt, a sudden strange gasp.

Henry glances around, wondering if he should take some things and slip out, but he feels impelled up the stairs, testing the steps for noise before setting down his weight. Although perhaps no one would notice the stairs creaking: the cries above are rising. Someone there is talking, too. A low woman's voice, saying, "Go on, go on, will you."

The stairs end in a short hallway with three doors—two closed, one open. Peeking around the frame of the open door, Henry sees a woman on a bed, sweating, groaning, her face taut with pain. Between her naked legs stands a second woman. "Go on," she says. "Out with it."

The woman on the bed twists her head, eyes open but unseeing, and Henry recognizes the deep-set eyes, the pointed face. It is Mary.

He nearly calls to her, but catches himself short.

He has seen births before, of goats and cows and dogs, but never a human person giving birth to another. Franklin said he would be an uncle. It will be a niece or a nephew. When the top of a head protrudes, Mary arches her back, and the nurse urges, "Go on! Go on!"

Henry creeps closer, into the room itself, and steps sideways into the shadowy nook made by a wardrobe. His foot nearly lands on something—a cat peering up at him. Henry recognizes her. "Tuesday," he mouths, making placating motions, fearing the cat will yowl and betray him. But Tuesday saunters away and disappears under the bed.

The room falls into a quiet that seems terribly perilous. Henry leans forward to see.

The nurse holds a little shape with one hand, dangling it by the feet.

"Boy," the nurse says. "A he."

She rubs the slick off the baby with a cloth and works the fluid out of his nose and eyes with her fingers, still holding him upside down. The cord from his belly dangles darkly. She rubs his back, until he breathes with a wet, wheezy gasp. His eyes startle open, and he stares.

The nurse rights him. His breath steadies and the wetness goes out of it. She hands a balled cloth to Mary. "Staunch your bleeding and you can hold him."

She sets the baby on a woolen blanket, wraps him snugly.

When Henry glimpses the child's face he whispers—despite the risk—"Mother!" The baby has her look for sure. "Your grandbaby," he murmurs, yearning to hear her.

But the only sound is a tiny sigh made by the baby as the nurse hands him to Mary. Mary stares at him, cooing, and he gazes glassily back at her. The afterbirth comes a couple of minutes later. The nurse knots two pieces of rawhide around the cord, near the baby's belly, then sets a knife between the two and saws through.

She looks down at Mary and the baby. "Well, there he is."

Mary peers suspiciously at her.

The nurse hoists a large pewter bowl from the floor. "We need clean water." She takes the bowl out the door, starts down the stairs.

Mary bends again to her baby. She looks extremely pale. Henry edges forward. "Mary."

Mary startles and makes a quick sharp sound before biting off her own scream with an audible click of teeth.

She and Henry look to the door. Faintly, the nurse utters a curse. Something rattles. But there is no sound of steps.

"May I hold my nephew?" Henry whispers, edging forward. He'd often wished for a younger brother. "I'd like to hold him. What's his name?"

"Henry," Mary says low. "Why are you here? Oh my God, Henry, how long have you been there? I can't believe you're here. You'll have to explain later. We have to go."

"But," Henry says, "you just had a baby."

"I know! And it's a boy. She's going to take the baby from me. I believe she really will. Or, my father will, he'll send his men. I don't know exactly how they've worked it out, but you're going to help me leave, with the baby." She struggles to move her legs over the edge of the bed while cradling the infant with both hands.

But the nurse strikes the stairs with clomping footfalls. Henry starts to back into his hiding place.

Mary thrusts the swaddled infant forward. "Take him," she says, in a scant whisper. "Run!"

Henry is happy to hold the baby. He gets both arms under the creature in an awkward cradle—his nephew seems incredibly tiny, no bigger than a muskrat—and retreats to the shadows as the nurse enters with the pewter bowl slopping water.

She stops. "By God," she says, staring.

Mary sits at the edge of the bed, glowering, empty-handed.

"Where is he?" the nurse cries.

Behind the nurse is a narrow path to the doorway. Henry takes a breath, springs forward, darts through.

He hears the water bowl crash. The nurse howls, "God damn it, my foot!" Then, "Dear Lord, it's a baby thief!"

Henry is already on the stairs, moving fast as he can in the dark. The baby makes a tiny cough as Henry reaches the bottom.

He glances down and finds the baby staring unnervingly at him with great black eyes. He grips the child to his chest with one arm like a piglet, gropes with the other arm for the front door. The nurse clatters on the stairs. "Baby thief! Oh my God! Baby robbery!"

Henry finds the door, fumbles the latch, shoves, steps through. Even amid the excitement, it makes him happy to be holding the baby, and he coos for his nephew as he steps into the street. He turns and runs around the corner. As soon as he's out of sight of the door, he presses his back to the wall, lays a hand lightly over the baby's mouth, and whispers, "Ssh ssh ssh."

The moon has not risen. By the glow of a couple of lamplit windows he can sense the edges of things. He doesn't dare look around the corner, but he hears the nurse at the front door. "Baby robber! Someone, help!"

The baby snorts under Henry's hand with surprising vigor. Luckily, the nurse couldn't possibly hear over her own yelling. "Baby stolen! Purloined baby! Thief!"

A couple of men down the street call, "What? What? What's wrong?" Henry hesitates, wondering if he should flee now. But his instinct says the baby needs his mother, and he will have to chance it. He returns to the servants' door, pushes through, moves again through the hall and kitchen to the parlor.

Mary stands at the foot of the stair, leaning on the newel post, breathing heavily. She holds a thing under her arm; it looks at Henry with green-glowing eyes. Tuesday.

The nurse is still shouting in the street. Mary doesn't seem to see Henry until he nudges her. "You have him," she says. "Good." She sets her free hand on Henry's shoulder and allows him to lead her back through the kitchen into the dark hallway.

The hall is narrow, and they must move one behind the

other. Mary leans on Henry's back. The clomping of the nurse comes through front door. Somehow she detects them in the hallway and comes at a run, shouting, "Miss Mary! You must return to the bed immediately. Who is there with you? Is that . . ."

Mary turns. Henry, glancing back, sees the silhouette of Mary's hands opening as she lofts the cat.

Tuesday, silent until now, yowls horribly in flight, and lands on the nurse with scrambling claws.

The nurse falls backward, shrieking, flailing. Mary shoves Henry along the hall. As they stumble outside he laughs and dances his feet. "You *threw* the *cat!*"

"Tuesday will never forgive me," Mary says.

Tuesday bursts through the doorway behind them and flies past, claws scrabbling, screeching as loud as anything that Henry heard at the Battle of Bladensburg. In an instant he vanishes into the darkness.

Mary sighs. She grips Henry by the shoulder. "We must hurry. That woman is quick on her feet."

They move between the looming shadows of houses for a block, then Mary draws Henry to one side. Beside a wall, gasping, she collapses. Henry crouches next to her. Scarcely a thing can be seen.

The baby rouses and cries, and Mary takes him from Henry. "He wants nursing," she says. She sounds dreadfully tired. Henry feels more than sees Mary beside him drop her gown off the shoulder and press the child to her bosom.

He does not like this, crouching in the dirt and dark to nurse a newborn, and he shifts his feet. "They'll be back with lanterns," he says. But there is nothing to be done, except to listen to the click of the baby sucking.

After a minute the baby pauses. Henry whispers, "We have to move on."

Silence. Then Mary says, "Henry, I can't. I need to rest."

"There's no time. There will be—" Henry says, leaping up. Then he remembers nothing for a time.

Mary hears a solid, hard, alarming sound break off Henry's sentence, hears him hit the earth like a sack of cornmeal.

"Henry?" Did someone strike him? She finds his shoulder and shakes him, but he doesn't respond. She feels for his heart—it's still going. Clutching the baby close with one hand, she reaches up with the other, and finds a timber jutting from the wall, a sort of saddle rest or sawhorse. Henry struck his head on it.

Mary settles back to the wall. She does not feel that she can possibly move much anyway. She worries for Henry, though. She once heard of a farrier struck in the head by a horse's kick who never woke again, although he lived six months on spoonfuls of milk and porridge.

Unable to carry her thoughts any further, she closes her eyes a moment, and thinks of nothing at all.

Some uncanny perception rouses her. She looks round, sees a lantern. She wishes that she had moved on while she could. The lantern is only a couple hundred feet away and sways to the side of the street to peer between buildings. Soon it will be on her. She might have left Henry here, but now she will be heard, and she has no chance of outrunning whoever holds the lantern.

She closes her eyes against it. She had really thought for a moment that she might escape with her son. Now, as she waits, time seems to revolve like water around a drain, moving and moving while scarcely drawing closer to its destination. She thinks of praying—her eldest sister is always praying, and Mary generally scorns anything her eldest sister does, but she can think of nothing to do but pray.

In her mind, she asks God's aid. Not for herself, she notes, desperately, but for her son. She could not bear to lose her son, and a son should not be taken from his mother. She would give anything, promise anything.

She casts about: what can she offer?

She peeks, sees the lantern has come yet closer.

What could she possibly offer God that would have any meaning to Him? She thinks, Forgiveness. Yes, forgiveness— even forgiveness she will give, she will promise.

The lantern sways nearer.

Help me, she pleads, moving her lips silently, and I will always forgive, forgive everyone.

Under Mary's hand, Henry twitches.

He shifts his feet, turns his head. He comes off the ground with a lurch, as if drawn up by the jerking of a string.

Mary says, "Henry?"

He touches his head, looks round, stares at the lantern, makes a little grumble in his throat.

"That's the nurse," Mary whispers. "Or one of my father's men."

Henry grimaces. "I'll lead them away." He stumbles into the street, draws himself up. "Oops!" he says. He cradles his arms. "Don't look at me! Nevermind me!"

He runs off, the lantern following. Mary can't see much, but she can see that it's a man with the lantern, not the nurse. She wonders how many are out searching.

Yet she doesn't worry now that anyone will find her. Instead she contemplates what she has promised. What exactly has she promised?

Some fifteen or twenty minutes later Henry returns—he surprises her, he's so quiet in the dark. "We have to go," he says. "They're all around here."

"I can't," she says and fights to stop herself from crying. Henry hesitates and, to her annoyance, stamps his feet. But she thinks, Forgive. And she lets him take her elbow and pull her into the street. She sways. Evidently it is possible to stand.

Perhaps it will be possible to walk, too. She pushes one foot forward, then the other.

Henry walks beside her, one hand on her elbow, the other to his head. "We only need a place to pass the night," he says. After a minute he adds, "In the morning I'll go find Franklin."

"Franklin is dead."

"He's dead?" Henry cries.

"They executed him."

"Oh, that. No, I saw him afterward."

"Saw him?" Mary stops. "Franklin? Be clear. You saw who, when?"

"But," Henry says, still walking, "Mother's dead. It's strange. And . . . "

"Be clear," Mary says, trailing him. If he'd stop, she would hit him. "Who's dead?"

"Mother's dead, but she still talks. Perhaps Franklin is dead, too. I don't know. I hadn't thought of that before. I saw him, but—" Henry seems frightened, breath short. "But, we embraced. So— I can see Mother still, too, but she looks dead and can't embrace me."

"You can see your mother where?"

"In a pickle barrel."

Mary shakes her head, dismayed, alarmed.

"Mary," Henry says, "are you dead?"

"You're raving," Mary says. "You're tired. You struck your head." Her own voice sounds small to her, and she peers around with dread. "Please, tell me if Franklin is alive."

"Mother's dead, of that I'm sure. She could say who's alive, who's not."

"Franklin, Henry. Is Franklin alive?"

"I *think* so."

"You saw him."

"I'm sure of that."

"You're not yourself, Henry," Mary says. "Not at all. You

don't usually think this hard." Mary focuses on the forward progress of her legs. She has hope for Franklin, but cautiously. What is wrong with Henry? The mention of Franklin cleared her mind briefly, but now exhaustion and pain roll back upon her. She mumbles, "I'm sorry about your mother."

"It's all right. I still hear her. I mean, I did."

A lantern light appears down the street. They shuffle away from it, round a corner. Henry says, "A church!" The moon now stands low in the sky, and she can dimly see Henry run up and knock, then rattle the door, without answer.

Another—or possibly the same—lantern appears. Mary hisses. They stumble away. A wet fishy smell comes by a breeze off the water. A small animal somewhere shrieks, dying in the grip of a cat or a rat.

She lets Henry lead because she cannot think what else to do. Henry's mumbling as he goes. It cannot be good for the baby, wandering about in the night air. She tries to think of forgiveness. If she falters in her forgiveness, she may yet be punished. Henry casts avid glances all around. What can he be looking for? She's so tired. She must not swoon. Her hips feel jellied. But she walks, because of her baby. She sees that everything she will ever do, she will do for him.

Franklin alive? Her eyes weep, which is an aggravation, because she cannot see, and things are difficult enough already. If Franklin's alive, she can forgive anything.

Then in her exhaustion even that thought fails and gives its energy over to walking, slower and slower.

She sits in the muddy street.

Opposite them is a large house, lights visible in several windows and surprisingly busy, with men moving in and out. Henry leaves her and goes to the door.

Presently he returns. "I know where to go. It's not far."

Mary's not sure: perhaps she's asleep. She's aware, vaguely, of Henry pushing at her back, then pulling at her arm. She's aware of Henry having one of his tantrums—the stomping feet, the dark face, the fists, so forth. It amuses her.

Until she notices a terrible absence, as if an organ had been taken out of her. She regains her feet before she even understands what has happened—that Henry has taken the baby.

She gropes after him. He trots ahead, shushing and holding her son in a ridiculous way. Mary, bent, stumbling, weeping, follows.

They come to another house, this one larger than the last, with lights in several windows, emitting various muffled indistinct noises, as if people are busy inside. Henry knocks, and the door swings. A woman in a black gown with lace gloves looks around, then down. Henry says something to her. She cocks her head, studying Henry, then the baby. She gestures inside.

They enter a small foyer lit by a smoky, low burning lamp on a small table. To the right stands a closed door, to the left extends a hallway lined with doors, and ahead rises a stairway. The sound of a chorus of drunks singing badly carries from upstairs. The woman says, as she disappears up the stairs, "I'll send her down."

"My son," Mary says, taking him from Henry. "Don't ever, ever do that again. Ever." She leans against the wall. "What is this place?"

"I know someone here," Henry says.

In the hallway, the nearest door opens. A man in an army uniform steps out. Behind him Mary glimpses a dead-eyed woman wearing only a light shift, seated on a rumpled bed.

"Oh my God!" Mary cries. The man leers as he brushes past. "These are whores! A bawdy house!" Mary shuffles backward along the wall. "I can't be seen here!"

"But that's why this is just the place," Henry says.

"You're mad!"

"No one will ever look for you here."

Mary feels she might fall to the ground and die.

Steps sound on the stair. "Too bad!" a voice calls. "Too bad for me that you keep turning up. Good thing you don't need any help."

Mary peers at the girl as she comes down: a little, bony whore.

The task of forgiveness presents itself.

Henry says, with diffidence, "Hello, Abigail."

The whore looks at Henry as if he is the least of all the smallest things in the world. She turns to Mary, and her expression conveys the idea that Mary is, possibly, yet smaller. But when she notices the baby, her brows lift. "How old?"

"Not a day in this world," Mary says.

"Well. You're in some fix? Too bad for you."

"Abigail—"

She cuts him off. "Too bad for you, but a nut like that needs warming and shouldn't be in the streets, I suppose. Come on."

Henry wakes, looks round, rises from the floor. Mary sleeps with the baby on a bench covered with horsehair cushions, the only furnishing in the little whitewashed room. Light comes in by a small window of rippled glass. Somewhere outside, a cock crows. The room has one door, and through it comes faintly a moan.

Henry watches Mary and the baby a moment, but soon grows bored.

The door doesn't open easily—he has to push hard, and the moan comes again. A leg blocks the door. He squeezes through and finds the hall full of bodies and empty whiskey bottles. There are a score or more men entwined and atop one another, this man's head on that man's chest, another man's foot on someone's ear. All are asleep. Most wear army uniforms, or parts of uniforms—some are missing jackets, missing boots, missing pants, using their shirts for pillows. Whiskey bottles lie all about.

Henry closes the door, high-steps over bodies. At the end of the hall he stops, shakes the last man awake, asks about Franklin's regiment, the 5th Maryland.

The man squints. "A young one for whoring, aren't you?" He flops one hand vaguely. "East."

Outside Henry finds the city freshly washed by a heavy rain, a loamy smell rising from the slimy churn of the street. Abigail is perched on the wide front step before the door along with a half dozen other young women chattering and laughing. They watch people go by in the street. One of the girls has a boiled chicken in her lap, and she's pulling the feathers. Abigail is idly collecting feathers and setting them into the mud at her feet, as if creating some strange flattened feathery creature. The girls have knowing faces; their hair is uncovered; several wear bright clusters of false jewels. They shift about, stand, flounce their skirts, sit again. One girl winks at Henry as he circles around to stand before Abigail.

He waits until she looks up. "Look who's back," she says. "Again. She can't stay here."

"We'll pay."

"Then pay."

"Soon, I mean."

The girls laugh. One, rolling her eyes, says, "Don't you know, dear, tomorrow's money isn't money at all?"

Abigail says, "Didn't you get anything at the battlefield?"

Henry scowls. "I couldn't, because of some things that happened."

Abigail hoots mockingly. "Too bad. Your friend will have to leave."

The girl beside her leans forward. "There *are* ways. She can earn her roof."

The girls nod, watching Henry.

"She needs to hide," Henry says. "They'll take her baby from her."

"Who's going to take the baby?"

"Suthers, her father."

Abigail recoils from the name. "Jeremiah Suthers? From Alexandria? That's mad. What's he care about a baby?"

"It's his grandson."

Abigail shakes her head. "That's mad," she repeats.

"So?" Henry kicks at the feathers in the mud. "Suthers takes what he wants—money, babies, anything." He searches the faces of the girls. He cannot tell what any of them are thinking.

Abigail shrugs. "I know Suthers is something in Alexandria, but this is Baltimore."

"You have to help her!" Henry cries. He backs up a step. "She needs help. I'm going to find the baby's father—my brother."

"Come here, imp."

Henry spins, runs.

"Ungrateful goblin!" Abigail calls.

"Goblin!" The other girls shout. "Goblin! Goblin! Goblin!"

Something whacks Henry wet and hard between the shoulder blades—a handful of mud and chicken feathers. At the corner he stops to look back, and the girls seem to have already forgotten him. They sit in the sun, languid and bright as a row of cats on a roof beam.

The Philadelphia Pike rises to a high point atop the ridge of hills on Baltimore's east flank. From here Henry can see on the slopes below a series of defenses that appear fairly impressive, if rather ramshackle. A pair of rough forts stand at either end of the north-south ridge, and a dozen cannon aim outward from each of these. Scattered between the two forts are chains of redoubts and batteries with various cannon, and also breast-works, flèches, traverses, palisades, and deep ditches filled with stakes. Around, upon, and among these are parties of soldiers, thousands altogether, some in drill, some cleaning weapons, some digging further lines of trench or heaving logs into walls.

A soldier moving mud with a whale spade tells Henry that the 5th Maryland have been sent toward North Point, on the peninsula between the Patapsco River and the Back River, to meet the redcoats.

Henry follows the road downhill. Below the fortifications, men for a mile and more around work with axes, saws, picks, and rakes to cut trees, clear brush, and beat down the late season corn to open the lines of sight and remove cover.

Henry trots on. If there is to be fighting, he does not want to miss it. He turns onto the peninsula road, and soon he's into the old woods, which grow thick and silent here, and he is alone.

The forest is cut by shafts of light slanting down. Mosses grow on the boles and the road. Swaths of ferns spread under the trees. For a time he walks beside a long still pool that shows himself back to himself. He alternates walking with trotting at a wolfish pace, sweating lavishly. Trotting has the happy effect of outdistancing the worst of the mosquitoes.

The day has tipped past noon when he hears the heavy crack of cannon. Soon, through a break in the trees, he sees wraiths of smoke easing into the sky.

He passes a small, solitary tavern. An entire regiment of American troops waits here, peering down the road. Their banner says they are the 6th. Henry circles around. The cannon are firing faster, and shells explode in a great clamor. Henry wets his feet in a creek, regains the road, runs through the speckled light that reaches the ground, rounds a gentle curve.

A line of five American cannon spans the road amid a tremendous bank of smoke, and when the cannon fire the smoke flashes with red light and more smoke joins the general haze and the cannon leap backward several feet. The crews wrestle the guns forward, sponge out, load, ram, and fire. Beyond the cannon the road opens into farm fields, and as Henry approaches he can see the American regiments spread like wings to either side of the cannon, positioned behind a split rail fence along the edge of the field.

And coming toward the Americans, not a hundred yards away, are the British in a line of faded red jackets stretching the full width of the field, thousands of men.

Henry's feet vibrate with excitement. Covering his ears against the steady blast of cannon, he casts around for a place to hide until the fighting passes. But then he notices the twentieth or so soldier to the left of the roadway—a very large man, squeezed into an American blue jacket.

An officer screams, and the Americans right of the road fire, hundreds of muskets discharging with a sound like a giant steel boot stomping gravel. Another officer screams, the giant boot stomps on the left of the road, and a billow of smoke engulfs Franklin's big shape.

For Franklin's first shot he had packed in a musket ball transfixed by a two-inch nail, a hunter's trick for creating a massive wound. It had probably been wasted, the distance too great to hit anything except by luck, even with Franklin's rifle. He works at reloading with an ordinary ball while watching the oncoming British. Prime, shut pan, cast about, load, pour powder, shake cartridge—

Until now there was nothing for Franklin to do but to watch, and the redcoats have been a dreadful marvel, marching in column into the far side of the fields, a half mile away, then moving and wheeling in big blocks of men, individual units progressing to new positions like sliding panels, swinging to an angle on the flanks like a gate on a hinge, methodically assembling themselves into precisely the shape that pleased them.

American cannon caused only ripples here or there along the lines of red. And meantime a series of carts appeared from the far woods and trundled behind a cluster of farm buildings. A few minutes later the British began lighting off rockets. Franklin had seen the rockets at Bladensburg only at a distance. Here they arced low and straight toward him, making weird sounds, like children with whooping cough. One skidded through the grass, and stopped a dozen feet away, frothing itself with smoke, spinning in place like a beheaded chicken. The British artillery began setting up, and they were bigger than the American guns. When one fired, it did so in apparent silence—smoke flung out of the barrel like a bundle of rags. The boom came seconds later. The crash of the shell came yet later, with a noise like an iron kettle smashing as it flung metal and made a burned place in the grass. The British artillery concentrated first on the American cannon, firing with the perfect regularity of a tolling bell, and Franklin wished he had been positioned elsewhere along the line, away from the road and the cannon.

But perhaps it was for the best, because after they struck among the American cannon for several minutes, the British guns swung and struck a hundred feet to the left and walked down the line that way, with steps that shredded men, blinded them, set their ears bleeding. Nothing could be done, only wait, and watch the movements of the redcoats, as precise and inexorable as a huge spring and gear driven machine.

Haystacks stood scattered around the fields, and some of the rockets fell short and set them afire. The fires made their own wind, sweeping cinders upward, which then fell into other haystacks. The American cannon, trying to reach the rocket tubes, hit the farmhouses and set those burning, too. Smoke piled in a dense haze, and it hurt Franklin's eyes to watch the British line—at first he wasn't sure if they were moving. He could see only a shimmering of the rough red stroke between the green of the field and the green of the trees. But presently they grew bigger, gained detail. They sent skirmishers ahead, to cover behind the burning haystacks and take shots while the main line came relentlessly on, with a little bow or flex here or there as a reminder that it was made of men.

Now the smoke from the Americans' discharge thins, and Franklin can see the redcoats are nearer, can see them stop, raise arms—

The entire long, long red line fires at once. It is as if he is before the firing squad again: a great black maw opens to swallow the world.

A scream erupts beside him—it is John Thaddeus, a mole-eyed man, the best maker of fires that Franklin ever met, able to build a ripping flame in an open field in a downpour. Thaddeus writhes on the ground, and Franklin winces, horrified, but continues the steps of loading. Push empty paper into the muzzle, draw ramrod, ram down, level powder, ram wadding, return ramrod.

The redcoats advance now by alternate half units—it is as if only the white squares in a checkerboard row move ahead, crenelating the line. The forward units halt, raise arms, fire— then begin to reload. Meanwhile the rear units start forward, pass through the first line, advance ten paces further, halt, aim, fire. The first line, now reloaded, starts forward.

Franklin fires. There's so much smoke swirling that it's like shooting into a fog bank. Each blast from the redcoats rouses fresh screams, and the American line around Franklin begins to draw together into clumps and clusters. But the officers shout and curse, and the men stay in place along the fence.

The redcoats are near enough that Franklin can see the gilt on their chin straps. The Americans fire raggedly, as fast as they can. The British still fire on command. They loom in the haze like phantoms, and their muskets make red tongues of flame that churn the smoke. Wadding falls from the muskets still smoldering and lights further fires in the dry grass. As Franklin finishes loading his third round, he cannot see the redcoats at all. Some of the men around him are lying down, trying to aim underneath the smoke. Franklin glances back, slings his rifle, turns, runs to the woods. During the long wait he had identified a likely spot—a hickory tree with an opening in the branches toward the field.

He comes first to Henry.

Henry stands in the underbrush, tattered, face so begrimed that the whites of his eyes gleam startling and wild. He smiles like everything's going just as he hoped.

Franklin stalls, gapes. "Henry!" In a rage, he seizes Henry by the armpit, pulls him squirming to the hickory, flings Henry onward into the woods. "Go!" Franklin starts climbing. "You little idiot!"

Franklin climbs with the quick steady confidence of a bear. As he moves upward, Henry shouts, his words lost in the smash of another British volley. Franklin yells, "Go! Why won't you go?"

"You're a father!" Those seem to be Henry's words amid the general pandemonium. Franklin hesitates. "You have a son!"

Franklin's heart surges—but it is a thing to contemplate another time. "I'm glad!" he shouts. "Now go somewhere safe!"

He swings to plant the brass nails of his boot on a branch and levels his rifle. Here the thickest writhing smoke lies below, and he can sight the length of the redcoats' line, less than fifty feet beyond the Americans. An officer leads the British, wearing a red silk sash tied around his waist, his saber shoulder-high, flashing arcs in the sun to cadence the march.

Franklin pots him. He begins reloading as the officer's shining saber twitches, droops, falls.

Henry retreats a few paces, ducks behind a large old oak, considers himself safe enough. Why, he thinks, the dead here will be all in a nice row, not scattered hither and yon, as they were at Bladensburg.

Peering about, however, he notices a human shape bent at the foot of a nearby tree. And another such shape further to the left, and then he spots a pair on the right, lumped shapes in tattered clothes, secreted in the brush.

Looters! Henry scowls, hating them.

The British have nearly reached the American line. In the road, the cannon are already gone, leaving only the pieces of one that was hit by a British shell, scattered like a beetle picked apart by idle boys. The line of redcoats discharge another round with a colossal crash. A patter of American shots reply amid the shouts, scarcely intelligible, of an order—the American blue coats turn, run.

They race past Henry with faces blackened by powder burn, wide-eyed, openmouthed.

The redcoats swarm the fence, roaring oaths and huzzahs. Most of them pause to prod the American bodies and peer into the trees. Behind them the smoke roils over the fields; the haystacks and farm buildings burn in a vast conflagration.

A shot sounds away down the tree line, then another, nearer. Henry worries they are shooting looters—but no. The redcoats are firing upward, into the trees.

A body in a blue jacket topples and his musket falls, but his foot catches in a crotch of the tree, and he dangles.

Franklin is overhead, although he's worked himself around the trunk so he can't be seen from the field. Why doesn't he flee? But then Henry sees that a number of redcoats, from the direction of the American left flank, have already circled deeper into the woods.

Another treed American shouts his surrender. The British jeer, then shoot him. The body lands with a dull slap.

Meanwhile, one of the redcoats approaches Franklin's tree— Franklin has his rifle on the man, but the shot will betray him.

The situation makes Henry furious—furious with Franklin, furious with the British, furious with Mother, Father, Suthers, Mary, babies, cripples, cretins, everyone. Hugging himself, Henry trembles with frustration until he can't bear it.

Then, unable to think of anything else to do, he stands up, in the open.

The nearest redcoat, pimpled and thick-faced, chuffing heavy breaths, staring upward, doesn't notice.

So Henry says, "Hello?"

The redcoat swings his musket on Henry, fires.

The shot snaps into leafy earth, well wide. Henry ignores it. "Excuse me?" he says, staring around. He touches the still raw welt where he struck his head the night before. "What now? What happened?"

The redcoat calls, shakily, "Only a boy! It's just a boy."

"Must've hit me on the head," Henry says. "That one hit me on the head." He points to the nearest looter, cowering in a mud-spattered jacket. The looter startles.

"What?" the redcoat asks, looking at the looter, at Henry.

"Or maybe it was those two," Henry says, pointing to the pair to the right.

They jump up, a man and a woman, lean, haggard creatures, and they back away toward the road, muttering, "No no no no no no."

The redcoat looks around, bewildered. Several other redcoats, curious, are drifting nearer. Henry edges toward the smoky open fields. "They were talking together. The lot of them. How do I know which one hit me?"

Everyone stares at Henry.

"I think they were all arguing about important papers," he says. "Or maps. Army maps, I think."

"These people?" The redcoat gestures at the disheveled looters. "Arguing about army maps?" The redcoat laughs. "Come now. I don't believe that."

"That's right!" The first looter—a tall, emaciated man with a wispy billy goat beard—aims a shaking finger at Henry. "He's a liar!"

The redcoat turns his bayonet on the looter. "Now quiet down, you. The boy's a liar, but he's not a good one."

The pair of looters by the road take this chance to bolt. The pimpled redcoat wheels and shouts, "Come back!" Several redcoats go after them. The billy goat looter then sets out running in the other direction. The pimpled redcoat spins and shouts after him, too.

The redcoats all around are in an uproar. "Papers! They have important papers!" someone yells. More looters pop out of the bushes, from behind trees. The redcoats shout and chase after this looter and that one. One of the redcoats fires a shot, narrowly missing another group of redcoats, and they berate one another. An officer wades into the scene, bellowing, waving his sword.

Meanwhile Henry watches Franklin drop from the tree, bend low, and dart into the woods.

"Ha! Ha!" Henry cries, to pull attention from Franklin's direction. He dashes into the open field, rushing straight past two redcoats—they're fighting over a bottle of whiskey amid the American dead and pay no heed to Henry. Henry scampers on, toward where the smoke is thickest, calling, "Ha! Ha! Ha!" like a maniacal bird.

He doesn't look back. Franklin should have a good chance to slip off. Henry worries for him, but exasperatedly. By now the bodies are well looted, and it's Franklin's fault that he's missed his chance, again.

Weaving between burning haystacks, he runs to the far side
of the field.

There he stops to catch his breath and look around. He
wonders if Radnor is here. As he searches the scene for black
soldiers, an idea resolves itself in his mind.

Radnor sits at a campfire more than a thousand feet from
the little Quaker meeting house where the surgeons have set
up, but he can hear quite plainly the screams of their patients,
can see the pile of arms and legs mounting beside the meeting
house door.

Radnor's unit advanced on the left flank of the battle, where
they met little resistance, but the day's march and the excitement of the fighting have been utterly exhausting. The other
Colonial Marines lie here and there on beds of leaves and pine
needles, but Radnor finds he cannot sleep to the sound of the
butchering of living men. He gazes dully into the fire.

Around midnight the surgeons are still at their task. Rain
clicks and ticks in the leaves above. Presently the rain grows
into a deluge that beats Radnor's fire down. But it is a kind of
relief, because in the downpour he can scarcely hear the men
losing their limbs. He begins to think that even in the rain he
might finally sleep a little.

Incredibly, however, he hears a whippoorwill.

He casts his gaze a moment toward the watering, black
heavens and listens as the whippoorwill grows louder and
louder, then wild and implausible, more like a swine call.

Finally he rises, stalks across the fresh mud, finds the boy
peering from behind the dripping branches of a low willow—
he's vague in the dark, but Radnor can see he's hatless, skinny,
forlorn, touchy looking as a bedraggled cat. "Boy," Radnor
says. "Why're you here? You'll wind up with your bottom
cheeks filled with shot. You're not so good at sneaking around
as you think."

"I can't hear Mother anymore," Henry says.

"I'm sure she's been given a heap of thoughtfulness by the pickling you put her into."

"And, Radnor," Henry says, "Suthers said that he's my father."

"He did, did he."

"You think it's true? Suthers is my father?"

"Your mother had many hard days. Mr. Phipps had other comforts. Who knows but what might have happened on one night or another when Phipps was away."

Henry says nothing.

"I never had any father I can recall," Radnor says. "But seems to me that it doesn't matter to God, and shouldn't matter to you. Your father is who treated you as his son and who you treated as your father. Consult your own heart."

"I'd like to kill Suthers, I think."

Radnor shrugs. "You already burned his house to the ground. That why you come for me? To tell me about your mother and Suthers? I'm finished with Suthers."

"I found this."

Henry presses something into Radnor's hand. A stick. Irritated, Radnor nearly casts it aside—but his fingers detect the notches. "Where'd you get this?"

"What's it say?"

"It says, 'Whoever finds this is a chickenheaded toad.'"

"A whatheaded what?"

"Actually, it's considerably more vulgar. Hollis is something of a joker."

"I hoped it would say something helpful."

"Well."

"I found it in an old cabin, away in the woods. Suthers took me there, with a hood over my head."

"I know it. Suthers took us there to work on the roof and the wall chinking one winter, years ago."

"Did he hood you, too?"

"He hooded Charles and me. But not Hollis. At the time Hollis could still see a little, but he let everyone believe he'd grown completely blind. I know where that cabin is."

"How can I get there?"

"Why would you want to?"

"Well, I left something there." Henry glances around. "Mother's bible."

"I've known dogs who're better liars than you, Henry," Radnor says. "I ought to go get some sleep."

"There's two sacks full of coin! Gold and silver!" Henry bursts out. "Suthers hid them near the cabin. It's a fortune, enough money to buy out my father and buy your brothers' freedom, too."

Radnor turns the notched stick in his fingers and half-listens as Henry tells a story about some outlandish robbery in Alexandria. The problem is what to do if this money is real.

He pockets the stick. "Give me the other one," he says. "The one I gave you in Washington."

Henry searches his trousers and comes up with the stick. Radnor takes it and feels over the notches with his thumb, then pulls his knife from his belt and begins to cut on the reverse side.

Radnor feels Henry's touch on his sleeve. Radnor shakes him off. "Did you hear me?" Henry asks. "I'll buy them out. Your brothers will be free men."

"I know where Suthers would've hid it," Radnor says. "We got around out there more than he knew."

"Tell me!" Henry cries.

"No," Radnor says. "I won't. I'll give you this stick, and you're going to take it to Hollis and Charles."

"You won't tell me?"

Henry's voice breaks on the last two words, catching Radnor's attention. It makes him uneasy for the boy. "Be strong," he says.

"I need you to be very strong now. Hollis and Charles can tell you where it is, but you'll have to strike a deal with them." He bends close, to peer into the faint night-gleam of Henry's eyes. "If there's as much money as you say, this will be complicated. Suthers won't make it easy. Maybe others will have to be involved, too. I don't know. Likely nothing now will be easy. But possibly we'll both get what we want." He works at the stick by feel. "First, you'll take this message to Hollis and Charles. Then, they'll decide what to do."

"I don't know how to find them," Henry says, sounding sulky.

"After sundown, go to the far point at the end of that spit of land in the swamp south of Suthers's house, where the sassafras grows. Light a small fire. Hollis and Charles will find you. You'll have this stick, and you'll give it to them, and then you'll talk to them about what to do."

"There's nothing past the sassafras but swamp," Henry says.

"You can do as you're told this one time. But, Henry, they'll need to know that once you have the coins, you won't just go off with the money, that you will come back to them, that you'll help them. It would be a bad risk for them to go after the money themselves, but they could try. They'll want collateral, to ensure your return." Radnor considers, shakes his head. "I'm not sure what it could be. Think on it. Bring something to them to hold."

"I wouldn't betray them."

"Perhaps, but when the stakes are such as this, trust is a fool's currency. I'm taking an awful chance already. Hollis and Charles are property and fugitives, and you might turn them in for a reward, you might make them show you where the coins are by putting a gun in their faces. If you did so, I don't think they'd tell you anything, but you might try it. I have to trust you, that you'll honor your word."

"On my mother's soul," Henry says.

Radnor thinks, A child's oath on a pickled soul. But his brothers are at risk every day, and if nothing is done, then eventually they will be caught and returned to slavery, or killed. Radnor grips Henry's shoulder—a thin, bony, wet shoulder. The boy is such a dubious vehicle. "Be strong," he repeats. "Henry, see this through, and I'll be eternally grateful. I'll be indebted to you."

"I wish you would just tell me where it is." Henry groans. "Give me the stick."

Through the night and the rain Henry tracks the road, mostly by the feel of the ruts underfoot. In the rain it is as if he is stumbling along troughs of porridge.

He comes upon a party of sodden soldiers working by lantern light in a dim, fulvous scene, wielding axes and saws to fell loblollies, sycamores, and blackgums into the road. They are ancient trees with trunks as big around as wagon wheels, and when the wood gives way they fall through the night-dark air with mysterious, tortured sounds—the screams of old hard fibers parting, the clash of branches, the collision with the earth.

As the day grays into daylight the rain slows and stops, and Henry emerges from the forest and turns onto the Philadelphia Pike. He's come to the foot of Baltimore's fortifications when a tremendous crash rolls out of the south, followed by a low, long boom. Crash and boom, cannon and mortar—they repeat over and over. Then the rockets join in with their whooping cough noises, tracing smoke trails over the horizon in long high curves. The British ships in the bay are bombarding Fort McHenry.

Henry asks among the American fortifications and eventually finds Franklin in a muddy spot behind a fragile palisade of boards pried off of some house or barn. Franklin lifts Henry and crushes him to his chest, as if to squeeze the water from him. "Where have you been?" he asks. "What's happened to you?"

When he drops Henry, Henry's inertia pulls him straight down onto his seat in the mud. His worries seem to follow down on top of him. He sits in the wet, exhausted and bitterly troubled. He feels he may sit here and say nothing forever.

When finally he glances up he sees Franklin's expression—confused and fearful—and it reminds him of how Mother's silence makes him feel, and he becomes a little frightened of himself. He opens his mouth, and in a rush he tells Franklin of Mary and the baby, of escaping the nurse and hiding Mary at the whorehouse, of finding Radnor, and what Radnor said.

Franklin's gaze lowers under a weight of consideration. Henry remains in the mud, sets his head on his knees. The roll and roar of the bombardment two miles behind him goes on and on, while he sleeps without dreams.

Men call and curse, run with heavy, sucking steps. A series of shells explode on Fort McHenry in fast succession, like a roll on a great drum. Henry lifts his head. He feels as if he slept only a minute or two, but the sun's height says it's been a couple of hours. He stands to peer over the flimsy palisade—red figures tremble in the distance on the Philadelphia Pike, the same road he came down earlier.

"The redcoats are here," Franklin says. "You ought to go."

"We should both sneak away," Henry says. "When the redcoats have the city, we can take what we want."

Franklin draws back his shoulders. "Behind us are families, mothers, children. If Baltimore falls, the redcoats will ransack and burn it all. My wife and child are there. Besides," Franklin says, "I would certainly be shot for deserting again. But you must go."

"I will."

Henry means it as he says it. He thinks of rousing himself to stand and go, expects his arms and legs will raise him up. Yet he doesn't move. He sits studying the mud. He listens for Mother. Nothing. He has not heard her in a great while, and he feels as if she has abandoned him.

He says, "I'm tired of being alone."

Franklin rests a large hand on Henry's head. For a moment he stands like that, thinking. Finally Henry twitches irritably under him.

"All right," Franklin says. "If the British come near enough to shoot at, I'll tell you you have to go. But Lord knows you probably won't do it."

Nearby a man leans against the palisade, and a section of mud-stuck boards topples, slides downhill.

Henry looks at the men scrambling to recover the boards, peers at the long and lengthening column of redcoats on the pike, says, "We'll never stop them."

Franklin replies only, "Henry."

As the morning becomes afternoon, the red line makes a right turn off the road and caterpillars across cornfields. They are some two miles away, well past the reach of the American artillery, but everything they do can be seen plainly. They come to another road, which also slants into Baltimore, and the red line bends onto it, toward the city.

Away to Henry's left, American troops hurry to form battle lines across the road, and in the fields on either side.

Bugles call thinly. The redcoats halt. British officers trot up and down, bunching, consulting, dithering. Finally, bugles and drums sound, and the red bodies about-face, and the line returns the way it came, up the road, back into the fields, toward the Philadelphia Pike.

"They've gotten lost," Henry says.

Franklin studies a moment, shakes his head. "It's like a wrestler circling, looking for an opening, a stumble."

The redcoat line returns to the Philadelphia Pike and stretches across it. They step into double ranks facing Baltimore, a formation that circuits an imposing breadth of the horizon. Bugles, drums: the vast line sets forward.

A few American cavalry burst out of the fortifications. They rush downhill, shouting and whooping, until, some three hundred feet from the redcoats, they rein up, watch the red line a moment, then turn and circle back. A minute later they reappear, rush the British line again, halt and turn back again. They remind Henry of dogs flinching from a bear.

The redcoats have closed to within a mile, and the American artillerymen stand leaning over their guns with lit match cords, but the British bugles sound again. The red line quivers to a stop.

No one moves. The only sound is the boom-crash-whoop of the bombardment of Fort McHenry. Minutes ease by.

Henry twitches in aggravation. "What're they doing?"

Franklin turns to look back at the city. He examines again the line of redcoats. He contemplates the sun's location—a hand's breadth over the horizon. "Maybe," he says, "they're going to wait until night."

Morley has crept a little distance away from his crew. He squats behind a berm, where he can edge back and forth and peer over now and again. There's nothing to be done but wait, and he hates cowering in a huddle with the others. He mutters imprecations, encouragements, invocations. Characteristically, the American earthworks are deplorably constructed, their cannon are a melange of French antiquities, and they neglected to bombproof the powder magazine, so they decided to take out the barrels of powder and put them here and there all around. Madness.

Morley is soaked through; the rain resumed around the time it fell dark. Rushes of wind drive it into his eyes, but he can see the British mortars fire with gouts of flame, and the burning fuses of the mortar shells rising, until finally they slow, turn, and come down. Those shells, Morley knows well, weigh 200 pounds. But he isn't especially fearful. The British fire from two miles away on ships that roll with the swells. Some rounds have crashed into the fort, but most go long or drop short.

And there's a rocket ship sending over rockets driven by long burns that shine off the ceiling of clouds with the color of a nice Spanish wine. But, while the rockets make a spectacle, they are basically harmless and ridiculous.

Indeed, in spite of all, as Morley twitches and moves back and forth behind the berm, he feels rather cheerful. The characteristics of war that he dislikes are the monotony, the slogging about at the behest of half-wits, the want of drink, and the dismal remuneration. But the fighting itself is a fine thing. He knows his business with a cannon, and it is a pleasure to enact his part in a crew, to feed the roar and spasm of a great machine, to propel many pounds of metal into objects far away.

It is irritating, however, that the British vessels carry guns with greater range than any of the cannon at McHenry, so they can hang beyond the Americans' reach and blast away with no risk to themselves.

There's nothing to do, but his nerves are ablaze. He's edging further and further out along the berm, whispering to himself, when he comes to the body.

He touches the hair, the face—it is a woman. Earlier he saw a woman bringing water and food to the men. She had a large wart on her cheek like a hairy insect. But otherwise very demure and rather pretty. She must have been struck by a bomb fragment as she crossed the open stretch between the fort and the earthworks, then pulled herself here to the berm, unseen in the dark.

Is she dead? He touches her throat. She is wet, chilled, dead. It's too bad she's dead. He reaches to see what she has in her clothes.

A rocket passing low sheds a stark light. Morley glances round—the lieutenant is only some twenty feet away, staring.

"You!" The rocket light vanishes, and the lieutenant's voice roars from the dark. "*What* are you doing?"

"Just found her, sir. She's expired."

Two mortar shells explode in rapid series, flashing light and cutting off talk. Morley ducks, but the lieutenant lurches closer.

"Your hands! In her . . . places!"

"Not at all," Morley cries, indignant. "Why, not a dead woman! I only wanted to examine what she carried, to be sure it would be returned to her family, of course."

"Liar! I saw you hawk-eyeing her!" the lieutenant says, voice breaking. "Charlotte." Another mortar shell explodes as he casts a wild look toward her. "Charlotte Malker has been aiding men in this fort for years. Years. And she and I— And you— You. You!"

"I'd give immediate physical defense to my honor, sir, if I could see you," Morley says, backing away.

"That you would touch Charlotte that way—" It sounds as if the lieutenant has bent to the ground beside the body.

Morley backs further away. It's damnably hard to see. He pauses for a flash of light to show him the scene. But time passes, and no light follows. Morley stands and looks out to the bay, but it's dark. No muzzle flashes, no rockets. "Ho! Ho!" Morley says. He moves toward the crew. "They've stopped!"

He pushes through the men and scrambles atop the earth-works. "Why stop?" He peers into the rain and darkness. A faint wide luminescence arises, as if exhaled by the bay water itself. That is all he can see. "They're about something, aren't they? Why should they stop? Because they fear hitting their own." Voices elsewhere in the fort cry out, too, words lost in the rain slosh.

Wiping the wet from his eyes Morley stares into the darkness, muttering. The silence bears on. He sees something, perhaps—he rubs his eyes, squints.

A moment later he is sure. The rain-beaten water reflects as pinpricks the downcast light of several shaded lanterns moving into the Ferry Branch, toward the rear of the fort. "There!" he shouts. "To the west! Swing the guns west!"

Someone in the crew has lit a little, low lamp. Morley sees wet faces gaping up.

"There they are!" he shouts in fury, jabbing his finger. "West! West!"

At that instant, an emplacement of American guns in a muddy battlement a few hundred feet further down the Branch blaze into the night with a fusillade of six or eight cannon at once. The discharge parts the night as Morley points, and for a flicker, the British vessels—a spread of barges, launches, gigs, and a schooner—show against the black waves. "There! There!" Morley cries.

The British vessels return fire toward the battlement, and their muzzle flashes betray them unmistakably. "There!" Morley shouts one last time. He jumps down, casts around for the lieutenant, sights him still crumpled over the woman's body. Morley shouts orders. "Shield the vents from the rain and check the priming!" He takes charge of sighting the cannon. "We'll wait on a flash, then reply before they can move away in the dark!"

Cannon erupt up and down the earthworks in chains and pulses of terrific noise. The dozen British vessels in the Branch return fire, and one launches rockets whooping toward the fort. Morley laughs at the rockets and sights another round. When the American cannonballs strike the water, white spouts tower up, visible only for the length of a muzzle flash, so that they seem never to fall.

Henry and Franklin stand in the mud peering toward the yellow points of the British campfires, which continue to burn despite the rain. "I don't know where they're at," Franklin says, "but they're not at those fires."

For a time the bombardment of Fort McHenry stopped. Now it has resumed, with a new tone. For the first time the guns at the fort are roaring in reply to the British.

The palisade men check their powder against the damp. "Radnor's out there," Henry says. "I don't want to shoot him."

Thinking, Franklin twists a finger in his ear. "There'll be lots of them. If I see Radnor, I suppose I'll shoot a different one."

"Do you think he'd kill us?"

"I don't know. It's a war."

"It seems an awful jumble, if we're to shoot at Radnor."

"He joined the enemy."

"Wouldn't you, if you were a slave?"

"That's not the question in hand."

Henry kicks at the palisade. It wobbles dangerously. "What's the question in hand, then?"

Franklin wipes rain from his eyes, says nothing.

Radnor, too, hears the change at Fort McHenry.

"It's the Americans firing now," the marine beside him says.

For hours now they have stood in the middle of a mile-long column in the mire of the Philadelphia Pike, thousands of waterlogged soldiers, bayonets at ready. They have been told they will knock a hole in the center of the American line, then roll them up in either direction.

The British fleet resumes its bombardment of Fort McHenry. The explosions of the big mortar shells make an especially monstrous noise. Radnor guesses the order to advance will come soon. He stands ready.

He waits.

Waits.

A command passes up the column, shouted from officer to officer. The shouts are made strange by the rain and nervous excitement; Radnor steps forward, jostling the soldier in front of him, before he understands. The order is to about-face.

They move back along the Philadelphia Pike, back down the North Point road, back into the forest, retracing the way they came.

Radnor stumbles, exhaustion heavy in every bone. He'd looked forward to the fighting, curious whether or not he would die. Now he must figure out how to carry on.

CHAPTER 6

The wind and rain die. Dawn lights the sky with purple and amber.

Henry wakes, shuddering in the marvelous warmth of the sun. After a moment he recalls where he is, notices a silence. The bombardment of Fort McHenry has stopped.

He stands to look over the palisade. The red line is gone. Franklin grips his shoulder. "They tried to send troops in boats to sneak around the far side of Fort McHenry," he says. "They were caught and turned back, and now the redcoats are gone. The Virginia and Pennsylvania regiments are chasing them, down North Point."

Looking at the empty fields below, awash in the rosy morning light, it makes Henry mad. "What a sorry sort of war. I haven't been able to do any good looting at all." Henry takes off his shirt, irritably wrings out a dribble of water, puts it on again. "Maybe the redcoats are circling around, setting a trap."

Franklin stares off, considering. "Maybe. But if I were a British admiral, I wouldn't let up on Fort McHenry for a minute, unless I was done with it. Can't bring ships in to help while the fort is there."

"If you were an admiral, I'd be a muskrat stew," Henry says. He feels shifty, bored already. He can't stand to idle here. "I'm going to find Charles and Hollis."

"You mustn't go alone." Franklin bends to Henry. "We must stay together now."

Henry puts out his tongue, backing away.

"Maybe, if you won't stay," Franklin says slowly, "I'll have to come with you."

Henry feels he would like that, and yet to hear Franklin say it only makes him madder. "Don't be stupid," he says. "You can't come. They'll set up the firing squad and really shoot you."

Mention of the firing squad strikes Franklin hard. He recoils, turns to gaze toward the fields where the redcoats were.

Henry takes a step backward.

Franklin stands still and quiet, looking off.

Henry whispers, "Sorry," and slips away.

Morley walks the Baltimore streets, penniless, contemplating the caprices of providence. By every right, he ought to be hailed a hero—he, the very pivot on which the Battle of Baltimore turned! With his command of batteries at Fort McHenry, the British flanking maneuver in the Ferry Branch was repelled! That he—he! one of Wellington's Invincibles!—should do such a thing for the American rabble! And that they should be so ungrateful!

Here is a tall freckled woman looking at sweet rolls in a window. Morley says hello. She glances at him, appears alarmed, hurries away.

Morley thinks of following her, but his spirits are too much diminished. This morning, after they'd run a preposterously large flag up over the fort and everyone was in good cheer, the lieutenant who had impugned him over the dead woman's body had stomped over and said he believed that Morley ought to be shot. But the captain had seen Morley directing fire during the fight and instead ordered a discharge, free and clear. When Morley asked for his pay, the lieutenant began to scream and wave his arms like a bear fighting bees. "You will not have your pay! Go!" He drew his saber. "Go! Before I open your head!"

So Morley slouched away, to the city, where he plods with little attention to direction. What does it matter, in a benighted, unjust world?

Until he sees the boy. The boy is headed away from the innumerable masts at the docks, passing right by the busy market and its stink of fish, walking fast with strides as long as his boy legs will swing. "Henry!" Morley calls, chasing him down. "What now! Where to? Wouldn't you know, in gratitude for extraordinary service, I've been granted an early release. Freed to seek my wealth as I see fit. Truth is, no one in the army ever gets rich. Let's put our minds to the task. Let's make plans!"

Henry shies like a nervous animal. "I can't," he says. "I'm going home. My brother says I must."

"What? What?" Morley cries. "Go home? Surely not. To what? What of your father?"

"If the British have gone, Franklin will be released soon," Henry says, edging further back. "He'll come home with his wife and baby. I have to prepare things for them."

"That sounds dreadful," Morley says indignantly. "There's no profit in it. Surely you don't want to go?"

"Franklin says I must." The boy shifts from foot to foot, color rising to his face.

"Ah!" Morley's instincts have quickened. "Perhaps I will accompany you."

"Oh, no," Henry says. "Our farm's a meager place, muddy, poor, thick with mosquitoes and pestilences."

Morley squints at the boy. He remembers well the coins that Henry described.

"I'm sorry," Henry says.

"Sorry!" Morley says. "No need for apologies! I wish you all luck, my little friend. I predict a great fortune in your future." He watches how the boy jiggles faster. "But, for now, family. Yes. It is the most important thing, after all. I'm sure you are right to do as your brother says." He takes the boy's hand, shakes it enthusiastically. "Godspeed!"

Henry heads away fast, nearly running. Morley watches him until the angle of the street takes him from sight.

Some five miles outside Baltimore Henry finds an abandoned encampment—it appears refugees from the city passed the night here, leaving behind broken biscuits and a bit of cooked squash, which Henry devours. He lies back, sleeps where he is.

He wakes mid-afternoon and travels several more miles before the sun falls behind the rim of the earth. He finds a place to lie down in a little hidden opening in a patch of pawpaw, tries to sleep, but for a long time he cannot. He listens for Mother, but hears only crickets and the scuttlings of tiny creatures.

The following day he walks through an intermittent drizzle of rain, soft as a patter of gnats on the skin. It keeps the road mud fresh. The animals are quieted by the silent rainfall, making a silent world, broken only by the fall of water off branches and leaves. Henry thinks about what Radnor said about collateral, something for his brothers to hold in exchange for the location of Suthers's cabin. It seems impossible. He possesses nothing of value.

Few people are on the road. He sees no one for an hour, and then another. But glancing back, he thinks he sees a distant shadow, disappearing.

And a mile later, deeper into the forest, surrounded by heavy gray misting air, turning, he sights a glisk of movement far back on the road.

"Mother?" he says. He has not heard her in such a long time.

There seems to be a faint murmuring. Perhaps it is only the vaporous noise of mist on the trees. He pushes his pace. What if Suthers sent one of his men after him? What could Suthers guess about Henry's intentions? He has the impression that Suthers might instinctively know Henry's thoughts and plans, by means of some terrible blood connection.

But, worse, what if it is Mother following? Grown impatient, she loosed herself from the barrel; she walks the road behind him—for what? To bring him to her, to the realm of the dead?

Surely she wouldn't do that! But he trots more quickly. Why couldn't Mother rise up and wander about, if she wants? It's horrible to think that she might have set out following him in agony and wrath. He might never be rid of her.

For a time he runs, until he's lost his wind, and he slows to breathe. Soon he has a feeling at his back again, like lye on his skin. Turning quickly—he's certain he sees a shape in the far road. He runs ahead, darts into thick brush, enters an open airy place under the canopy of the trees. Birdcalls sound far overhead. Drips of water strike the ground with startling crashes.

He picks up a heavy fallen limb. The earth lies soft underfoot, lightly scattered with leaves. He stomps ahead, creating a trail of footprints deeper into the forest. Then he circles back to hide behind a tall old maple, gripping the limb.

He waits, and the longer he waits the more he fears it is Mother, somehow lurching after him. If it is Mother, nothing will save him. He would be pleased to hear her, but to *see* her up and about is entirely another matter. He once saw a boy nail a frog to a tree to watch it spasm and strain; Henry's heart feels like that frog, nailed to a rib.

A moth lands on his arm, rises away again. A mouse scuttles in half-rotten leaves. He hears nothing for a long while. Clouds part and sunlight comes down in canted lines. Just as he thinks he has slipped away unnoticed, and he can escape through the forest, the brush behind him rustles.

A step squelches in the wet earth. Someone is following his false trail. He hears a heavy breath, very near. More steps. By the sound, Henry is sure: this is not Mother.

A shadow cuts into a line of sunlight at Henry's feet, and Henry steps forward, swinging hard as he can, working the weight of the branch like an axe.

He aims for head height, but because Franklin is so big, Henry's blow strikes him in the chest.

"Oof!" Franklin says and falls to the ground.

"Franklin!" Throwing aside the branch, Henry yells, "I'm sorry! I'm sorry!"

Franklin sits up, wavering. He wheezes. "You idiot."

"Me!" Henry cries. "You, creeping around, jumping at me—"

"Jumping? Who jumped?" Franklin pulls up his shirt, studies his chest.

"You'll be fine," Henry says. But he is trembling. "You shouldn't have followed me. They'll shoot you."

Franklin shakes his head. "Had to."

"No! You didn't!"

"I couldn't let you go alone."

"You left me alone to go to the army."

"I left you with Mother and Father."

Henry regards him silently.

Franklin thinks. Finally he says, "Perhaps you're right. But if I was wrong to leave you before, it would be doubly wrong now."

"I don't need your help," Henry says, backing away.

"Henry—lots of folks are quicker than me," Franklin says, "and you're one of them. But I am your brother. You can think up ways to leave me behind. But I am your brother. You're quicker, but I'm stronger. I can help you. That's the how of how it has to be."

There's an odd little noise—Mary is coming up, and the baby at her chest is mewling.

"Them too!"

Franklin nods. "I couldn't leave them in that whorehouse."

"Already taking care of two hem-tuggers," Mary says. "Might as well three."

They make a motley assembly. Franklin has his rifle and that night they eat a possum he shot, and a turtle that Henry found in black still water beside the road. While the meat cooks, Henry spends several minutes wondering over the pattern on the turtle shell, like a map of some other world. Mary says turtle meat isn't any good to eat unless ground and put into a soup, but Henry happily gnaws the stringy flesh.

Franklin refuses on principle to take anything from the farms that they pass, but when Henry appears in the morning with eggs, late season corn, and a piece of broken crockery holding a few spoonfuls of goat's milk for Mary, Franklin bends his head and says nothing.

Mary keeps pace with the two brothers, but she lacks color, and when they stop she settles heavily and stares unseeing. She will not let the others carry the baby. The baby is strangely quiet. Even when hungry he makes only small animal sounds through scarcely parted lips. Yet otherwise he appears healthy and keeps his eyes open a great deal and gazes with more understanding than seems usual for an infant only days old, unable even to hold up his own head.

The next afternoon they are walking beside sycamore and hackberry lining a shallow muddy pond—an egret stands in the water, white as cotton, neck like a feathered snake—when Mother shouts, The baby!

Henry nearly jumps out of the rope belt cinching his trousers. He looks around. The others are staring. Even the baby recumbent in Mary's arms stares.

"Did you hear?" Henry asks Franklin.

Slowly, Franklin shakes his head.

But Henry hears her. She sounds now faint and far off, as if calling from beyond a hill ahead. He sets forward again, walking with one eye closed to listen, happy in his heart. He never could predict Mother's exit from the black spirit, anymore than he could predict when it would begin.

The baby, she calls. It'll have to be the baby.

He puzzles over this until it occurs to him what she means. Then he stops. "The baby?" He grinds his nails into the palms of his hands, stomps a foot. "No."

Mary says, "What is it, Henry?"

He starts forward again, brooding.

Franklin walks beside him. "Tell us," he says.

Henry says, "Seems that turtle has grown quarrelsome with my innards."

Franklin looks doubtful.

Henry ignores him. The baby—offer the baby? He feels a terrible loneliness, although Franklin walks just beside him, and Mother hums again.

Next afternoon, they arrive at Suthers's estate. Mary gazes at the pile of black char where the house stood. "How did this happen?" she asks.

"Redcoats," Henry says.

She looks him over. "You know something about this, don't you?"

Henry shakes his head, avoids her gaze.

In the orchard one of Suthers's horses is pulling apples off the low branches. "Libro!" Mary says. She hands the baby to Franklin. Libro is a dun colored pony with one white stocking. He's uncombed and muddy with a deep raw scratch on his flank, and he whinnies and shies, but Mary talks low and hums, and soon she has a hand on his neck. "Poor Libro," she whispers, examining his scrape. Presently he allows her to mount and ride bareback to the hillside cabin, Henry's home.

Franklin stares at the pile of pickled vegetables on the ground, stares at the hole in the cabin ceiling, stares at the spot below the hole. Weather has come in and muddied the floor, but the impressions where the cow fell and scuffled are still apparent. A sparrow flits in through the ceiling and lands on the mantle, and finally Franklin stirs, goes to the chest against the back wall, drags out Father's old, ill-assorted set of carpenter's tools. They are wrapped in a swath of oiled canvas. He takes the canvas to the roof and nails it over the hole. It covers the hole incompletely, so he takes up a bedsheet too.

Coming back into the cabin, Franklin says, "We have to find Charles and Hollis."

"We make a fire at the point in the swamp." Henry takes a breath, adds, "At first light."

He watches Franklin warily. Franklin only nods.

Henry and Franklin clean the cabin to make it passable for a night. Mary binds a poultice to the scrape on Libro's neck, then cooks a supper from a few things out of the untended weedy garden and some salted pork that Franklin finds hidden in the barn.

After nightfall, Henry lies awake.

About midnight he hears Mary rise to suckle the baby, shush him to sleep, bed down again.

He waits for what seems to him half an hour. Everyone breathes evenly. A scant light hovers off the low embers on the hearth.

Mother says, soft as a hum, Now now now.

Henry rises, stands gathering courage, heart a-going. Franklin smacks his lips. Mary nestles close to Franklin, on her side, curled tight. Beside her the baby sleeps wrapped in a strip of cloth, incredibly small.

Henry lifts him carefully, the small warm bundle of baby, happy-making.

The baby doesn't stir. Henry cradles him in one arm, goes

to the door, eases the door open, steps through, eases the door shut, walks swiftly away.

Mosquitoes throng the night. A waning moon stands a quarter way up the sky. Henry does his best to keep the insects off the baby, and he collects a few sticks as he walks.

At the end of the point he places the baby on the damp earth, gathers a few more branches, assembles a pile. He has brought flint, steel, and char cloth in his pocket. Soon a fire burns hungrily. He picks up the baby again and finds him silent but open-eyed. "I'm sorry," Henry says to him. "But it's for your grandfather, and it won't be long, I promise. You are my nephew, and I won't let anything bad happen to you."

He stares into the swamp. When a cloud blacks the moon he can see nothing past the light thrown by the fire. Small sounds rise from the water and reeds, little splashes, rattles, gurgles, peeps, whispers. Henry waves at the mosquitoes. "Likely," he says, "you will grow up big like Franklin, and you'll understand what it is to have a father, and what you would do for him, even if Father is a shirker and a talker and a drinker and a gambler and maybe in a way not your father at all. Still, he is your father. You're no bigger than a possum now and know even less than a possum, but when you're bigger you'll see."

The baby closes his eyes and sleeps again.

A moment later, a hand taps his shoulder.

Henry startles, yelps, nearly drops the baby.

It is Charles. He looks at Henry curiously, at the baby, at Henry.

"I've seen Radnor," Henry says. "Only a few days ago. He's well. I expect he's halfway to London now. He told me how to find you, so that I can talk to you and Hollis." He hands Charles the stick that Radnor notched.

Charles examines it, peers again at the baby.

"This is Franklin and Mary's boy. Where is Hollis? I'll explain to you both."

Charles makes a tongueless huffing noise. He removes his hat, dips water into it, puts out the fire. He takes Henry by the shoulder, guides him along the point, into a canebrake.

Henry sees dimly a little flat-bottom boat. Charles points for Henry to sit in the bow, then pulls a rag from his pocket, draws it over Henry's eyes, ties it. "Suthers did this too," Henry says, vexed. "I'll soon be as used to it as your brother." He hears a pole come off the bottom of the boat and slip into the water, feels the boat slide.

The baby squeals, a strange sound in the swamp's immense solemn quiet. Henry shushes him. Soon, Henry worries, the baby will be hungry.

They glide with only a whisper now and again as the boat touches reeds, or a plash as the pole cuts the water.

He listens for Mother. She sounds a faint hum, happy, it seems.

Perhaps an hour has passed when he feels the boat scrape to a stop. Charles unties the blindfold. It's very dark. Charles leads him along a gentle uphill slope, out of the swamp, through a few trees, then into an open area. Ahead is an orange glow that seems to smolder in the earth itself. Henry scents woodsmoke and hears an eerie singing of several voices at almost a whisper, slave songs he's heard before in the fields, but transformed now by tone and place, made unsettling and spectral.

The light and song emit from a deep, square hole, about three feet across. Charles leads him to the edge, where Henry sees a ladder. Charles points to it. Henry settles the baby in one arm, grips the ladder with the other hand, descends.

He passes through a layer of earth upheld by beams and comes into an open space. The singing stops. Henry gapes. He says, "I didn't expect—" He tries again, "I didn't know."

Henry has heard stories of a hidden place in the swamps where fugitive slaves live, sleeping by day and traveling by night on hidden waterways and Indian trails to forage and to trade with slaves on the farms. He never expected to find himself inside such a place. A small fire tosses wavering light in an underground chamber double or triple the size of Henry's home. Areas for sleeping pallets on the floor have been divided off by sheets of homespun. Also hanging from the overhead beams are herbs, hams, and a chain of sausages. One corner is filled with cooking supplies—pots, crockery, knives, vegetables piled on the floor and on slats of shelving. A chicken wanders about. But mostly the space is crowded and warm with people, a score or more, including several children, an old woman with milky cataract eyes, a tall sinewy woman toddling a baby on her knee, and, seated in the middle near the fire, a giant man who seems heavy and rooted as an old worn mountain. His round face is marked by burn scars on one side like a spatter of lacquer.

They gaze at Henry from all sides.

Despite the hole in the ceiling it is smoky, and Henry's eyes water. The giant burn-scarred man shifts a little closer to Henry. "Who're you?" Despite his size, his voice is soft, lilting. He sounds genuinely curious.

Henry's mouth clicks, dry.

"What is it?" Seated to one side, face turned blindly to the fire, is Hollis. "Who's here?"

"It's a white boy," the giant burned man says.

"Carrying a white baby," notes the tall woman holding her own baby, in a tone of grim wonder. Her child appears only a couple of months older than the baby that Henry carries.

Charles makes a heaving sound that might be a sigh. He communicates through a combination of hacking noises and quick, tapping finger touches on Hollis's hand. Hollis says, "He says Radnor sent him." He turns to Charles. "It's a trick.

You were followed." Charles shakes his head, grunts, gives Hollis the notched stick.

Henry feels a grind of unease in his stomach, and the baby has begun making small movements in his arms. "I wouldn't tell anyone of this place," Henry says to the people looking at him. "Father always said black men should be free, and if Suthers's property walks off, it's nothing to me."

Hollis rubs a finger over the notches in the stick on one side, then the other. "It's dangerous for you to be here." He doesn't turn his blind eyes to Henry but speaks as if to the fire. "Never had any white person here before. Some folks have lived here for years. Saul—" Hollis nods in the direction of the giant man, who gazes contemplatively at Henry. "Saul first dug this place out, and no one knows how many years he's been here, because he won't say. They've taken in Charles and me. We're their guests." He scowls. "I think Charles shouldn't have brought you."

"I came because Radnor sent me."

"My beloved brother Radnor is a proud, high-minded fool, and you are a boy with clabber for brains, carrying a baby for I cannot imagine what reason. The sensible thing to do is to feed both of you in small pieces to the snapping turtles."

Henry shakes his head, irritation overwhelming his worries. "No one knows exactly where I am, but my brother has some idea. This baby is my brother's son and Suthers's grandson. If we vanish, Suthers will have parties of white men searching all through here."

Hollis says, "Now you threaten us."

"I didn't begin the threatening," Henry cries.

"Saul," Hollis says, leaning back a little, "what do we do with him?"

Saul gazes at Henry, and the others watch Saul. Saul nods to Henry. "Go on."

Henry explains about the coins that Suthers has hidden,

and his encounter with Radnor. "Radnor said you would know where the hiding place is. It is an enormous fortune. I can buy you and Charles free, and buy my father out too. Now that you know the coins are there, you could go after it yourself, but I can travel there freely, without risk, and I can negotiate a price for you with Suthers. Also, if you go to Suthers with the coins, he will simply put you back into slavery and take the money for himself."

"He might do much the same to you."

"I won't let him have the money until the terms between us have been completed, and he'll not abuse me for it because he thinks that I'm his son."

Hollis cocks his head and squints his sightless eyes. "He told you that."

"Do you think it's true?" Henry asks.

"Your voice is very like his. You bite your words like him."

A terrible dismay comes on Henry: his own voice a traitor to him.

Saul stirs, rises. He is so tall that he has to bend his head under the ceiling. He gazes at the baby that Henry holds. The baby, with his large staring eyes, seems to gaze back. The only sound is the settling of the fire.

"You can feed me to the turtles if you have to," Henry offers. "But please, not the baby. He's a good baby."

"He looks," Saul says in his soft voice, stepping back a pace, as if to better see the baby, "like a surprised badger."

The baby wriggles, begins to cry.

Henry tries to shush the baby, but he only grows louder. After a minute the tall woman holds out her hands. "He's only a few days old, isn't he." She rocks the baby a moment. "He's hungry."

"It took us a while to come here."

"Well," the woman says, unsmiling, "it will not be the first time I've nursed a white man's child."

"If you obtain all of this money," Hollis says to Henry, "you will simply keep it to yourself."

"I brought the baby, my brother's baby," Henry says, "for you to hold against my return."

Everyone laughs. Saul's laugh is like the sound of someone chopping wet wood.

"You're mad," Hollis says.

"Radnor said you wouldn't trust me if I couldn't leave something that you knew I'd return for."

"The baby!" Hollis cries. "By God."

But Charles coughs and taps on Hollis's hand. And then the others begin talking all together in confusion.

The discussion goes on and on. Henry sits to one side, watching, wondering what it feels like to be eaten by snapping turtles. Faces loom in and out of the firelight as they talk. Saul says little. He sits like a tree amid chattering birds. The tall lean woman argues against Henry's plan. But it seems there are too many people here—so many slaves have slipped away in the war's turmoil and found their way to this place. Freedom for Hollis and Charles would create needed space.

They fall to whispering, and Henry cannot hear. He dozes.

Someone touches Henry's hand. He looks up and finds Saul gazing down. The firelight gleams on the scars on his face. Hollis too has his blind gaze on Henry. "I've told them," Hollis says, frowning, "though with great reservations, that your mother aided us, once. That, perhaps, you might do as you say, assuming that any sensible person could possibly think of trusting a scrawny white boy."

"Mother thinks," Henry says, "that a family should be together. And Father said you should be free."

"Never said it to me."

"Well, he needed his luck to turn."

"I don't think that bears on it." Hollis shakes his head. "And I also don't think that's what he needed." He sighs.

"Almost surely we will regret it, but we'll keep the baby against your return. If needed, we'll deal directly with Suthers."

"Suthers shouldn't be trusted."

"Nonetheless. Charles will take you to where you met him and indicate to you where to go. On the seventh night after tonight, Charles will come for you at the same place. If you're not there with the contract for our freedom, then we'll approach Suthers."

The baby is in the tall woman's arms. She scowls at Henry as Henry kisses the fuzz atop his nephew's head. The baby stares with his great, dark, uncanny eyes. They seem to accuse, with terrible gentleness. Henry wrenches himself away. He isn't at all certain that this is the right thing to do. It requires all of his will to move up the ladder.

As they come out of the ground, it's still dark. Henry dons the blindfold. Charles poles the boat. Mother says, The substance of things hoped for, the evidence of things not seen.

Henry isn't sure what she means by that. He feels too low to ask.

When they land, Charles removes the blindfold. The day's first light simmers on the horizon. Charles draws a map in the dirt. Henry asks some questions, and Charles draws some more. When Henry nods, Charles departs.

As Henry comes into the garden, Franklin appears out of the far wood. "Where've you been?" Franklin is running, shouting, shaking, eyes agog. "Someone's taken the baby!"

Henry looks at the ground.

Franklin seizes him by the shoulders and lifts him, vibrating, to eye level. "Help us find him!"

"He's—"

"What?"

"He's being minded."

"Wait." Franklin lifts Henry further aloft while he thinks.

"You took him? That's what Mary said, that you took him. She said, Henry's gone, baby's gone, Henry must've took the baby. I said she was wrong. You took him?" He grips Henry's shoulders painfully.

As Henry explains what he's done, Franklin takes on an expression of horror. Henry trails away, exhausted and sick in his stomach.

"Henry," Franklin says, "you have to take me to my son."

"I don't know how. I was blindfolded. We have to find the coins."

"Put him down," Mary says. She has come up behind Henry. She may have been there for a while.

Franklin looks at her, looks at Henry, drops Henry.

Mary springs forward and sets into Henry with a series of blows and wrath that knock him to the ground. He curls on himself.

"Henry took him," Franklin says.

"That's what I told you," Mary says. She kicks Henry in the ribs. Henry closes his eyes, tries to call to Mother. But his mouth is in the dirt, and he cannot speak.

When nothing more has happened for some time he looks up with one eye. Franklin and Mary sit wretchedly watching him.

Henry feels fortunate; when he saw the look on Mary's face, he expected worse. Now she's grinding her teeth. "Forgiveness," she says bitterly, as if it were the name of an enemy. "But why?" she says. "*Why?* Your father will only go into debt again."

Henry says, without thinking, "His luck is due to turn."

Franklin looks at the ground. Mary's eyes bulge.

"And it's what Mother wants," Henry says.

"Henry," Mary says, "your mother *is dead.*"

"He still hears her," Franklin says.

"She doesn't talk as much as she used to," Henry says.

"She's dead," Mary says, "and my child is worth ten thousand talking corpses."

"He's got no sense," Franklin says. "Things have gone hard on him. He's seen too much. He's only a boy."

"How do you summon them back?" Mary says. "Hollis and Charles know me. They'll listen to me."

"They'll return in a week. They won't come back any sooner. And we need to have the money then."

"I'm trying to forgive you, because I made a promise," Mary says to Henry, "but I don't know." She bores into him with a look that could kill small animals. "If this doesn't come out right," she says. "I'll—"

She twitches, turns, rises, sets away, leaving the brothers to follow.

Mary, riding Libro, sets an unsparing pace, keeping the Phipps brothers always at her back. Franklin carries his army knapsack with flint and steel, some rope, a little salted meat, a wooden canteen. The place indicated by Charles's map is along a stream feeding the East Branch, an isolated place, but not far away. Looking at the map scratched in the dirt, Henry thought first that there was a mistake, but Charles insisted. It seems that Suthers rode him around in a great circle. The stream they crossed, where Henry nearly fell off, was likely the East Branch. Henry doesn't know where the crossing that Suthers used might be; he decides to cross at the bridge at Bladensburg, and then find a way north to the road where he abandoned Suthers.

In the long sloping meadow over Bladensburg where the battle was fought, Henry turns for the orchard.

"Mother?" he says. "Mother?"

She says distinctly, Henry!

"Mother!" He bursts for the apple trees. Franklin calls after him, but Henry runs, heedless.

He finds the chokecherry patch, and the cart and the barrel—the barrel lies on its side in the cart, the lid wide open. He can't see if Mother is there until he circles around: she's tumbled half out of the barrel, looks like something that floated up out of a bog.

Franklin says, "What's that?"

"Someone must've found the cart—" Henry says, panting, vastly relieved. The brine has all run out; the ground below is still damp. Flies are gathering. "They looked inside the barrel, saw her, ran off. Why, it must've happened only a short time ago, or the animals would've gotten into her by now. We're lucky. Oh no! Where's the dress?" For a moment he panics and looks frantically. He finds Mother's gingham in a ball, tossed on a the ground a few feet away.

Franklin's gaze moves from the dress to the body. "That's—"

Mother says, Henry. Don't, don't leave me.

Gently, Henry puts her back in, rights the barrel.

You've left me too many times, now, Mother says. You have to take me.

Franklin, wide-eyed, says, "That's her?"

Henry says, "She says we have to take her with us."

"She's dead, Henry."

Henry closes the lid. Mary comes up on Libro. "What's that?"

"She looks dreadful," Franklin says.

"You have rope," Henry says. "Rig a harness. Libro will pull."

"Pull what?" Mary says.

"It's Mother," Henry says. "Do you want to see?" He moves to open the lid again, but Franklin stops him.

"This," Franklin says, "will haunt my sleep."

"We will not," Mary says, "slow down to drag around a dead woman in a hogshead."

It's awfully important, Mother says. You must bring me with you.

"We have to take her," Henry says. "Someone found her. They'll be back. Or they'll tell someone who will come back. Not for her, but for the cart and barrel, and then what'll they do with her?"

Franklin stands looking hard at the barrel.

"Most likely," Mary says, "they'll give her a proper burial."

"She wants to go to sea," Henry says, "with her family around."

Franklin sighs. "I'll rig up the harness."

Mary purses her lips, and it seems she may cry. "I've joined a family of deranged people."

But after a moment she climbs down and helps them rig the rope harness.

Henry finds a cart track, then an old Indian path, and Franklin helps to shove the cart through the brush and out of ruts, until they come into an old weedy road. It looks familiar to Henry, and soon they come to the peddler's camp—the wagon with the drawers is here, and Hy and Dosia. They hail Henry with pleasure. Dosia runs into the road to kiss his cheek, and she invites them to come eat. "We are blessed with many fish!" Hy calls.

But Mary scowls and won't slow Libro.

They cross a shaded, narrow, fast stream on a mossy old log bridge. They turn upstream, and the road is forced to swing out wide around a broad low swampy area where the red-winged blackbirds trill to one another. They pass the pond where Henry watched the newts. They pass the place where Henry left Suthers.

From here Henry doesn't know the land, and Charles's scratchings in the dirt seem terribly vague. They turn onto something hardly more than a deer trail to stay near the water.

It is slow going. The day reaches mid-afternoon. They move alongside a fast stream. Franklin shoves the cart while Libro pulls. "This is mad!" Mary cries. "Leave the cart. No one will find it here."

Mother says, It's just ahead.

Henry says, "It's just ahead." Hoping it's true.

It is. A few minutes later Henry sights a cabin above the stream—old, mossy, and settled into the earth like an egg in a nest. He's never seen it from the outside before, but he's sure this is it.

Charles's indications in the dirt showed a hiding place in the creek below the cabin. They find a little bluff over the water, and the creek running about fifteen feet wide and up to three feet deep at the middle, with tawny water, at bottom, showing a few stones and snagged branches. Henry can see no bags.

On the water's edge he removes his boots, rolls his trousers. Underfoot he feels smooth stones and a fine silt that rises in turbid swirls. He crosses the creek, feeling step by step with his toes for the bags.

Franklin joins him. Mary ties Libro above on the bluff, then she too comes down into the water. The three of them move back and forth like herons stalking crayfish, Mary with her skirt pulled to her waist, all straining to see through the silt and the rot flowing ceaselessly from the swamps.

An hour and more passes; the skin on Henry's feet puckers. Despair, all day a small hard seed in him, begins to open. A horsefly bites him on the neck, and he cries out with frustration and splashes about, kicking up the silt.

"Stop that," Franklin says.

"I don't think it's here," Mary says. "We've been all through here. Maybe it's upstream."

"Charles drew an arrow straight to the water."

"This is madness. How does Charles know what my father did that day?"

Henry reaches down to probe between rocks, comes out

with a black leech on his finger. He tears it free, grinds it into a rock. "When he came back into the cabin," he says, "Suthers's trousers were wet up to here." He indicates his knee. "His sleeves were wet too." He peers into the water again, reaches in, begins to turn over the larger rocks.

Libro neighs, yanks at his tether. "Libro, please!" Mary calls.

But Libro whinnies and pulls the tether again. Mary climbs the bluff to tend to him.

Henry flips several rocks. Coming to one that he cannot lift, he summons Franklin, and Franklin raises it high and hurls it at the shore as if to stave in the brains of the world.

Henry points Franklin to another stone, and another.

They have done this several times when Franklin stops, bends. "There's a hollow place."

He reaches deep, strains—rises up, with two streaming canvas bags.

"That's it!" Henry cries.

Franklin opens a bag, peers inside. He laughs.

Henry shrieks, jumps, whoops, splashes water to all sides.

"Mary!" Franklin yells. He peers again into the bag. "I've never seen so much money."

It is then, as if dictated by the inexorable mathematics of luck, that things begin to go wrong.

Franklin, turning to look for Mary on the bluff, stumbles and drops one of the bags. He goes down into the water after it. At the same time, Henry hears Mother yelp with alarm. Henry shouts to her, "We have the coins! See!"

But Mother is shrieking. Franklin comes out of the water with the bag and yells. "Mary!"

She doesn't answer.

Franklin runs for the shore as best he can through the water while carrying the heavy bags. He's on the sand below the bluff when Mary comes into view. She cries out—a strangled, inarticulate, indignant noise.

Behind Mary is a very ugly man holding a pistol.

"Morley?" Henry says.

"My boy!" Morley cries. "So pleasant to see you. A delight. Wonderful. Tracked you around for days. Not bad scouting work for an artillery man. Lost you for a bit, at times. A few times. Sometimes I wondered if perhaps I had misread the situation. But I counseled myself patience. I nearly lost your track again today. But now, we are here." Theatrically, Morley levels the pistol at Mary's head. "Be so good as to tell the big one to send up the bags."

"You keep the coins," Mary says to Franklin.

Franklin says, "He'll kill you."

"Indeed," Morley says. "I'll send a ball through her brains."

"Keep those coins for our child, or I swear I'll kill you," Mary says.

"I'm going to throw them," Franklin says to Morley.

"I'm going to kill you!" Mary shouts.

Franklin throws the sacks, one after the other.

Mary hangs her head. Morley grabs the sacks and ogles the contents.

Henry has been gaping, but now he yells with frustration, pounds his feet in the river, punches himself on the top of the head. "You can't do this, Morley! It's not fair!" He comes out of the water and starts up the bluff, but the muddy loose earth crumbles under him.

Morley unties Libro, swings up, jams his heels into Libro's flanks. Libro snorts and kicks before he starts forward.

"Libro!" Mary calls. She's standing where Morley left her. She whistles sharply.

Morley has the pistol in one hand while with the other he strains to balance the two sacks of coins atop the horse. He kicks and bellows, "God damn it!" But Libro wheels round toward Mary.

Libro doesn't move any closer, however. He only stands

trembling while Morley works him with his knees. "Shake him off, Libro!" Mary calls. "Throw him!" Libro bends his knees and vibrates like a frightened rabbit. Morley looks down fearfully. Mary shouts, "Throw him! Throw him!"

Morley glances around wildly and his gaze falls to the pistol in his hand, as if he had forgotten it. Scowling, he aims at Mary, and fires.

Mary falls, making no sound. The discharge startles Libro: he shrieks and rears while Morley bends over the sacks and clings desperately. Libro comes to ground, leaps, and races into the woods with Morley riding almost sideways, his head narrowly missing the first tree that goes by.

Franklin finally reaches the top of the bluff and runs to Mary, bellowing like a wounded bull. Henry follows.

As they near, Mary pushes herself to sitting. "I don't think it hit bone." Her left leg bleeds from the thigh. "Libro was always a stupid one," she says. She grimaces at Franklin and Henry. "You have to go."

Franklin stares aghast. "We must bind it."

"I'll do that. You can catch him."

"He has Libro," Henry says.

"It doesn't matter. You'll take the river to the bridge and catch him there. He has to follow the road around the swamp, which will take him much longer, and he has to wrestle Libro back first. He's going the wrong way just now."

"We have no boat," Franklin says. "And I'm a bad swimmer."

Mary says, "The barrel."

"The barrel?" Henry says. "Mother's in the barrel."

Mary pushes to her feet, hobbles two paces, then screams with pain and frustration, grabs her leg. She glares at Henry. "Don't act the ninny. Go!"

After opening the latches, Henry takes a breath. "I'm sorry," he says. Mother says nothing, which worries him. But he topples the barrel onto its side on the ground. The body doesn't come out. Franklin takes the barrel from him, lifts it upside down, shakes it.

Still Mother stays inside.

"She's swollen a bit," Henry says.

Franklin jolts the barrel again, and Mother slides out.

She lies on the ground, lips pulled from leering teeth, neck swollen like a goiter, skin of her hands limp around the bones, eyeballs low in the sockets.

"Mother?" Henry says. When he found her spilled out at Bladensburg, he had somehow set her back into the barrel without really examining her condition.

She stares, hideous and silent.

Franklin starts to close the barrel, but Henry stops him, puts Mother's dress inside, then seals it. "Mother," Henry says, "do you mind if you are left here, a little while?"

She says nothing.

Henry cringes, but turns away. "She wants us to get the coins and her grandson," he says.

Franklin rips a board off the cart for an oar. They roll the barrel into the river, and Henry climbs atop with the board while Franklin hangs off the side by one arm.

The water runs narrow and swift here. There's little use paddling, and Henry watches the land slide past. Franklin asks, "Do you hear Mother now?"

Henry shakes his head. "I don't know why, but she's quiet."

After a while Franklin says, "Do you think you really have gone mad?"

Henry says, "No."

Franklin considers. "Isn't that what a madman would say?"

"No," Henry says. "If you ask a madman if he's mad, he'll say, 'Handsaw!' or yip like a fox or blow his nose on your foot."

The stream discharges into slow water, spreading into a

206 - NICK ARVIN

wide area of reeds and cattails on either side. Henry pushes
with the board. Franklin kicks his feet. For more than an hour
they work grimly onward. Henry streams with sweat, and he
finds mosquitoes in his nose and ears. At times the water is
shallow, and Franklin puts his feet down and pushes the barrel. They climb over a beaver dam, Franklin carrying the barrel. Here the stream narrows again. Soon they see the log
bridge that they passed over in the morning.

Franklin lifts the barrel onto shore. They climb dripping to
the road. "He may have already gone by," Franklin says. "He
may go a different way."

"He doesn't know this territory well. He'll stay to the
road."

"I don't know what to do about his pistol," Franklin says.

"All you have to do is hide in some bushes and jump on
him."

"I can't jump on a man on a horse."

"He'll climb down."

"Why would he?"

Henry opens the barrel, takes out Mother's gingham dress.
"He was cursed with a poverty of will against the tender sex."

Henry plucks a raspberry with his right hand, eats it. His
left hand is full of berries. "It's difficult to pick these berries,"
he complains. "If I pick all the berries there won't be any
berries to pick, and he'll be suspicious. But if I don't pick
berries, he'll be suspicious."

"Hush," Franklin says.

A hay wagon dragged by a mule trundles up the road.
Henry slowly picks a berry. The wagon driver, a shirtless man
smoking a clay pipe, stares at Henry, but says nothing. In a
moment he vanishes down the road.

With a finger Henry pokes berries, this one, that one, this
one again.

A jay disputes with smaller birds overhead. Two squirrels chase each other round a tree, scrambling, chattering. Henry looks at the road.

"Don't!" Franklin whispers.

Hooves thud on the log bridge. Henry bends to the berries, picks one. The hoof falls continue at an easy gait, muffled by the moss between the two tracks of the road.

Just behind Henry, the rider stops.

"A long way out from anywhere, aren't you?" Morley calls. "Quite lonesome here. Not safe, for a girl like yourself. Perhaps I can offer assistance?"

Henry says nothing, works at the berries. Morley's horse—Libro—snorts.

Morley dismounts. "Come. Let's not be uncouth." Henry hears him step nearer. "What are you playing at, dear? I do like games, of course." He comes closer. "No reason to be fearful." Henry fumbles a berry. "No reason," Morley says, "to be fearful." The steps come very close. "Lady, you are rude. Quit your picking and lift your dress to receive your punishment."

Franklin bursts out with a bear roar that startles Henry so that he nearly falls onto his face.

Morley shrieks with surprise. Franklin grips him from behind in a hug that pins Morley's arms, squeezes his chest, pulls him off his feet, purples his face.

Morley makes little piping baby bird sounds.

Henry looks Morley over. He sighs, scuffles his feet, grimaces. "Franklin," he says, "let him down."

Franklin says, "He shot Mary." He continues to squeeze.

Something in Morley's back or chest makes a little wet pop. Morley twitches, drops his pistol.

"I know," Henry says, "but think of honor and such."

Morley's ugly face shades to green.

"He shot Mary," Franklin repeats. "A defenseless woman."

"He was a friend to me," Henry says, "when I had no friends." He is looking Franklin in the eye.

Franklin winces. He jerks up, then slams Morley down.

Morley collapses onto hands and knees, gasping.

Franklin picks up the pistol and examines the priming. Henry goes to Libro and takes hold of the rope round his neck. The bags of coins are tied across Libro's back.

"Should we put him into the barrel," Franklin says, "and into the water?"

"Somehow," Morley wheezes, "things always turn against me in the end." He tries to stand, but groans and drops to his hands again. "I think you've broken one of my ribs."

Franklin kicks him in the ass.

Henry says, "I thought you were a friend."

"I am," Morley says. He sits, and, groaning, stretches one leg in front of himself, bends the other. "But a man must also strive."

"That doesn't make sense!" Henry cries.

But Morley is looking past Henry. "The horse," Morley says.

"Libro?" Henry turns. Libro is working peaceably at the grass. Henry has the rope. "What of him?"

He turns back, and Morley is drawing the flashing metal of a small knife from his boot.

Henry shouts as Morley turns on Franklin. Franklin begins to raise the pistol, but Morley strikes first, driving the knife into Franklin's stomach.

Franklin says, "Oh!"

He drops the pistol, sits in the grass. He looks at the knife, his hands spread around it.

Henry twists Libro's rope reins in his hands, the sight of the knife in Franklin like a fragment of dream, everything quiet around it.

Morley bends for the pistol.

The silence in Henry's mind bursts, and he rushes forward. He is sure that the pistol's priming has been ruined by being dropped.

But Morley swings up the pistol, cocks, fires—it discharges, to Henry's immense surprise. It feels like hot sand thrown in his face, with a bright flash and a blast and a quick sharp whistle.

He staggers. But there's nothing more, no pain, no lifting away from life. It comes to him that Morley has missed, that the whistle was the ball whining past. He sets his feet and bares his teeth, feeling made of rage.

Morley lifts the pistol like a hatchet, and as Henry springs, he brings the pistol down onto the crown of Henry's head.

Henry crumples.

Then, on the operation of some reflex, he rises up again. He sways on his feet, black shapes swirling before him like ash over a fire. Amid these black fragments stand three Morleys, left, right, and center. Behind the three Morleys sit three Franklins. The three Franklins set three big hands to the three knives in their three stomachs.

They pull out the knives.

"Morley!" Henry cries. "Please!"

"I think I'd best to leave you both dead." The left, right, and center Morleys look regretful as they raise the three pistols to club Henry again. Behind the three Morleys, the three Franklins stand up. "Sorry for this," Morley says, "but I can't have you arranging for highway robbers to jump at me from the bushes all the rest of my life."

The Franklins turn their knives around. Henry stands wavering as the three pistols pause high, then start down toward him, while at the same time the three Franklins press the three knives into the three Morleys.

The pistol bounces off the side of Henry's head, driving him to the ground and filling the world with swarming darkness.

When it slowly parts, before Henry, only a foot away, sits

Morley, twisting his arm to grope for the knife in his back. Dizziness makes the world spin and expand and contract in stutter steps. Henry's anger has vanished, leaving the scrapings of grief. Morley gives up on reaching the knife in his back and sags.

Henry pushes forward and takes Morley's hand.

Franklin stands alone, wavering over them.

"You might have let me have the coins," Morley says.

"You stole them. It made me angry."

"I suppose you mined the metal from the earth with your own hands."

"That doesn't make it yours!" Henry says. He begins to weep.

"It's all right, my boy," Morley says. All the strain falls from his face. He looks remote and kindly and almost not ugly. "Find good use for those coins." He peers skyward, and he's quiet, and then, as he sits there, he's dead.

Franklin settles to the ground, and the three are in a circle, so that it is as if they sit in parley with the dead man.

Libro, with the coins tied to his saddle, browses the grass beside the road.

When Henry recovers a little he is flat on his back, and when he looks at the world it pulses. Morley has toppled onto his side. Franklin sits gazing blankly. He's pale, sweating, shivering. While struggling they have ended up a distance from the road, in the tall grasses and brush.

"We need to get to the roadway," Henry says, "where a passerby will find us."

He makes an effort to rise, but nausea pushes him straight down again. Darkness cuts into the limits of his vision, and he struggles to fight it away. When he tries again to stand, the darkness nearly closes out everything. He settles to the ground and yells with frustration.

Franklin stands slowly, sways over Henry. "I'll lift you."

"You can't. Look at you."

Franklin ponders. He says, "I won't leave you."

"Just go into the road."

"If I die there," Franklin says, "how will they know you're here?"

He lifts Henry by the armpits, and, staggering, carries him to the road. Then he settles to his knees, puts Henry down, falls onto his side.

Henry sits with legs before him on the moss of the road while the sun moves overhead. "Stay close," he says to Libro. "Don't go wandering." Libro lifts his ears and looks at him, then goes back to grazing. Henry cannot hear Mother at all. Darkness creeps a little into vision, then more, then yet further, and Henry knows he cannot keep it away.

The scratch of a rough mattress wakes him.

He resists waking for a long time. Waking seems to pull him from a feeling of wonderful ease and peace, a feeling that his mind and spirit are fully his own, that everything is strange but not evil, and there are voices—Mother's, but also Morley's, and many others, a world of voices, and he feels no obligation to name them, or understand them, or reply to them, and he has only to listen to them, as if listening from another room to a conversation of many, many happy voices.

But finally this feeling recedes, turning unreal, and he wakes in a little structure, some sort of pig shelter, smelling of stale manure and musty hay, with slatted walls pierced all over by white lines of sunlight. Poking and scratching his back is a straw tick mattress. He watches motes of dust make desultory explorations of one shaft of light then another.

Turning his head, he finds the bulky shape of Franklin, a white bandage wrapped around the middle of him. Franklin's eyes are closed, and his chest moves shallowly, with a quiver in each breath.

On Henry's other side is a low doorway. A woman steps through. She kneels beside Henry, looks into his eyes. "Do you recognize me?"

Presently, he does. "You're the peddler's wife. Dosia."

Dosia tells Henry that Mary limped along the river until she found a leaking canoe hidden on the bank, rode it downstream, found Henry and Franklin in the road, mounted Libro. She had come into Hy and Dosia's camp to ask for help.

Mary paid a farmer from the coins to let them use this shelter. She paid a doctor to look at them. She has been hobbling all about, Dosia says, although the doctor said she oughtn't on her injured leg. Henry and Franklin have been lying here for two days.

"Will Franklin live?" Henry asks.

"He felt the brush of the wing," Dosia says, cheerily, "but he's not dead. As for the future, it's outside our knowing."

Mary puts her head in the doorway, measures Henry with a cold look. "Can you get up?"

He pushes onto his elbows, and the nausea rushes on him again, though it isn't so terrible as he remembers in the road. "I'm not sure," he says. "What must we do?"

"My son, you idiot," Mary says. "We must regain my son who you gave away."

Attempting to stand makes Henry violently ill, and he collapses.

As he lies in the pig shelter, the hours move curiously, light and dark swallowing each other. At moments when he grows angry and raises himself, nausea like churning water pushes him back down.

He worries he may never be able to stand upright again.

He listens for Mother's voice. Only once, for a moment, is

there a sibilance at the limit of perception. But then he wakes and realizes: a dream.

Franklin occasionally opens his eyes, looks around, says a few words, smiles. He will swallow a little broth. Mostly he sleeps, or anyway lies resting with his eyes closed. Sometimes Henry thinks he seems to be improving a little; at other times he thinks not.

One morning he sits up and his head swims, but the feeling subsides. He crawls from the shelter, stands, wavers a moment, walks a circle watching his feet, raises his head. The peddler's wagon stands nearby. They are encamped beside a stone chimney that stands naked in the grass, the final remnant of some vanished homestead.

Mary comes and looks at him, then goes away. A few minutes later she returns, leading Libro, the bags of coins tied across his saddle. "I've waited for you; I don't know why. It's five days since you gave away my son." She mounts. "We have to hurry to strike a deal with my father."

"I'll ride in front," he says.

"No, you won't," she says, seizing Henry's hand and pulling him up behind.

They ride for Alexandria, and Henry cannot muster a dispute about his position—Libro's every step makes his mind wobble like a table with a short leg. A warmth radiates from the place where Morley struck him. He tilts his face and watches the treetops and clouds, because it helps to even out the jolting of the road, until a flock of crows wheels overhead, making him dizzy. When he shuts his eyes against the feeling, he seems to go out of himself.

Washington still smells of char. Mary stares at the blackened buildings, but doesn't slow. They pay the Potomac ferry from the coins, cross over, ride on.

Judging they are near Alexandria, Henry says, "We need to hide the coins."

"Why?" Mary asks.

"We can't go into Suthers's office with the coins in hand. He'll simply take them."

"He's still my father."

"You know he takes what he wants," Henry says.

Mary watches him scrape a hollow amid a stand of dogwood, drop the bags in, and shove a section of half-rotten log over to mark the spot.

At an inn they pay for feed and board for Libro. Henry leads Mary through the streets toward the waterfront. Approaching the tall brick warehouse, Henry slows. "It'd be best to watch for a time," he says.

"Watch for what?"

He has no answer, but he feels uneasy. He leads the way to a little burn-scarred house with nothing but weeds before it. They sit on a charred timber where they are hidden by the weeds.

The afternoon proceeds slowly. A dog snuffles around them. A couple of men enter Suthers's office, leave again.

"We're dithering," Mary says. "We don't have time."

"Just a few minutes more," Henry says. But he wonders if he is afraid. Usually, if he notices that he is afraid of a thing, it makes him angry, and he will run right toward it. Now—thinking of Suthers turns something inside him, winding his guts like a winch. But he isn't certain if this feeling is fear, or something else.

Whatever it is, the way he is thinking about it starts to make him angry, and he is about to stand out of the hiding place when a tall rawboned figure appears in the street, limping, his face so terribly damaged that for a moment Henry stares unrecognizing.

Henry had assumed that Lodowicke died after he was thrown from Suthers's wagon. But here he is. On the side of his face where the redcoats' bullet struck there's a large red hole of scarred flesh, and the eye above this hole is lifeless and rolled, the eye-white turned the yellow-orange of a harvest moon. He swings one leg like a board.

He goes into Suthers's office.

"Let's go," Mary says. Henry says no, not until Lodowicke leaves. "We waited until he arrived," Mary says, "and now you want to wait until he leaves?"

Lodowicke comes out only a moment later. When he's vanished down the street, Henry stands. "Let's not dally forever," he says.

Mary snorts.

Henry crosses the street rubbing his head with a sense of furious trepedation, kicking the dust as he goes.

Light penetrates into Suthers's office through a single window to show a few shelves of books and papers and an enormous polished oak desk. Suthers stares across its expanse. Henry feels he has seen more hospitality in the face of a copperhead snake.

"Mary," Suthers says. "Henry. How interesting."

Henry explains that they wish to purchase the slaves, Charles and Hollis.

"Those two are not currently in my possession, as I think you are aware."

"That doesn't matter," Henry says. "We'll pay for them."

Suthers gazes flat at them. "You know where they are, I suppose. Why do you want them?"

"We have our own reasons," Mary says.

"And where did you find such money?"

"There have been opportunities," Henry says. He shifts his feet. "A war is like a rich man dancing with a hole in his pocket . . ."

The door behind him opens. Lodowicke steps through. He's as tall as the door in his hand. He closes it and stands scanning Henry and Mary with his good eye, saying nothing.

Suthers says, "Henry."

Henry turns to him reluctantly.

"My coins?" Suthers says.

Henry says nothing. He looks at the floor.

Suthers laughs. "My coins," he says. "You've somehow gotten your hands on my coins. And Hollis and Charles are involved, too. You wish to buy my slaves from me with funds that you have stolen from me."

Henry straightens. "It's no matter to you where the money comes from."

"You're a considerable little devil," Suthers says. Henry isn't sure if the narrow of Suthers's eyes is anger or humor. "Do you know, Henry, that I sat for a day and a half in that road where you left me? And why do you need to buy the slaves?"

"We think that men ought not to own other men as property," Henry says. "We'll free them."

"A matter of principle."

Henry nods.

Suthers, smiling, shakes his head. "You're a bad liar, Henry."

"It doesn't matter, Papa," Mary says. "Any more than it matters where the money comes from. We're asking if you'll sell the slaves."

"It is uncommon strange," Suthers says, "to be offered money that is my own for things that I do not have. I expect I'd be a fool not to sell." He tilts his head. "As a man of business, I'm not known to be a fool, am I, Mr. Lodowicke?" he says, not looking at Lodowicke.

"No, sir."

Henry proposes a price of one thousand dollars for the two slaves, which is at least twice their value.

Suthers shakes his head. "There are eighty-nine pieces of gold and three hundred fourteen pieces of silver. You will return them all to me."

"They're not worth half the silver!" Henry cries, dancing with vexation.

Suthers shrugs. "Go to the slave market. Buy some others."

Mary touches Henry's shoulder. "Henry," she says.

Henry squeaks, "It's too much!"

"We have to pay this," she says.

Henry's head hurts. Mary and Suthers look at him, and the silence in the room presses him. He cannot hear Mother. His own thoughts seem to dart out of sight. He turns to escape Suthers's gaze and finds himself looking into the hole in Lodowicke's face.

Mary says, "We have no choice."

"Really," Suthers says, "if I let you spend a single silver coin on Phipps—that's what you want to do, isn't it?—I would feel I had entirely failed you. We are agreed?"

Henry whispers, "All right."

Suthers opens a drawer in the desk, flourishes vellum and quill, writes a contract, signs it, shows it. "You hand me the funds: I hand this to you."

Mary says, "We'll bring the coins to the common at five o'clock."

Suthers shrugs, nods. Lodowicke steps aside from the door.

As Henry and Mary move into the street, Henry fills with despair.

"Mother?" he says.

Mary looks closely at him.

He ignores her. "Mother? We'll find another way."

Mother is silent. The place where Morley struck him on the head hurts. He feels abject and lonesome. "Mother?"

He looks around with dark apprehension, as on occasions in the deep woods when he could neither see nor hear anything unusual, but some unnamed sense made him sure that a panther was stalking him.

As they go about retrieving the coins from under the rotten log, Henry watches to see if they are followed. Mary is grim. They walk quickly. The absence of Mother's voice feels like a heat in Henry's head.

Suthers and Lodowicke already stand at the center of the common. Mary's hurt leg scuffs in the grass. The day is fine: a few other people are about, taking the air. A man sits reading a book. A little boy runs past, rolling a barrel hoop.

Suthers and Lodowicke bend to each other, talking quietly. They glance up only as Henry and Mary come near.

Henry throws the two bags down with a feeling of vexation, but then considers that this throwing down may not have been the best approach, so he puts a foot on top of a bag. Mary says, "The contract, please, Papa."

Suthers says, "Good day to you, children."

Henry kicks the bag. "Here," he says.

"There's no great rush, is there?" Suthers asks. "Between us, as men and children of commercial enterprise?"

The silence in Henry's head generates mounting heat. He feels sure that things have already gone wrong, somehow. "The contract!" he cries.

"I tore it up the moment you left my office."

The silence in Henry's head is like a flame.

Suthers points a thumb over one shoulder. "You see the man with the delightful Corsican hat with the feather."

They see the man.

He gestures over the other shoulder. "And the man with the silver-handled ebony cane." He points past Henry. "And the man with the impressive white mustache." He points past Mary. "The seated gentleman with the red leather-bound book."

Lodowicke stumps around to stand close behind Henry and Mary.

"Those're my men, and I've only pointed out half of them.

This is my city. You want to cheat me, you'd best do so somewhere other than Alexandria. You believe that standing here on the common gives you any power over me? You're wrong. You have nothing. You'll give the coins to me, then you'll lead me to my grandson, and then I'll decide what to do with you."

Henry looks round at the men Suthers pointed out. They all watch him. He has been a stupendous fool. Why did he suppose they could trust Suthers after an agreement was struck?

With a cry of rage, Mary starts forward—but Lodowicke reaches with a long arm and knocks her to the ground. She howls, pushes herself up, and Lodowicke kicks her in the side.

She lies clutching herself. Suthers says nothing. He looks at Henry. Henry's head feels like it is in an inferno of silence, and his fury strains in him—his feet twitch, his teeth ache; he wants to hurtle forward. But he will only be struck down. By an immense effort, he remains where he stands.

"Now," Suthers says, "you'll explain to me why you want to buy those slaves."

Henry resorts to truth. He tells Suthers that Hollis and Charles helped him find the coins, and they are holding the baby against his return.

Suthers's lip curls. "And all this is because you would free Phipps? My boy, there are times and reasons to bear certain risks, but this? For *Phipps*? No. Even if you were to succeed, Phipps would drink and gamble himself back into prison before the new corn is out of the ground."

Henry can scarcely hear him through the pain of heat in his head. Mother has gone forever. He has lost his chance to free Father. His nephew will be trapped with this man.

"I'll take the coins," Suthers says, "and you'll tell me how to locate Hollis and Charles, and I'll have them whipped until they are dead, and I'll reclaim my grandson to myself."

Henry wavers on his feet. Mother, he thinks. Mother? But she's not there, and he's alone; there's only him.

And he sees what he can do.

"Me," he says. The heat in his mind is already dying. "You have a son."

Suthers shakes his head. "I have thought of it. You have spirit. But you'll simply run off. I should have taken you away long ago, but your mother said no, and I deferred. It's too late now."

"I speak like you," Henry says. "I'm sized like you."

Suthers hesitates.

"What?" Mary interrupts. She has stood up. "Wait."

"I don't like it," Lodowicke says. Suthers tightens his lips, but Lodowicke goes on. "He'll betray you."

"What do you mean, 'You have a son?'" Mary says.

Suthers gestures silence. "I'll talk with the boy," he says. "Wait over there. Take her."

Lodowicke scowls, twitches, seizes Mary by the shoulder, drags her off. "Henry!" she cries. "You should've told me."

"Your proposal is: you work for me, and meanwhile I'm to lose my slaves," Suthers says, "and I'm to be paid in coin stolen from me for the privilege? It's out of the question. You must have a means to signal or contact them. That's all we need. A trap can be set. We'll recover my property and my grandson that way."

"I won't tell you how to find them. I gave my word."

"You've given me no reason to think you trustworthy," Suthers scoffs, "or anything except a thief. I'm also doubtful that you like me in the least."

"I want to learn to seize chances as you do."

"I don't know." Suthers shakes his head. "Look at how you stumble from thing to thing on instinct."

"Yet I got the coins."

Suthers laughs. "Yes, yet you're a fool. You were a fool to come here. By the way, if such a situation were ever to arise again, you should engage a lawyer to convey your messages. I cannot abide lawyers, but they do have certain uses."

It makes Henry angry. "I'm a fool, but you want the baby?" he cries. "Have you seen the baby? He's helpless and hairless and useless as a slick kitten, and he'll be that way for years! You'll grow old waiting for that baby to become something useful. And who knows what you'll have then? He may have the falling sickness. He may be a caitiff or simpleminded. The baby cannot help it if he grows into any of those things. Neither can you."

"So I should take you in hand?"

"Yes!"

"I don't know if you can unlearn Phipps's habits."

Henry asks sullenly, "What habits?"

"An aversion to difficult work. Always reaching for the easy chance."

"I'll work, if that's what you want," Henry says. "I'm tired of ill luck."

Suthers studies Henry, and Henry looks back at him. "I like you," Suthers says, "and it's true that I don't know what kind of man the baby will turn out to be." He gazes away a moment. "My own father was a plague on me. To be a son ought not to be a slave. Let's say that in exchange for Hollis and Charles, you owe the coins and a further debt to me that you must work off. Let's say that the term of your debt to me is six years. After that time you'll be your own man, and if you don't feel that I am father to you, then you may do as you like. If you don't care for our business, you may leave it."

Six years sounds like a long time to Henry. But he doesn't think of saying no. "All right," he says.

"I'll grant you even Phipps's debts," Suthers says, "then send him away, because otherwise his plight will be in your mind. You'll see him freed this once, and then you'll be done with him, and your days will be with me. You'll learn my business. You'll learn how I think. Phipps will dwindle behind you. You'll look back and see him as a small, ludicrous figure on the horizon. As for the business—I've seen how your mind turns. I think you'll find it to your liking."

Henry understands: it's a trap. One that he has already entered. Suthers let him come in by his own way.

Henry says, "You'll also get my brother out of his trouble with the army."

Suthers shrugs. "We'll send them all away, all the Phippses, and now the negotiation is complete. You'll promise me six years."

"Yes, sir."

"Then," Suthers says, "you can choose who your father is. I'll tell you now, there's a question under the question of the father you choose, and that question is: what kind of man do you want to be?"

Franklin has contrived a rope sling to enclose the barrel, and he has weighted it with a stone the size of a pony's head.

They ride in a borrowed rowboat. A wind drives choppy waves, making them plunge down and up. Franklin grips his seat with his hand. His injury has left him pale and thin, although at this moment his pallor is tinting green. Henry sits with his feet on the barrel, to keep it from rolling. Phipps works the oars. Henry has noted—an internal observation of his own instincts—that the name in his mind now is not Father but Phipps.

In the distance, on the beach, waiting, are Mary and the baby. Franklin has been granted his army discharge and one hundred sixty acres in the new state of Ohio. He plans to take Mary, the baby, and Phipps.

Also on the beach are many bottles of whiskey and a troupe of drunks that Phipps brought with him from the tavern. Henry does not know how he paid for the whiskey. They had gathered around Mother's barrel and one man, a purported reverend who only looked like another drunk to Henry, had stood with his hands out, eyes rolled, mumbling. "I'm a resurrection, and life; he that believe in meat, even dead, will live: Live and believe and, uh, don't die."

Phipps announces that they've gone far enough. To roll the barrel and the stone out of the boat requires the full strength of the three of them. Phipps, in the vigor of his efforts, somehow gets a hand entangled in the rope sling—the barrel goes over, and Phipps is pulled after, making a small yelp, looking surprised. Then stone, barrel, and man vanish as the water closes.

Henry and Franklin gape as a few bubbles appear.

"It might," Franklin says finally, "be honorable if he stayed down with her."

"Give me your knife," Henry says.

Franklin gives him the knife; Henry sets it in his teeth—he has seen crabbers go after tangled lines this way—and dives.

He nearly collides head-on with Phipps.

Phipps climbs into the boat laughing. He pulls Henry back in. "She didn't want to go alone!" he says. "But Franklin, you'll never make a seaman. Those knots are loose as an old hinge. I slipped onc in an instant."

A soft wooden noise of collision sounds against the boat. They discover the barrel floating beside them. The sling has fallen away entirely, and the barrel bobs rather merrily at starboard. Henry regards it suspiciously. "Mother," he says, leaning over the barrel, "we're all together, and you're to sea. You can go. Why don't you go?"

Phipps says that they must bring her back to shore and locate more rope. Henry strips his clothes and goes back into the water to push the barrel into the boat. But without the sling, Phipps and Franklin have difficulty gaining purchase on it, and Franklin hasn't all of his strength. He trembles over the water. Finally Phipps calls Henry back into the boat, puts a hand on the barrel, shoves it toward the open horizon. "Go on, my love!" he cries. "Go! Go! Your labor here is done! Enjoy the everlasting mercies that you have earned!"

"This isn't proper," Franklin says. "She'll float around out there."

"She might like that!" Phipps says. "Yes, I think so." And he sets to the oars.

Returned to the beach, Franklin stumbles over to where Mary sits with the baby. Phipps claps Henry's shoulder and says, "A perfect day! Gulls croaking in a blue sky! A mild breeze off the water!"

"Why did she come back up?" Henry asks, still dismayed.

"She was ever active," Phipps says.

"Except when lying abed," Henry says.

"And what blame would attach to that? Her life was more toilsome than she ever deserved."

"But why?" Henry asks, with a stirring in his gut, feeling mean.

Phipps, however, doesn't notice. "Poor fortune," he sighs. "Lamentable fortune has been our lot. Of course it must turn."

Henry supposes there is nothing to say to this. He is not disappointed, however, since it never crossed his mind that the experience of prison might better Phipps. When Phipps was paid out, Franklin gave him several dollars. By the next morning all of the dollars had either been converted into drink and drunk, or turned into empty air by the alchemy of the faro table.

Phipps wanders away toward his friends, but a moment later he circles back. "Son." Phipps squeezes Henry's shoulder. It seems to Henry that people are always grabbing him as they speak to him, and he pulls away. "Mother has gone," Phipps says, "and I must be more of a father to you than ever before."

But he is full of whiskey and tight as a ringbolt, and Henry knows that any promises will soon be forgotten. "I'm going to work for Suthers," Henry says, "in Alexandria."

"What! No! Not at all. Now that I'm out of prison, I'll provide for you. We'll work your brother's farm. We'll build ourselves up."

"I've already decided."

"No, you haven't, no." Phipps waves a hand. He stumbles a step, though he is standing still. "We'll talk of it tomorrow."

Henry has already told Franklin that he intends to honor his oath and work for Suthers. Franklin thought on it for several minutes, then said, "It was a promise made under threat, so it's not binding."

Henry shook his head. "I'm sure he would kill me."

The night darkness seeps into the sky, fills the water, rises onto the beach. The men from the tavern grow drunker and drunker. They yell and caper and laugh. In a warbling tone, one of them offers a new tavern song he heard.

Oh, say can you see by the dawn's early light
What so proudly we hailed at the twilight's last gleaming

Someone brings out a fiddle. Another plays a Jew's harp. The others drink and dance around a fire. Even Franklin is a little drunk and dancing.

Henry watches while the others fall asleep, sprawling here and there on the sand. He looks out to sea and thinks of Mother carried on the circulation of the great currents, and thinks perhaps that is not so bad after all.

Finally, only the baby lies awake beside Mary, staring at Henry. Henry kneels close, lets the baby grip his finger, and shakes his hand solemnly. He salutes the great sleeping shape of his brother and gazes a moment at Phipps, curled on his side near the fire. Then Henry departs to present himself at Suthers's office.

Epilogue

Henry's days are full; he often wobbles at the limit of exhaustion. If he has a minute, he curls in a corner to nap. Sometimes he sleeps on his feet.

For his few hours of rest at night he has a backroom pallet in a house that rents to sailors and dockworkers, dozens of them, who keep strange hours. Various men constantly come and go from Henry's shared room, but there is one man who Henry sees every night—Rion, a small, limber man, with a birthmark across his eyes like a raccoon mask. Rion knows that Henry is Suthers's son, and he says, glowering, "I suppose if I did anything against you, I'd find myself in considerable pain, or considerable dead." Rion rises before dawn and goes to the docks, and Henry goes with him. They join the work gangs, loading and unloading boats. Henry is the smallest and youngest, as they often remind him with foul words while sending him to the smaller boxes and crates.

Sometimes Rion sets a crate aside from the others, and soon it vanishes. Sometimes a passerby leaves a crate or a hogshead beside the docks, and Rion lifts it and places it among the others.

At sunset Henry leaves the docks to report to Suthers's warehouse. Lodowicke sits in a corner and tells people what to do. He tells Henry what to do. Most nights this involves working one of the gambling tables—dice or faro or backgammon. The dealers tell Henry to watch for cheats, to bring drinks, to retrieve whiskey from the warehouse. Sometimes he is sent to collect bets at a boxing match. Sometimes he is told to sit outside a house and report if anyone leaves, and, if so, where they go.

The docks grow increasingly busy. When Henry begins, the British still control the Chesapeake, and goods must be moved by small boats that slip through the blockade by nighttime or bribery. And some shipments, operating under arrangements of third-hand payment, are sent out for intentional capture by the redcoats. But the British are withdrawing pieces of their fleet, and by the end of 1814 the fortifications on Tangier Island have been abandoned, and all of the former slaves there have been evacuated. Only a half dozen British light frigates remain in the area, and even these are not inclined to engage a well-armed privateer.

On an evening in February word arrives that the war is ended. The church bells clamor, and enormous crowds parade and dance in the streets with lamps, torches, and bottles of whiskey. Henry dances too at first, but ends up watching drowsily from one side. He falls asleep with his back to a haberdasher's shop. When he wakes a couple of hours later, he returns to the docks. He can't see that anyone gained much by the war, excepting the smugglers like Suthers, the slaves like Radnor who joined the redcoats, and the looters who did their work better than Henry. And Charles and Hollis, who departed for Philadelphia, where Hollis said he knew of a friend of a cousin who is a free black and owns a ropewalk. "Cables, spun yarn, rigging, marline, log-lines, lead-lines whipping twine, and drum lines," Hollis said. "Don't have to be able to see to walk the ropewalk. Just count your steps."

The war's end doesn't slow Suthers's enterprises. It seems there is always smuggling and bribery to be done, if not to evade the British, then the collector of customs. And while Henry's work is exhausting, he's delighted by the sights and things and people and smells and sounds. The great ships moving in and out of the harbor. The piles of goods and tumult and cries on the docks. The bars with oil lamps hanging low over battered tables, smoking and stinking of whale oil. The men with monkeys and parrots. A camel with two humps. A living headless chicken that takes water and corn into the hole in its neck. The tones and rhythms of a dozen different languages. The sailors' chants. The men on the docks talk of Savannah, of Boston, of the Northern Lakes, of China, of Madagascar, of wan sea monsters and golden mermaids, of mountains that reach the clouds, of landscapes of sand, of floating islands of ice, of cities filled with silver and music, of jungles filled with incredible beasts. A knowing grows in Henry—it feels sure as knowledge—that one day he will go to see these things.

Henry works seven days a week. Sundays he helps to set up the horse races at a muddy, egg-shaped track a mile outside the city. And Lodowicke's debt collections often occur on Sundays, because men are most likely to be home. Lodowicke says, without further comment, that Suthers calls these excursions "hygienic events." He leads Henry to a house, sets Henry to stand as lookout, then goes to the door. If a knock is not answered, Lodowicke—skilled with a pick, and with the long crowbar he often carries to these appointments—enters regardless.

Henry stands at the side of the street, unsure what he should watch for. And what should he do if the to-be-watched-for appears?

It doesn't seem to matter. Perhaps he is here to learn some other lesson. The hygienic events mostly pass quietly. On occasion Henry hears breaking crockery, furniture, glassware. Sometimes he hears a sob, a scream. He listens, waits, watches the passersby.

Over time, he notices that there are fewer passersby, and he realizes that people seeing him now circle wide, or turn back.

He's become known, his presence in the street like a sign, advertising Lodowicke at work.

Henry can imagine Lodowicke working on Phipps, a notion that flutters his stomach. But the trepidation of the people in the street amuses and irritates him. He puts out his tongue. He stares until they look away.

He sees Suthers at the faro games, at the horse races and boxing matches, but they only talk once or twice a month, when Henry is summoned to supper. They eat at Suthers's desk—roast pig or fricasseed chicken or alamode beef or boiled brains, with baked beans, cooked dandelion, mashed potatoes, rennet pudding, a jug of beer. Henry eats until he might burst. Suthers talks of his operations and plans, of how money flows through Alexandria, and how it always eventually passes over the docks. He talks of the value of goods, of land, of reliable men, of the character of the gamblers, the merchants, the boxers, the horses, the card dealers, the ship captains, the prostitutes, the dock workers, the sailors, the city councillors. He seems to know everyone. Henry asks about this. "I'm always watching," Suthers says. "But anyone can watch. The crux of business is to know when to act."

Henry supposes this is how a father is meant to be, but maybe he preferred the old one. On a few occasions, Suthers says nothing at all as they eat, and this reminds Henry of Mother.

The seasons turn; summer becomes winter becomes summer. One warm evening Henry climbs a cobbled street uphill from the docks. The night's faro games have ended. Henry is thoughtless with exhaustion. He stumbles, catches himself. Away toward the docks someone sings. Nearer, a baby cries. A drunk lurches past, breathing hard.

A movement catches Henry's attention. He looks up. A bright star flashes overhead. Not a second later, another falls down more slowly, fainter, seeming to pulse, and vanishes behind the roof of the house before him.

More follow. Henry watches them go. He recalls a similar night years ago with Father. Or, rather, Phipps.

Then he continues to his pallet and collapses into deepest sleep.

He wakes before dawn and finds that Rion is gone. He rises, dresses, walks to the docks. The sky is only beginning to lighten. Rion stands with a cluster of men, talking low. One notices Henry and stares. Soon all of them stare. Rion crosses over, leans close. "Lodowicke wants to see you."

"What?"

"What?" Rion sneers. "What?" He turns.

Henry enters the office and finds Suthers alone at his desk, facedown, unstayed. Henry's breath stops. He doesn't think of saying hello: he can see that Suthers is dead.

He edges nearer. In the side of Suthers's neck are the flat lips of a knife wound, seeping blood.

Then he turns and discovers Lodowicke on a stool in the corner.

"I killed him here," Lodowicke says, "so that everyone can see him ended in his throne."

The lid of Lodowicke's dead eye twitches. He rises. On his belt he carries an ivory-handled knife and a leather cartridge box. In his hand is a pistol. He opens the cartridge box, begins loading the pistol.

"It's been coming due ever since he abandoned me over the side of that wagon." Lodowicke contrives to shape his ruined face into a type of smile. "You have the intellect of a rabid squirrel, but I don't dislike you, Henry. You and I both were wronged by him. You're freed now. Fly off." Lodowicke primes the pan on the pistol and pulls back the frizzen. "One thing I've never killed before is a child, but if you're still here when I finish loading this pistol, I'll kill you." He pushes a powder charge into the pistol barrel, ball, wadding. "Suthers chose to trust me rather than to put his own hand to the blood of the business. 'Hygienic events,' indeed. That's a mistake I'll have no trouble avoiding." While Lodowicke is speaking, Henry's indignation flares and mounts. Soon he is full of fury, with a roaring mind and vibrating limbs. He says, "He was my father!"

Lodowicke ramrods the pistol barrel. "I'll tell you what I believe. A father is only one more person who will betray you. Better to live as if we're orphans."

The rage is too much, and Henry leaps.

He crashes bodily into Lodowicke, which is much like running into a barn wall. Lodowiche grunts, grips Henry by the arm, flings him.

Henry bounces off the desk, drops to the floor. With his breath gone, he lies in a jumble of his own limbs, his vision aswim with luminous shapes. But he has hold of the thing in his hand, the thing he wanted, the ivory-handled knife from Lodowicke's belt.

Yet as the room spins he has difficulty sorting out his arms and his legs, which one goes where, what to do with them to make his body rise. When finally he stands, Lodowicke brings back the cock of the pistol.

A horrible scream erupts.

Henry wonders, Am I screaming? But he is not. It is loud and piercing as needles thrust into the ears. He says, "Mother?"

Lodowicke, however, seems not to hear the scream. "Mother?" He snorts. He pulls the trigger. The flint snaps, throws sparks—

Nothing.

"Damnation," Lodowicke says. "Of all the luck."

The scream fades.

Henry raises the knife.

"Boy," Lodowicke says. But Henry thinks he detects a twitch of hesitation. He knows Lodowicke's work. Lodowicke wins by intimidation, by striking first. Ever since Lodowicke was thrown off Suthers's wagon, he has moved a little clumsily.

Henry rises on the balls of his feet. He may be quick enough to get under Lodowicke's reach.

Later—years later—he will wonder if Suthers had lived a little longer, might he have done differently, might he have grown more accustomed to the violence, might he have loved Suthers more and felt obliged to avenge him?

Instead he looks into Lodowicke's good eye, and, at the behest of an obscure feeling, as if the faintest end of Mother's scream wrapped a thread around him and drew him back, he steps away. Perhaps it is only that he likes Lodowicke a little, or understands him a little, which might be the same thing.

"I'll go," he says. Somehow his anger has turned sad.

Eyeing Lodowicke cautiously—but Lodowicke only seems to slump—Henry circles to the door, and he goes.

The first two days Henry walks. For twenty dollars he buys a tin water bottle, small pan, butter, salted beef and tripe, and a Harper's Ferry rifle with shot, wadding, and flints. He shoots squirrel as he walks. On the third day he finds a pony offered by a tavern-keep who took it in exchange for debts, a bright bay gelding, four years old, with a star on his forehead and mild mannered. Henry pays twenty-five dollars.

He follows the Wilderness Road cut by Daniel Boone through the Cumberland Gap to the Ohio River. He ferries across on a raft and continues onward, into vast forests.

There are oak and hickory, beech and maple, hemlock and pine, trees of astounding girth that rise seventy feet and more to the first branches, where they weave together in a dense canopy. The shadowed space below lies open as a park, and the road is a faint track through the leaf litter. Scratches show where the turkeys have been searching for food. He sees bear, deer, fisher, and, across a grassy meadow, on a hill, a group of elk. Some days he sees no people at all. He has heard horrible stories of the Indians, but the only ones he sees are a family idling outside a trading post. They wear white men's clothing and eat sunflower seeds.

Sometimes he stops and listens for Mother, a habit that won't pass.

He rides a rough path over a rise, passes among a number of dying girdled trees, and enters an open field. Against the trees on the far side stands a small, square cabin built of logs, a wooly thread of smoke rising from the chimney.

The dogs sight Henry first. They rush toward him, barking. Between three dogs there are ten and a half legs. Henry leans down to hold out a hand. They sniff it, wag their tails, trot with him toward the cabin.

The baby is alone outside, naked, a great fat child assembling on his head a mud hat. Sighting Henry he shrieks, rises, waddles to the cabin.

Phipps appears in the doorway. He whoops, dances, weeps. He has grown a huge gray beard. "Father," Henry says.

Franklin runs up, drags Henry off the pony, throws him in the air, catches him. Even Mary—pregnant, Henry observes—hugs him, briefly. The baby stares from the cabin doorway and laughs.

Only a few dozen people live within fifty miles. Franklin has talked with all of them, made himself clear: no one should give Father so much as a half-cent if they expect to be repaid, and neither should they give him a drop of whiskey or anything else on credit. This has been fairly effective, Franklin says, excepting the night when Father traded away the clothes he wore and stumbled home naked.

Father looks thin, unkempt, and mumbles into his beard. He seems unsettled and hesitant amid the new circumstances. He doesn't speechify or announce his opinions as he used to. He works harder than Henry has seen him work before, but that's not much. He is often not looking at what his hands are doing. He gazes off at one thing or another—the prints of a cat in the mud, the leaves of a tree in the wind, the horizon. Does he hope to go there, or expect to see something coming? His attitude seems to suggest the latter, and that what he might see is likely to be of doubtful fortune.

The baby has a name at last, which is George, named for the only president of whom Father approves, "Even if he was another damned Virginian." It amuses Henry that a baby should be named after a president, and calling the baby George makes him laugh, and George likes the laughing, so they laugh at each other in mounting hilarity. George seems to have his father's big body and his mother's dark eyes, but also a confidence of his own. He puts a frog in Franklin's boot. He laughs when Mary scolds him. He is no longer so solemn as he seemed when he was tiny, but still he seems never to blink, could stare down a wolf. Scattered around the cabin are the toys that Mary has brought him: nests, snake-skins, the delicate eggshells of songbirds, the skull of a vole, pretty stones, pieces of wood, flowers. Also in the cabin, besides the dogs, are a cat, a squirrel that sits in the rafters and scolds the cat, and three mice named Speck, Speckle, and Fleck, kept in a box.

Franklin has planted acres of corn and potatoes. There is also flax, wheat, rye, geese, pigs, chickens, turkeys, a milking cow, and a vegetable garden. Franklin and Mary rise before the sun, and when there is moonlight they work well after sun-down. The skin of Franklin's face, neck, and hands is tanned deep brown. It seems as if he has been doing the work of two or three men. Mary comments on it to Henry, shaking her head. "A man is not a waterwheel," she says. But to Henry's eye she works as hard as Franklin.

Franklin mentions that occasionally she takes George and goes wandering in the forests of walnuts, cherries, and oaks, that sometimes she is gone with him the whole day and into the night.

Henry supposes the farm may become quite profitable, but it will need a decade or more. It seems to him that the others all look a little strangely at him, excepting George, who directs toward Henry the same unnerving stare that he aims at everything.

Henry lasts two weeks.

Franklin plans to dig a well beside the house, but for now water must be carried uphill from a spring nearly a mile away. Henry has carried up a pair of buckets for the animals, and his arms feel as if they may fall off. More water is needed for the laundry. Henry contemplates the buckets to be filled. He can endure the work, but it seems so dull. Mary shucks corn behind the shed. Franklin, in the far field, grubs potatoes. Most of the harvest is well in hand. He can hardly bear to think of the monotony of a winter in the little cabin. The edges of the leaves on certain trees are tinting red and gold. Returning through the mountains will be difficult when the hard cold arrives.

As Henry stands looking at the buckets, Father wanders up. He stops suddenly, as if surprised to find he is not alone. "Well, Henry," he says. "What does Mother say just now?"

Henry says, "Nothing."

"Surely something? She always did talk."

"No," Henry says crossly.

Father squints, frowns. "My boy, you never could tell a tale." He ruffles Henry's hair. "Certainly not to your father. Be straight. What does she say?"

Henry scowls, backs away a pace. But something in Father's gaze makes his anger turn melancholy. Father, away from gambling and drink, with nothing much around but forest for a hundred miles—it's as if in this place he doesn't know who he is, how to be. As if he were a lost child. And Henry has a strange new fear, that this anger turning to melancholy is how life will go, that this is the feeling of growing older.

He studies Father's face, the watery pale eyes, the gray conflagration of his beard, the sagging bellies of flesh below the eyes. Father looks as if he doesn't expect his luck to turn. Or as if his luck did turn, and perhaps he wishes now that it hadn't.

"Mother says," Henry says, "that your luck is bound to turn soon."

Father grins. "She has always said so."

"Father," Henry says. His own melancholy makes him angry.

"Yes," Father says.

"I'm going to move on soon."

Father nods. "Of course. Anyone can see that."

"What I mean," Henry says, "is now." He realizes it in saying it. "I'm leaving now." All he wants to do is run.

Father says something, but Henry pays no heed. He is rushing away.

It feels good to rush. In the cabin he seizes his rifle, some food, a jacket. He takes out Franklin's quill and ink and starts to scratch a short note, but the ink splatters, and in frustration he throws the pen aside.

In the door sits George, watching, gnawing a turnip.

Henry tickles George, saying, "George! George!"

Both laugh.

Henry steps outside, saddles his pony, mounts, and departs.

ACKNOWLEDGEMENTS

Thank you to the friends who read versions of this book and helped shape it: Amanda Rea, Erika Krouse, Jeremy Mullem, Thomas O'Malley, and Jacinda Townsend. Thank you to Eric Simonoff for his faith and effort on behalf of this book; to Michael Reynolds and the team at Europa Editions for making *Mad Boy* a reality with such care and enthusiasm; and to Jay Kenney for creating the incredible map in the front pages of this book. Thank you to the many historians who have documented and analyzed the early years of the United States and laid the foundations for this story; I am particularly indebted to the work of Alan Taylor and Neil H. Swanson.

And thank you to Rachel and Cade for your support and patience with the quiet madness of a writer's life.

ABOUT THE AUTHOR

Nick Arvin's *Articles of War* was named one of the best books of the year by *Esquire, Detroit Free Press, Rocky Mountain News,* and *The Independent.* It won the American Academy of Arts and Letters Rosenthal Family Foundation Award, the American Library Association's Y.A. Boyd Award for Excellence, and was selected for the One Book, One Denver reading program. He is also the author of *The Reconstructionist* and the forthcoming collection, *In the Electric Eden.* Arvin lives in Denver.